GLIMMERS OF
THORNS

EMMA SAVANT

To my husband,
for all the kisses.

CONTENTS

ACKNOWLEDGMENTS

As always, my first and deepest gratitude goes to Elayne Morgan for her sharp eye, thoughtful comments, and entertaining marginalia.

My husband holds me together. These books would not have happened without him, and I am so grateful I will probably make him cookies.

And, of course, thanks to The Cat. Can't write without a cat.

CHAPTER ONE

The weather might have been gray and drizzly outdoors, but inside Wishes Fulfilled, it looked like the Easter Bunny had ingested an entire craft store worth of glitter and then thrown it up all over the walls.

Despite it being emphatically winter, Lorinda was determined to "put a *spring* in our steps!" This meant daffodils nodded on every desk, pink and purple glitter floated down from the ceiling and dissolved just above our heads, and the occasional overpowering scent of freshly mown grass wafted through the office.

Lorinda, I was starting to realize, had seasonal depression, and we were all going to feel the effects of it.

And we weren't just getting the effects of one holiday. Since it was actually December, the place was also full of candy dishes loaded with Christmas treats that were not doing my blood sugar any favors.

I ducked into my cubicle and sat down immediately to dodge a hot beam of sunlight. Rays kept bursting from an enchanted disco ball in the corner of our open office, flashing around the room in blinding golden beams. I liked sunshine as much as the next person, but this had to be the world's worst delivery system.

Everyone wanted elf magic during the holidays, which meant a slow month for us. To fill the time, I helped Tabitha prep the Magical Moments packages we'd be offering around Valentine's Day. Magical Moments weren't exactly a godmother's bread and butter, but the work—mostly setting up flawless enchanted environments for romantic dinners and proposals and the like—was easy and didn't require me to make a whole lot of choices.

After my Little Mermaid case, that was something to be grateful for.

The stack of papers on my desk, on the other hand, made my stomach squeeze a little. A glittering lavender sticky note curled up from the top of the pile. Lorinda's sharp, swooping handwriting read: *New cases. Look through and see if anything catches your interest. I suggest a Tom Thumb or Frog Princess; the variety will be good professional development.*

I did not want good professional development. I did not want any professional development. I just wanted to keep my head down and get on with my life.

Before I'd skimmed even half the pages in the pile, Lorinda was there.

"What do you think?" she said.

My phone, sitting on my desk, buzzed. I caught the name *Lucas* before the screen went dark again.

"Lots of good cases here," I said.

"There really are," she said. "These are all about right for your skill level, and you'll have plenty of opportunities to expand your skills. It's good to get a real breadth of experience when you're first starting out. Did you get a chance to look at the Frog Princess case? Not a frog this time. The enchanted prince, our client, is actually her guide dog. It's got the potential to be a really lovely romantic Story if we handle it right. He's been with her for years and she has no idea. The real challenge is going to be helping her realize that he's genuinely cursed into dog form *and* genuinely committed to her, not just transfigured so he can watch her change clothes, if you get my drift. We had an awkward mix-up with that one back in the—"

"Lorinda?" I interrupted.

She blinked. "Yes?"

"I think maybe I'm not ready for another case just yet," I said.

She looked over her silver reading glasses at me. "What's that?"

EMMA SAVANT

"I'm really busy right now," I said. "I just signed up for an intensive study program to prep for college and it's going to be taking up a lot of my time."

I bit the inside of my cheek and hoped she wouldn't ask for details. The "intensive study program" was actually a botany course offered for free online from a major university. I had a feeling Lorinda wouldn't take that too seriously, and I wasn't great at lying to other faeries.

But she'd already jumped way ahead of me and was racing ahead with her delighted assumptions.

"Oh, of course!" she said. "You've got all sorts of entrance exams coming up, don't you? Your father made a point of letting me know you were going to apply to his alma mater. In Austria, isn't it?"

"Yeah, the Imperial College of Faeries," I said.

Which I was not applying to. Dad knew that, but he hadn't acknowledged it. The closest we'd gotten to a conversation on the subject was a pamphlet on the College that he'd left on the kitchen table for me to find.

I flinched as another ray of sunlight swept over our heads.

"That's the one," she said. "Such an exclusive school! You must be very excited. Of course you ought to focus on your prep course. But when summer comes, I hope you'll do us a favor and take on one last case."

She winked.

I forced a smile and tried to suppress the guilt that bubbled in the bottom of my stomach. Fortunately, she was too wrapped up in her own excitement over my future to pay attention to how I felt. I jumped in before she had a chance.

"I'm happy as Tabitha's assistant," I said. "I think shadowing one of her cases would be a good compromise."

My phone buzzed again. Lorinda looked at the phone. Her eyebrows went up like we'd all just had a wonderful surprise.

"That must be your young man."

She winked again, and I did my best not to cringe.

The worst part was that, once she'd bustled back out and I'd had a chance to check my phone, it was "my young man." Not that he was mine, or a man, for that matter—but he was close enough to both that it made my stomach flip over. I had three texts.

Lucas: Mind if I swing by and take you to lunch? I'm downtown and craving Chinese. Also I'm pretty sure I saw a magician.

Lucas: Maybe not a magician. Maybe just a guy in a top hat.

Lucas: I'm outside.

I shot up and grabbed my coat way faster than I'd planned. If he was outside, that meant two things. First, he was here and we were going to lunch. Second, he was standing not a hundred feet away from the Oracle's Fountain, and I didn't want him anywhere near that thing. I flew down the hall and into the elevator.

He gave me a smile when I got out of the elevator, but not a hug, and I was half relieved and half disappointed. He eyed the Fountain.

"Let's get out of here?" he said.

"Fast," I said.

The water was still and quiet, as it had been since October, but I knew what was underneath it, and I knew she was probably watching us. I clutched one hand around my purse and took comfort in the barely-there weight of the silver ring beneath my shirt.

We walked down the sidewalk, close enough that every step was almost enough to make us touch.

"Sorry," Lucas said suddenly. "You didn't have lunch plans, did you?"

"I was probably going to skip it, honestly."

"I'm glad I caught you."

The air around him frizzed. He was as skittish as I was, and the thought did nothing to settle my nerves.

It wasn't like I didn't see him every day. We had classes together, and it was impossible not to run into him in the hallways sometimes. But hanging out outside of school was different. We were alone here, and it made me feel way too exposed.

"So you saw a magician?" I said.

"I don't think so," Lucas said. "He was doing card tricks on a street corner and he was a little too good. But then he did a trick I already knew."

"I didn't know you did card tricks."

"Just one," he said. "And really badly."

A laugh burst out of me with way too much force. I choked it back down. He pretended not to notice.

We'd been so normal once. Intellectually, I remembered what it was like to be comfortable around him. Emotionally, I couldn't even remember what "comfortable" felt like.

And yet, we couldn't stay away from each other. This was the second time this month he'd taken me out for lunch. I couldn't really blame him. Discovering an entire magical world living under his nose was bound to send him for a loop; no wonder he wanted someone there to answer his questions. And I was the only one who could, because there was no way I was letting a third party get involved. Lucas wasn't even supposed to know about our world, and I had a feeling the Oracle wouldn't back us up if we tried to explain to the Council that *she'd* exposed it to him.

"Where are we going?" I asked, at the same moment he blurted, "You smell like grass."

It took me a second to realize he was not, in fact, talking about marijuana.

"My boss," I said. "She's made the whole office smell like a lawnmower just came through. She's not really a winter person."

"It's not bad," he said. A flush covered his face and a wave of nervous energy rolled off him.

This was getting ridiculous.

"You said Chinese, right?" I said. Anything to keep the conversation going.

"Does that sound okay?"

"Food sounds okay," I said.

I kept forgetting to eat these days. In between the Oracle, Imogen, work, school, my parents, and Lucas, my brain was on constant overtime. I didn't have the mental energy left for remembering regular meals. Now that I was paying attention, though, I realized I was starving.

The little place Lucas led us to was busy with the lunchtime rush. An older woman seated us and left us with menus. I liked the noise in here—silverware clinking and quiet conversations. It made it harder to hear my heart pounding in my chest.

"I have to tell you something," I said.

Lucas leaned forward until I could see the tiny crease between his dark eyebrows. I flicked my fingers out. A bubble of silence sprang up to shield our conversation from any eavesdroppers.

"I got a call from Isabelle," I said. "She wants to meet up with me."

His eyes widened.

Months ago, on a single horrible night, Lucas had been introduced to our world, my Little Mermaid client had found an unsettling happily-ever-after, and the Oracle had stolen my best friend, Imogen, away from me. The next morning, I'd met a woman named Isabelle, who seemed to know even more than I did about the trouble the Oracle was causing throughout Portland.

Then she'd disappeared to France for a plant breeding course at a Glimmering university in Europe. I'd had no idea plant breeding courses even existed at Glimmering universities.

"She's back in the country," I said. "And she wants me to meet her at her work tomorrow."

"That's good, right?" Lucas said.

His face said he knew it wasn't. And of course he knew. My faerie features were probably broadcasting my worry to the entire restaurant.

"She told me not to tell anyone," I said.

Lucas frowned. "Isn't that dangerous?"

I picked at the edge of the paper placemat in front of me. It showed sketches of the animals of the Chinese zodiac, one after another in a giant wheel. I wished life were as predictable as it looked on this placemat, one thing following another in a predetermined progression.

"I don't think Isabelle's working for the Oracle, if that's what you mean," I said. "She just sounded worried. I probably shouldn't even be telling you, but—"

I cut myself off. My gaze shot up to meet his.

He wasn't challenging me, just listening and waiting for me to have the answers.

I had no answers.

"No, it's not dangerous," I said, with more certainty than I felt.

A younger waitress came by and gave us two glasses of ice water. Lucas thanked her and reached for his, but I caught his wrist before he could touch the glass. The heat of his arm through his jacket burned into my palm. Humdrums didn't have magical auras. Even so, they sometimes felt too warm or too cold or too electric just the same.

Especially when I was nervous.

I gathered energy in my free hand and swirled it till it felt hazy and unclear. The glasses dimmed for a moment when I threw the energy over them like a cloak.

"Sorry," Lucas said. "I forgot."

I couldn't imagine how it was possible for him to forget. I'd been putting blocking spells on every bit of clear water that crossed my path for months now; I didn't even step into the shower these days without putting a shield over the shower-head to prevent the Oracle from being able to see through any water that came through it.

What freaked me out was that these spells were becoming second nature. This time last year, I'd had to shut out all distractions and focus all my energy on getting a single charm to work. Now, I barely had to think.

I'd spent my entire life being proud of how Humdrum I was for a faerie, and now, here I was, showing off my magic for Lucas like some kind of show pony.

And he looked fascinated. He stared at me like he was trying to see inside me, and I couldn't stop a tiny thrill from going up my spine.

It was a thrill I did not have time for.

"Anyway," I said, forcing my attention back to the conversation at hand. "Isabelle's still kind of upset about what happened at the Fountain. Understandably."

"I'm still trying to figure that one out myself," Lucas said.

"What's to figure out?" I said. "The Oracle showed up and Imogen lost her mind." I couldn't stop an edge of bitterness from entering my voice.

I could still see her, walking away from me and into the dark rippling water.

EMMA SAVANT

It wasn't as though Imogen had gone forever. Within days, I had run into her in the hallway at work. I'd almost collapsed with relief, but she'd walked past me like I wasn't even there.

A few weeks later, I'd overhead her mom talking to mine when Mrs. Dann came over to borrow some golden apple juice for a potion. Mrs. Dann had seemed normal—happy, even— and chattered on about Imogen's upcoming departure to Institut Glänzen, the university Imogen had cheated on her exams to get into.

She hadn't been to Humdrum school lately, though. She probably thought it was beneath her.

Lucas rubbed the back of his neck and looked out the window. I felt my face flushing pink.

"At any rate, I'll keep you posted," I said. "On Isabelle, I mean."

Lucas smiled and nodded, but he seemed a million miles away. I changed the subject to our weekend plans and gossip about Tabitha's latest cases at work. Neither of us mentioned Isabelle, the Oracle, or Imogen again.

CHAPTER TWO

The heavy December sky loomed down like it was trying to intimidate me.

"You're too late," I muttered. "Already in way over my head."

The car had been idling for five minutes in front of the empty fenced tennis courts, and still the fluttering in my stomach wouldn't settle.

No one but Lucas knew I was here, and the temptation to back out and drive away overwhelmed me.

After all, the Oracle hadn't made a peep since the stupid night everything had gone down. If not for the persistent reminder that Lucas was now part of the Glimmering world and the constant gap in my life that used to contain Imogen, it would have been easy to pretend things were back to normal.

There'd been a rumor that a Humdrum woman had abandoned her apartment on the other end of town after the pipes kept bursting at three in the morning on the dot, but that was it.

Unfortunately for me, that was enough.

I'd been hearing those stories for a long time without taking them seriously. All it had gotten me was a brainwashed ex-best friend, a stressful side gig as the Faerie's Queen's informant, and a whole lot of stress.

I turned the ignition off. The engine wound down to silence. Thunder rumbled in the distance.

After the way the Oracle had royally screwed with my Little Mermaid case and brainwashed my best friend, I was more than ready to tear her limb from watery limb. The problem was that the girl marching into the Oracle's Fountain to take her down was Daydream Olivia. Real World Olivia was too nervous to get out of her vehicle.

There was relative peace as I sat here in the imaginary safety of my car, but it wasn't going to last. I felt it in the air and my memory of her voice ringing in my ears: *War is coming. I want you on my side.* Every second of silence was one second closer to the hammer falling.

A heavy raindrop landed on my windshield. I scowled at it and pushed my door open.

The public rose garden where Isabelle and I had agreed to meet was deserted this time of year, and no wonder. From where I stood at the top of cement stairs leading down to the garden, the place looked deserted. Hundreds upon hundreds of gray-brown rose bushes spread out below me, indistinguishable from one another, each one nothing more than a lump of dark twigs unceremoniously lopped short for the winter.

I walked down the steps and shoved my gloved hands deeper in my coat pockets. The garden was abandoned, with Isabelle nowhere to be seen. A raised bed of miniature roses hunkered down in the cold. I touched the handle of my wand, which held my hair back in a loose bun, and stretched out a finger toward the nearest bush. A single twig shot up and put out a bud, then opened with a flourish of red petals. It was the only spot of color in this whole gray-on-green landscape. I walked on.

"Olivia!"

I turned. The garden was still empty. But then, from over my glasses, I saw a curl of pink.

I pulled the lenses down to the bottom of my nose. Over them, a nebula of blushing light swirled up from between two rose bushes.

Isabelle came into view as I approached. She crouched between the rows and wore dirty brown overalls under a green jacket. A moss-green scarf tied back her soft brown hair.

"You're easy to miss," I said.

"That's on purpose," she said. "I try to not disturb the rabbits."

She leaned back on her heels and wiped her forehead with the back of one hand. Behind her, a small brown bunny leapt down the row of bushes and out of sight. I wasn't sure whether it had been startled my movement or by her energy. She looked calm, but inside, she was as freaked out as I was.

"What are you doing?" I said.

"Killing time," Isabelle said. She dropped a pair of hedge clippers onto the pile of twig clippings next to her. "I'm glad you're here."

I considered pointing out that she hadn't exactly been waiting on me. But I didn't know how much time we had, so I didn't bring up the subject of her plant breeding program, even though it was at least a thousand times more pleasant a subject than the Oracle.

I threw up a sound bubble that would protect us from anyone interested in eavesdropping. It glowed white everywhere my glasses didn't cover. I threw up a second bubble inside the first one, and a glamour inside of that one that would make it hard for passerby to notice us. The rain had left droplets of water everywhere. The Oracle could be listening or watching through any one of them.

"Do you want to go somewhere dry?" I said. I hit the last word a little too hard and gave Isabelle a meaningful look.

"No," she said, keeping her voice low. "I know what you're thinking, but Haidar and I have this place secured."

"Haidar?"

"My boss," she said. "He's a wizard."

"And he knows about the Oracle?" I said.

My skin tingled. Just saying her name made me cringe. It felt like it would summon her and make her come down on us, hard.

"I've left Haidar out of this," Isabelle said. "But he has reasons of his own for keeping it locked down. So let's talk."

This was moving way too fast. I crouched down beside her.

"How do you know you can trust me?" I said. "How do I know I can trust you?"

"Because, Olivia," she said. "We're both ethical people. And I saw what happened to you at the Fountain."

Inside my coat pocket, a spark of startled magic leapt from my fingertips.

"Wait, what?" I said.

"I was there," she said. "I'm sorry, I thought you knew. I'd followed Evan, and then I saw what happened with him and —"

Her nostrils flared and her cheeks flushed. Apparently she wasn't quite as over it as she'd appeared.

She cleared her throat. "I could tell you weren't happy when that faerie went into the Fountain," she said. "I think we both lost somebody to the Oracle. I'm willing to trust you for that."

I did not want to think about Imogen Dann right now. I nodded sharply, trying to send the memory skittering away.

A few more drops of water sprinkled down on my head. One landed on my nose, making me flinch. I raised a hand and flung it toward the sky. The ceiling of our little bubble hardened, and the drops stopped.

"What's your plan?"

She brushed her hands off on her knees.

"I don't really know," she said.

I touched my wand to focus my energy—I barely had to touch it for a second, now—and held my hand out over the ground. Steam coiled up from the damp earth, leaving the grass and dirt warm and dry. We both let ourselves drop to the ground. I folded my legs underneath me and clasped my hands on my lap.

"Maybe you'd better back up," I said.

She ran her fingers along a rose stem. The plant seemed to shudder and breathe under her touch.

"I've been watching the Oracle for a long time," she said. "A few years ago, I started getting reports from Glims that the fountains in this garden weren't calling up the sprites like they used to."

I glanced up. A large metal fountain sat in the middle of this part of the garden, its structure made of shining rectangular pillars over a small square pond. The other fountain, which looked like bird baths stacked on top of one another, was farther away. I felt magic from neither of them, but the sight still made a prickle run down my spine.

"Haidar and I have been enchanting the garden for years," Isabelle said. "I started working here when I was fifteen, years ago now, and Haidar's been here..." She frowned. "Longer than I have. I don't know exactly. We've been putting all sorts of spells on the property, adding a few each year and letting them grow together like vines. For the last few years, every time we put a new spell up, I'd hear complaints about people not being able to get sprites to appear in the fountains."

She gently snipped a stray twig off a branch. I winced, but the rose bush seemed to sigh in relief the moment the twig was gone. Or, I thought, squinting at it, maybe the breeze had made the few straggling leaves flutter and relax like that.

"I tried to find the problem, but there was none," she said. "The spells were working exactly as they should, and the fountains were working exactly as they should."

"The magic wasn't compatible," I said.

"And ours was stronger."

She looked over at the rectangular metal fountain. Her dark arched eyebrows drew together, just enough to make two tiny lines appear between them.

"The Oracle's servants couldn't get in, and that seemed odd. Our spells were created like a net, designed to let anyone with good intentions in and keep anyone with bad intentions out. It's been a nice thing for the gardens over the years. We attract the loveliest people on the loveliest days. You come here in spring and you can hardly believe someplace so beautiful exists. But the sprites can't get in anymore."

"Can they come in without using the fountains?"

"Not that I've seen," Isabelle said. "I told Haidar my suspicions. Must have been a year ago now, maybe more. He put extra enchantments on the garden to keep them out after that. I suppose I expected the Oracle to say something about it, to force a confrontation, but she's stayed silent."

"Talking would blow her cover," I said.

"Those were my thoughts," she said. "I've been keeping an eye on her for years, but then everything happened with Evan."

She stared vaguely into the rose bush as if her thoughts had become tangled in its branches.

My throat felt dry. I coughed into my elbow. She didn't seem to hear.

"I'm sorry about all that," I said.

She started and looked at me, eyes large and gleaming like ink in the gray light. "It's not your fault," she said. "I saw it coming."

"The Oracle, or—?"

"I knew Evan was seeing someone," she said.

I caught a wave of sharp pain off her, like someone had just socked her in the stomach. My own gut twinged in sympathy, but the tightness passed as she turned back to the bush and began stroking it again.

"I followed him, and I saw her, and... well, it wasn't hard to tell she was Glim. I felt water on her, like she was always swimming. I assumed the Oracle had sent her."

"She's a mermaid," I said. "Or she was, anyway."

The lines in Isabelle's forehead relaxed, but only slightly.

"I thought she seemed off for a sprite," Isabelle said. "She wasn't connected to the Oracle?"

"Not until the end," I said. "I was supposed to be her faerie godmother. She'd wished for Evan but I was trying to redirect her. Until the Oracle told me not to. It was complicated."

Isabelle sighed deeply but silently, like she didn't want me to hear.

"I assumed she'd been working with the Oracle from the beginning," she said. "Our spells have kept her out of our garden for years now. It's hard to think she hasn't noticed. I thought perhaps it was her revenge."

"It still might have been," I said. "It's hard to know *what* she's noticed. It's better not to underestimate her."

I'd learned that lesson firsthand.

The rain intensified over us, but we stayed dry. It seemed to be getting warmer in our bubble. I couldn't tell if it was our body heat or just my nerves.

Isabelle crossed her legs and looked at me. "I've been tracking reports of weird activity from her fountains since last year," she said. "I lapsed for a while when Evan and I got engaged, but then that fell apart and I've been tracking ever since."

"Even while you were in France?"

"My roses catch messages for me," she said.

She gave the bush next to us a fond smile. She and the plant appeared to be having a moment, but I couldn't help interrupting.

"Your roses what?"

"They listen," she said. "I asked them to watch the breeze for gossip about the Oracle. They catch the messages on their branches and I've been collecting them ever since I got home."

She leaned back and stretched an arm out behind her. It was immediately soaked by the downpour.

She felt around in one of the bushes. I tensed, but the plants didn't seem interested in scratching her. Instead, a tiny thorn glowed when her fingertip touched it. She pried it gently from the stem.

"Here," she said.

The thorn glistened with rain. The moment she dropped it in my palm, a whispery voice wafted past my head like perfume.

I helped an old Humdrum woman carry her groceries onto the train, a young woman's voice said. And nothing. I got one coin. Yippee. I mean, I didn't do it for the money, but when I was a kid, helping old Humdrum ladies with stuff was worth a lot more, you know? People better not whine about "kid witches these days" if they aren't going to give them the same rewards as the last generation, that's all I'm saying.

The voice faded, leaving only the sound of rain sizzling to silence above us and pattering on the muddy grass outside our bubble.

"You're going to have to teach me that," I said.

"It's not hard," Isabelle said. "You just have to build a relationship with your roses, that's all."

She took the thorn back from me and kissed it. The barb dissolved to dark brown soil between her fingers and she sprinkled the dirt on the ground.

"I've been getting a lot of messages like this. Not enough coins for helping Humdrums, too many coins for helping Glims, and even some reports of fountains malfunctioning."

Her voice turned ironic. "A couple of the ones downtown have been handing out coins whenever people scare Humdrums."

"The Oracle's been paying people to bait them," I said. "She wants to drive the Hums out of the city entirely."

"I wish I could be more surprised," Isabelle said.

"But you're not," I said. "Why? I sure was."

"The Oracle's been around for a long time," Isabelle said. "She lived in Bridal Veil Falls for years, and then she moved to the Fountain in the seventies. She's never been like the Faerie Queen. We don't know if there's only ever been one Oracle or if the role gets passed down like the Queen's does. We don't know her name. We only think she's a faerie because enough people have made assumptions and because the sprites follow her, and you don't hear of sprites following too many other forms of magic. But we don't know. We just think she's good because she rewards goodwill."

"The person with the job changes," I said.

Isabelle's eyes narrowed. "And how do you know that?"

"I heard it somewhere," I said. "I don't remember."

Unless Isabelle had been watching me much more closely than I realized, she didn't know I knew Queen Amani. And she wouldn't. We might all be on the same side, but Amani had asked me after the Fountain incident to continue keeping our connection to myself. The way she'd said it, I knew it wasn't just about her trying to limit gossip about her potential heir anymore. It was a matter of safety, maybe more.

"The Oracle rewards goodwill, but she also maintains balance," I said, trying to steer the conversation back to only mostly dangerous waters.

"She works for the happy completion of Stories," Isabelle said, and there was an edge of sarcasm in her voice. "But she doesn't get Stories. They change. Cinderella is assigned an impossible task until it just disappears from the Story. Stepsisters cut off their heels for years to get the slipper to fit until one day, that's just too messy and foot mutilation becomes optional. Cinderella's tree-spirit mother gives her advice and pretty gowns, unless of course she's helped by a faerie godmother."

"All Stories have variations," I said.

"Variations that have been working in the Oracle's favor a lot lately. You heard about Aster's case?"

"No," I said. I knew Aster, of course—she was a Wishes Fulfilled godmother—but we didn't talk much. "Have you been watching my work?"

"I've been watching all the fountains," Isabelle said. "Aster, your coworker, recently had a pretty typical situation involving a prince trying to guess a princess's unbeatable riddle."

I rolled my eyes. "Let me guess," I said. "The box with no jewels at all on it held the true treasure."

"Not quite," she said. "If he came up with the right answer, he could gain access to a magic fountain that happened to sit on the princess's family's property. The usual plain box was the right answer, but guess what was in it? A dozen fairies who hadn't eaten in days. When he opened the box, they flew off and attacked some poor Humdrum."

I winced. The tiny, glowing creatures we called "fairies" were actually hex moths—tiny, humanoid insects with sharp tempers and nasty bites. My great-great-ancestors had cultivated them and kept entire flocks for the potent dust that fell off their constantly shedding wings.

"The princess thought this was so hysterical that she granted him access to the fountain on the spot, and the fountain bubbled up a spray of gold coins he wasn't even planning on," Isabelle said. "And now some Hum is walking around Portland with itching fairy bites on his ears and can't remember where they came from, except he's starting to think that his apartment has bedbugs and maybe he should move."

"Let me guess," I said. "Far, far from the city."

"And everyone's surprised," Isabelle said. "It keeps happening. And the lines between good and bad are becoming sharper. Not so anyone's noticed, but it's happening. The Oracle is clearly marking which actions deserve rewards, and you know people are going to fall for it."

She reached out to touch a rose bush as if for support. The stress throbbing off her started to wash over me in waves. I surreptitiously put my hand on the ground and reached out toward the bushes, too. The earth beneath my fingers pulsed with a warm, steady heartbeat.

"No one is all good or bad," Isabelle said. "Goodness and rewards don't always go together. Beauty does not always mean goodness, and goodness does not always triumph. Stories are mixed." She stared at me, her eyes large and intense. "We've forgotten that, as a people. We've forgotten that beautiful people can be good *and* bad, and we've forgotten that leaders will not be good if we aren't watching their behavior and calling them out on their mistakes. We live in a culture of blind obedience, where everyone just does whatever the Faerie Queen says and whatever the Oracle says and never mind what they themselves think, and it's *toxic,* Olivia. We are living in a toxic environment where things are going wrong and no one is even bothering to ask questions."

She fell silent. Her chest rose and fell with heaving breaths.

She might be diving headfirst into dangerous territory, but apathy was never going to be one of her problems.

"You don't think we should do what the Faerie Queen says?" I said.

"I haven't watched her as closely as the Oracle," Isabelle said "But do you really think anyone with that kind of power can wield it without becoming corrupted?"

The question made me pause.

Amani was just as nervous about the Oracle as Isabelle and I were, but I could hardly tell Isabelle that.

As for power, I didn't know. I'd been offered the job, but I'd never thought about what it might do to me if I took it.

"She and the Oracle are close," Isabelle went on. "That's all I know."

"I think Queen Amani is different from the Oracle," I said.

"They're two sides of the same coin," Isabelle said. "We've forgotten the Stories, all of us. The Oracle and Faerie Queen have collaborated on everything since they first settled in this city. The Queen did high-level things and the Oracle had her boots on the ground. That's the way it's been for two hundred years. Why would that have changed now, just because they don't talk about their connection so much?"

"The Faerie Queen has changed maybe a dozen times in two hundred years," I said. "So has the Oracle, probably."

Isabelle wasn't hearing it.

"Doesn't it seem strange that the Queen hasn't said anything about the fountains?" she said. Her words tumbled over one another in their race to get out. "They both live behind water. They both hide from the world and don't bother to come down and speak with mere mortals. Aren't they a little too similar for your comfort?"

But Queen Amani *did* come down, I wanted to say. Amani was watching the Oracle as closely as Isabelle was.

"No one even knows who the Oracle is," Isabelle said. The rose bush next to her trembled in response to her fervent energy. "And no one knows enough about the Queen, either."

"My dad works with both of them," I said.

"And how does your dad feel about the Oracle lately?" Isabelle said.

I shrugged. If he had thoughts on the matter, he certainly hadn't shared them with me.

"That's what I thought," she said. "I know what I'm saying isn't going to win me any friends. A few hundred years ago, I would have been called to the Queen's court to stand trial for treason."

This seemed unlikely, but I kept my mouth shut. Isabelle had clearly formed her own opinions. She didn't need mine.

The problem was, her opinions made some sense. Unpleasant, unlikely sense, but sense. I stilled the impulse to touch the silver ring hidden underneath my shirt.

Isabelle fell silent and stared off down the hill. In the distance, Portland shimmered dull silver and chrome in the rainy light.

"Why are you telling me all this, then?" I said.

She didn't move, but her dark eyes grew so intense that she might as well have been an inch away.

"I saw you at the Oracle's Fountain," she said. "I saw your face when your friend walked into the Fountain and chose *her*."

I bit the inside of my cheek.

"Maybe that's not enough," she said. "I'm taking a big risk being honest with you, I know that. But I can't keep doing this alone. I need help."

"And you think I can help."

"I don't know much about faerie magic, but I did my research," she said. "You're the youngest godmother Wishes Fulfilled has seen in a long time. You must have something going for you. You work right across the street from one of the most important Glimmering spots in Portland. And the Oracle took someone from you, just like she took someone from me."

It wasn't much, as votes of confidence went. But Isabelle was right. She did need help, and so did I.

"What do you want me to do?"

Nerves fizzled off of her like static, and I braced myself for whatever enormous task she was about to give me.

"Keep an eye on her."

It was hard to keep a straight face. What Isabelle seemed to think was a dangerous new job added almost nothing to my plate.

I'd already been watching the Oracle for months, at Queen Amani's request. I'd kept her posted about gossip I overheard and rumors I picked up around town, seemingly unrelated things about a haunted building here or a Humdrum attack there. These things had been happening for years as isolated incidents. Only lately had a few of us started to see the patterns.

With Isabelle on board, my work hadn't changed. I'd just be texting two people now instead of one.

"Don't tell a soul about this," Isabelle said. "We can't trust anyone."

"You trust Haidar," I said.

"Haidar and you," Isabelle said. "And you have no idea how hard my heart is pounding now, just trusting you."

I did know. I'd felt it slamming and shuddering in her chest for the past twenty minutes.

"Don't worry about me," I said. I thought about Queen Amani, and Imogen, and the Oracle's voice echoing in my ears: *There is a storm brewing.* "I know how to keep secrets."

CHAPTER THREE

The front door slammed. I didn't need to hear the way it shuddered in its hinges to know that Dad was home. The air prickled like a storm was brewing, and it wasn't long before the storm swept into the kitchen.

"Where's your mother?" he said, barely bothering to glance at me.

"Shopping," I said.

I didn't clarify that she was downtown buying divination charms, or that she'd met with a new client today, a hundredth-generation princess living in the suburbs who needed help telling which of her household pets had swallowed her golden ring.

He opened the fridge and glared at the contents. "I heard you turned down a case," he said. His tone was cool, but I knew better than to trust it.

Instead of answering, I turned back to my laptop, where jewel-like green leaves in a photograph threatened to grow right out of the screen. *Imperial College of Faeries* was written across the top in silver letters, and underneath that, *Department of Magical Botany.*

Of *course* a magic-based study of plants existed. Of *course* I could study new species at a Glimmering university as well as anywhere else.

It blew my mind that I'd never connected these dots before.

My entire life, I had been more interested in plants than in magic. My faerie gifts seemed snobbish, secret, restricted only to the kind of people who had my parents' self-important approval. Plants, on the other hand, covered the world and were there for anyone to discover, no matter who their parents were or which Councils they sat on. All plants needed was dirt and sun and they grew, transforming from tiny seeds to complex organisms that could nourish or poison, all without a hint of a spell.

That had seemed like real magic.

I'd been so determined to slough off my Glimmering roots and reach for this real magic that I'd completely failed to realize there was some overlap between the two—and the overlap was *fascinating*.

"Between you and your brother, I'm not sure the Feye family name is going to mean anything after I'm gone," Dad said.

"Mmhm," I said.

How had it taken Isabelle going clear to Europe for me to realize stuff like this existed? I'd known she was going to Europe for some plant breeding thing, but it hadn't occurred to me to look Glimmering botany programs up until I'd actually seen her in her garden with her roses. Those rose bushes had responded to her as if they were not only alive, but conscious. I'd never seen anything like it.

Text ran across the page: *The magical properties of roses have long been known to Glimmering-kind. Though it is said that faeries have an inborn gift for the growth of these enchanted blooms, closer study will reveal that the current robust diversity in species is largely thanks to the work of a school of Spanish sorcerers which formed in the sixteenth century and continues to the present day. Once a year, the Imperial College brings one of these sorcerers to our campus to discuss Spenican roses and their unique contribution to the field of magic.*

"You're almost an adult, Olivia," Dad said. "You might not care about your future, but I'm your father, and it's my job to care."

"That's true," I murmured.

Our unique collection of rare snapdragons is among the most diverse in the world. Second-year students have an opportunity to grow these remarkable plants from seedlings. (Please note: Students must demonstrate firm control over the fire element before taking seedlings home. Students who do not pass fire certification will be required to keep their snapdragons in one of our four campus greenhouses.)

Dad shut the fridge door, and I heard the glug of wine being poured into a glass.

The conservation of magical plants is of vital importance to the next generation of Glimmering botanists.

"I guess I should be grateful that you're going to college at all, even if it is a Humdrum school," Dad said, his contempt lacing the word Humdrum with venom. "Daniel won't even be able to manage that much if his grades don't improve."

We work closely with Glimmer-aware Humdrum biologists to identify and cultivate new plant species. Each year, five students are selected from the graduating class to join a two-week international Glim-Hum botanical expedition.

"He'd better start working on them," I said. My eyes raced across the page.

A special series on the healing properties of herbs is available through a collaboration with the Department of Healing & Health Services... Past visiting speakers have included prominent ecologists… Field studies are integrated into each of our summer courses…

"Olivia," Dad said, his voice slicing into my awareness.

I looked up, surprised to see him still standing there. "What?"

"Are you listening to me?" he said. "Damn computers. Your generation has lost the ability to focus on anything."

"Sorry," I said. I couldn't stop myself from glancing back down to the page. "What were you saying?"

"What are you looking at on there?" he demanded. I reached out, fingers poised to minimize the screen, but he was behind my shoulder in an instant. I held very still, bracing myself for the "I told you so" and demands that I send in my application immediately.

Instead, he raised the wine glass to his lips.

"That would be a good choice," he said. "If your mom gets home, tell her I'm in my office taking a call."

He walked out of the room, taking his wine with him.

Since he wasn't going to force me, I clicked the link at that top of the page that said *Apply* in thin, elegant letters. I scanned over the requirements. Scores from a Gifts Elucidation test—the Glimmering world's version of an SAT or ACT, much more generalized than Imogen's specialist Proctor Exam had been—and an entry essay to be sent through the website using their JinxNet Spell Secure system.

My cursor hovered over the *Save* icon in the corner of the screen. Before I could talk myself out of it, I downloaded the application, then shut my laptop with a click.

I heard the front door open. My mom's energy floated in ahead of her, exuberant and unfamiliar.

Mom was going through some kind of midlife crisis. She'd started doing volunteer Quests and taking on paid freelancing divination jobs. When that seemed to be going well, she'd dyed her hair a vivid auburn. A week or two later, she'd joined a Rediscovering Your Inner Wild Woman group which, as far as I could tell, consisted mostly of middle-aged women doing weird spells and tribal dances designed to make their periods more magical or something. My mom had gotten weird.

I liked her better this way.

"Olivia," she called. "Come help with the groceries."

I hopped off my kitchen stool and went into the foyer. Reusable linen grocery bags hung from her arms. I took a gallon of milk from her outstretched hand and slid a bag from her wrist.

She swept ahead of me into the kitchen. A potted plant on the hall table curled a leaf toward her. I couldn't blame it; she'd carried some residue from the divination shop home with her and she reeked of magic. I liked the feel of it, but I knew Dad wouldn't.

I freed one of my fingers from the grocery bag handle and wiggled the finger toward her, funneling some of the magic off of her aura and into mine.

"Did you know the Imperial College has a botany program?" I said in an undertone as soon as we were in the kitchen.

Mom set her bags on the island and turned to face me.

"Really?" she said, like I'd just asked her to do twenty backwards somersaults for my entertainment. "You *just* realized this?"

"Why didn't you mention it?" I said.

She rolled her eyes. "I did mention it," she said.

"I don't remember that."

"Might have something to do with how your eyes glaze over whenever anyone says *Imperial*," she said. "I've brought it up at least five hundred times."

I frowned. I had no memory of this. "When?"

"I don't know," she said. "I started a few years ago? Three, maybe? And you said—" she paused, trying to remember. Then, in an overly dramatic voice I assumed was supposed to imply *teenager*, said, "Ugh, Mom, I'm not looking for some mediocre imitation of *real* Humdrum *science*, God!"

I was pretty sure my voice had never been quite that huffy. The words sounded like me, though.

"Well, then, yes," I said. My forehead felt hot. "I just realized this."

She pulled her now-auburn hair into a ponytail on top of her head.

"You going to do anything about it?" she said.

I handed her a carton of eggs.

"I don't know," I said. "Probably not. I don't know why I mentioned it."

When Dad came back into the room, I gave him a sidelong glance. He was grumpy about something, but the energy wasn't directed at me.

Mom stiffened.

"What?" she said. "What did I do now?"

"Not everything is all about you, Marigold," he said. He checked his watch, an ancient timepiece that kept track of time and of the lunar cycles. "I need to go into the office."

"You just got home," I said.

His jaw twitched. "I'm aware of that, Olivia," he said, in an exaggerated show of patience. "But Her Majesty, Queen Amani, has urgent business to discuss with me, and we are all subject to her timing."

I busied myself putting vegetables into the crisper, bending down behind the fridge door so he couldn't see my face.

She'd promised to keep our connection private. My stomach wobbled anyway.

"What kind of urgent business?" I said.

"Marigold, are you aware that Olivia has expressed an interest in the Imperial College?" he said, like I wasn't there.

"She mentioned it," Mom said.

She handed me the jug of milk. The handle was almost too cold to touch. I slid it into the fridge and cleared my throat.

"I'm also expressing an interest in your job," I said. "Why does Her Majesty want to see you?"

Reginald Feye was the master of the poker face. No one outside the family would have recognized the look of utter confusion that made his lips get tight. It was hard to blame him. I hadn't asked about his job in years. I'd barely asked him about *anything* in years.

"I'm curious," I said, like this wasn't completely out of character.

He frowned at me. "There have been some tensions between Glimmers and Humdrums in recent months," he said.

My stomach flipped over. This tension was exactly what Amani had asked me to watch for.

"I know," I said. "I mean, I've heard you mention it."

His dark eyebrows went up by just a hair. "Well, then perhaps you're aware that someone has been attacking the Humdrums," he said.

Daniel came into the room behind him. In his black turtle-neck, my skinny younger brother was like a shadow. He leaned against the wall and listened.

"Much to my surprise, the Council has so far been unable to locate the perpetrator. This is alarming, for obvious reasons."

Obvious reasons being that the Council was the greatest thing in the universe, according to Dad, and totally incapable of the failure that dogged us mere mortals.

"I just spoke with one of my colleagues on the phone and learned that someone has kidnapped a young Humdrum girl, and there's reason to believe a Glimmer is involved. Queen Amani wishes to speak with a select few members of the Council to determine how to proceed. She values our input." His chest swelled a little as he spoke.

Relief flooded me, followed quickly by something else. I hadn't felt the ring under my shirt glow warm, the way it usually did when Amani wanted to contact me. She hadn't texted, either. Normally, she let me know as soon as anything new happened with the Humdrums.

"Queen Amani relies on us," Dad said. "And while this is a great honor, it comes with its own pressures. The Council has been unable to determine who is behind these attacks, and Her Majesty is not pleased by our inability to catch the criminals."

His face tightened for a moment. "It appears she holds me and other Council leaders responsible."

"But it's not your fault," I said. Daniel raised his thin eyebrows.

"It is, actually," Mom said. "It's the Council's job to govern our world."

She pulled a cutting board out of a drawer, not looking at Dad.

"It doesn't help that people are starting to get suspicious," she said. "Some Glimmers seem to think the bad guy has the right idea, and some Humdrums are getting more and more skeptical that this is all chance."

"That's rumor," Dad snapped.

"A persistent rumor has just as much power as the truth," Mom said.

"It's virtually impossible to glamour the memories of every Humdrum who's been exposed to magic," Dad said. "If you think otherwise, I'm sure the entire Council would love to hear your suggestions."

"I'm not criticizing," Mom said. She dropped a bunch of carrots in the sink and pulled her wand out of her pocket. "It's a fine line. Even the best Erasers disagree on how to balance the glamour and removal of memories. We all know that."

"And with good reason," Dad said, as Mom waved her wand in a series of sharp flicks. The carrots began to shed their skin, the orange curls piling up in the sink.

He turned to me. "We haven't had to clean memories on this scale since riots in the nineteen-sixties."

Daniel sauntered forward and slid onto one of the stools by the island.

"I'll bet it doesn't help that Queen Amani still hasn't picked an heir," he said.

Dad cleared his throat. "That's true, though I don't know what you know about it," he said.

"Just gossip," Daniel said. "I'll bet that makes your job harder."

"Queen Phoebe had three potential heirs selected by the time she was Queen Amani's age, even if it took her some time to make her final decision," Dad said. He'd missed the sarcasm in Daniel's voice. "And, of course, there are people who hold me responsible for that as well, though Titania knows why. It's enough that they're angling for my job like vultures."

Heat started to rise off of him, a dry feeling I associated with irritation. I jumped up and went over to Mom.

"Anything I can help with?"

She took the hint. "Enough about politics, more about dinner," she said. "Olivia, pull the chicken out of the fridge.

51

Daniel, there's garlic bread in the bag on the counter. Turn the oven on. Reginald?"

"I'm going to the office. Don't wait up for me," he said, before she could give him an assignment. Not that he would have done it if she had. He gave me a quick appraising look, but I pretended to be busy.

A Humdrum had been kidnapped. My dad was being held personally responsible.

So why hadn't Queen Amani told me?

CHAPTER FOUR

The air froze the inside of my nose every time I breathed in. I buried as much of my face in my scarf as I could and hurried down the street toward Lucas, who looked just as cold as I was.

"You could have gone in," I said when I reached him.

His dark eyebrows tensed. "In where?"

"Um, right here?" I said.

He frowned. "You said it was a café. This looks like the wrong place."

"This is a café," I said, waving toward the windows. The words *Pumpkin Spice* curled across them, and the walls inside were the color of butterscotch. Hazy nebulas and constellations floated around the Glims who sat around the place, each unique aura a fingerprint of magic.

He glanced at the windows, raised his eyebrows, and looked back at me.

"Pretty sure that's a Lebanese restaurant."

Of course. I'd forgotten.

The Oracle had dropped Lucas in my world, and he'd found his way to Wishes Fulfilled the next day through the building's elevator. Humdrums—usually relatives of Glims—had to come see us now and again, so I knew getting to our office wasn't impossible for them, but it *was* hard. I'd started to assume he could find everywhere as easily as he'd found my cubicle.

I took my wand out of my hair and tapped its tip on the frame of my glasses. I forced my energy to merge with Lucas' for a brief moment, just long enough for me to get a taste of what it meant to live in a world without magic. I pushed his energy through my wand and into the lenses.

With full Humdrum vision, Pumpkin Spice wasn't even there. The windows of the Lebanese restaurant stretched in from one side, and the brick of the real estate office next door stretched in from the other.

The emptiness of his world relaxed me instantly, but we were both too cold for me to enjoy it. I let the spell fade and put my hand on Pumpkin Spice's door.

"Take my hand," I said. "And just trust me."

He reached out and took my hand. I stepped forward, trying to push as much magic back through my hand and into his as possible. As we walked through the door, he stumbled, then said, "Whoa."

The door swung shut behind us, and I let go.

The café pulsed with life, and the baristas at the far end of the room seemed up to their eyebrows in orders. There was nowhere to sit. I caught Elle's eye. She waved at me from across the room, then twirled her hand and thrust it toward us, palm out. A table and chairs sprang into being in front of us, tucked against the wall in what appeared to be one of the only free spaces in the building.

Her witch abilities had taken off since I'd first introduced her to our world. Now, she juggled the many demands of her business, made the best fairy dust-laced coffee on this side of Portland, and, apparently, had developed an ability to conjure furniture out of the air.

I slid into one of the chairs. Its back was carved with pumpkin leaves.

"Sit," I said to Lucas. He stared around the room, his eyes as wide as the coasters on the tables.

A moment later, Elle wove her way across the room, drinks in her hands. She'd gotten weirdly good at intuiting people's cravings, and now she set two steaming hot chocolates in pumpkin-colored mugs on the table. Mine smelled vaguely like oranges and Lucas' was topped with a giant swirl of whipped cream dusted with cinnamon.

I stood to give Elle a quick hug.

"This is Lucas," I said, sitting back down.

"No kidding," she said.

She eyed him up and down, not bothering with subtlety.

"Welcome. How are you acclimating, kid?" She waved a hand around the room.

I hadn't told Elle everything about the Oracle, of course, but she did know the Oracle had allowed Lucas into our world. She was probably the only person who had a clue what he was going through right now.

He cupped his hands around the cocoa. "A little over-whelmed."

"You seem to be handling it better than I did," she said. "Good job."

"This is your place, right? This is amazing."

"Aw," she said. "Thanks."

She smiled at him, then widened her eyes at me. We were going to talk later.

"I've got to get back," she said. "It's Crazy Town today."

She gave us a little wave and went back to the counter, where she was immediately busy throwing together drinks and calling out orders to her staff.

"She was my first faerie godmothering case," I said. I couldn't stop watching her. This was probably what it was like to be a proud mom. "Cinderella Archetype."

"What's an Archetype again?"

I swirled the cocoa. It left a thin brown film on the inside of the orange mug.

"It's like a stereotype," I said. "But not quite. She had certain traits, which meant her Story—her life—was supposed to include certain elements."

"Cinderella goes to the ball," he said.

"Prom, in her case," I said. "Which then turned into a dance at a geek culture convention."

Lucas' eyes widened. He'd gone to that dance with me, right after he'd gotten into an argument with his ex-girlfriend. He hadn't had a clue what was going on at the time, and now, I watched his face as the pieces clicked into place in his head.

"Your job is more interesting than mine," Lucas said.

I believed it. He worked part-time at a food cart.

A jingling bell followed by a freezing draft announced that the door had opened. I looked up and waved Isabelle over. She twisted her dark hair into a wispy bun as she walked toward us.

She unzipped her jacket and pulled off her gloves.

"Sorry I'm late," she said. "Missed the train."

"No worries," I said. "We just got here. Isabelle, this is Lucas."

She held out her hand and he shook it.

"Hi, Lucas," she said. "So you're a Humdrum."

She slid into her seat, not taking her eyes from him.

"Still not sure how I feel about that word," he said.

"What do you prefer?" she said. "Mundane? Non-magic being?"

"Person?" he said.

"We're all people," she said dryly.

She shot me a sharp look. "So, I have to be honest, I'm not really understanding what's happening." She nodded toward Lucas. "Why is he here?"

"He's my friend," I said. "He's involved in this, or he's supposed to be."

"Olivia's been telling me about what's been going on with the Oracle," he said, lowering his voice on the last words. "We think I might be able to help. As a... Humdrum person... I might hear things you won't."

Isabelle pursed her lips. "So how do you know about our world?" she said. "You've got a Glim relative?"

"No," he said. "Nothing like that."

I bit the inside of my cheek. This was going to be the hard part, and I wished Isabelle had at least given me three minutes to enjoy my cocoa before launching into it all.

There was no good way to say it.

"The Oracle introduced him to our world," I said.

Her lips pressed together.

"He saw everything that happened at the Fountain," I said.

"That's why you look familiar," she said, and not like it was a good thing.

"He was able to get past the Humdrum barrier," I said. "Imogen—the girl who walked into the Fountain—Imogen is his girlfriend. Was his girlfriend."

I felt my face go hot, for no good reason whatsoever.

"Wait," Isabelle said. "You mean to tell me that you're discussing our *concerns* about the Oracle," she said, putting the slightest emphasis on the word, "with someone who is in league with the Oracle?"

"I'm not 'in league' with anyone," Lucas said. His voice was instantly sharp.

"It sounds like you are," Isabelle said. She leaned back and folded her arms tight across her chest. "Olivia, can you explain this to me?"

"No," I said.

Lucas frowned at me. A tiny crease twitched between his eyebrows. He seemed to be asking a question, one I didn't understand. Isabelle had just cleared her throat when he spoke.

"I can," he said. "I think I can, anyway."

"No kidding?" I said.

"No kidding," he said. "I mean, it's obvious, when you step back and look at it."

News to me.

"I was dating Imogen," he said. His gaze flicked toward me and then away. "The Oracle wanted Imogen, and it sounds like the Oracle wants Olivia, too. But I think, if they'd been on speaking terms, they would have talked each other out of following her. They're smart, both of them, and they balance each other out. But if she could isolate them—either one of them—then…"

"She isolates her prey before attacking," I said.

I couldn't help staring at him. That had been freaking insightful, especially coming from a guy I hadn't thought was paying attention.

"The Oracle used me to break them up," he said. "Get a guy in the picture and it ruins female friendships."

"No, it doesn't," I said, but he laughed, without much humor.

"I've watched my mom do this a million times," he said. "Her friends practically disappear when a new guy comes into the picture, and she's not much better when she gets a boyfriend. If you want to make a girl feel lonely, throw a guy between her and her best friend."

He barely met my eyes, then stared down at his cocoa. Embarrassment flared from him like heat from a bonfire.

Isabelle continued to frown at him.

"The Oracle knew I liked Lucas," I said. The words came out in one long string. "She used that to divide Imogen and me. That and some other stuff. Not important."

The pieces clicked into place. It was so obvious. I couldn't see how I'd missed it all these months.

"By the time Imogen walked into the Fountain, of course Lucas could get through the Humdrum barrier," I said. "He'd been at the center of a powerful faerie's plans for months. He was already involved in our world; he just didn't know it."

"She probably didn't think it was worth kicking me back out after all that," Lucas said. "Unless you're right." He met Isabelle's gaze. "Maybe she does still have plans for me. But if she does, I don't know about them."

Isabelle leaned back in her chair with her arms still folded like a shield. She examined him for a long moment. Just when I was about to snap at her to get over it already, she nodded.

"I can live with that."

"Gracious of you," I said, unable to keep an edge from my voice. I rushed on before she could say anything about it. "Okay, so what are our next steps? What have you learned?"

Isabelle narrowed her eyes at me, but then shook her head. "I have some information about the Humdrum child who was kidnapped," she said.

She dug into her purse and pulled out a folded piece of paper. I touched the back of my neck and felt the thin metal chain that held Queen Amani's ring beneath my shirt.

Amani still hadn't called to tell me about the kidnapping. If she didn't think the Hum child was worth mentioning to me, maybe she wouldn't care about these details.

Or maybe I'd done something wrong at the Fountain. I hadn't been quick enough to save Imogen. How could she trust me with anything bigger?

But, to be fair, I hadn't told her about Isabelle yet, either. I'd been waiting for this meeting so I'd actually have something to tell. Maybe Amani was waiting until she had more information, too.

"Girl was three years old," Isabelle said, running a finger down the paper. "Daughter of a Humdrum guy whose stepsister is a muse. No clear motive, but it sounds like he and his sister didn't always get along. I heard he thought the Glim world was dangerous or something, but that's just rumor. I couldn't get a confirmation on any of it."

"Do you have their names?" Lucas said.

"Daughter is Maddy Barnes," Isabelle said. "Dad's Jason Barnes, Mom is Jessica Sullivan-Barnes. The dad's sister is Ruby Barnes, adopted by Jason's Humdrum dad when she was a toddler."

Lucas shook his head. I'd never heard of them either.

"Glimmering law enforcement talked to all of them, but their stories match," Isabelle said. "The parents were at the mall, and they turned around and the kid was gone. The sister was at work."

"Where in the mall?" I said, knowing the answer.

"Right by a fountain," Isabelle said.

I knew the one she was talking about. Imogen had always stopped there to say hi to the sprites and get fresh enchanted water for her cosmetics and spells.

Crackling and sparks filled the air as a wizard girl across the room started shooting fireworks out of her fingers toward an elf friend. The elf girl squealed and giggled. Behind the counter, Elle held a hand up in the air; a moment later, the fireworks had stopped and the wizard stared at her fingertips in confusion.

Elle caught my eye and winked.

"Do you want anything?" I asked Isabelle, gesturing at my hot chocolate.

Isabelle shook her head and tucked the paper back in her purse.

"No, I have to get going," she said. "Just wanted to make sure everything was going okay and keep you updated."

She gave Lucas another appraising look. Her dark, sharp features made her look like an eagle deciding whether or not to attack.

"Keep me posted if you hear anything else," she said, standing up. "I'll do the same."

Lucas and I watched her leave. Lucas' eyebrow quirked, his expression hard to read. I felt out into the air around him, searching for emotions, but I didn't come up with much. He was thoughtful, I could tell that much. What was hard to get at was the content of the thoughts.

I sipped my cocoa. It was perfect, as always. The tiniest refreshing hint of rainwater gathered on a new moon mingled with the orange and chocolate, keeping the drink from being too heavy.

"I have something else to tell you," Lucas blurted.

I waited, my mug halfway back to the table.

"It's really off-topic," he said. "Just, I've been talking to Aubrey."

I set the mug down. Out of everything I'd expected him to say, that wasn't on the list. Aubrey was his ex, the one before

Imogen. She was gorgeous, flirtatious, and kind of a nasty person when he wasn't around.

He tapped on his mug and didn't meet my gaze.

"She wants to get back together."

CHAPTER FIVE

Aubrey wanted to get back together with Lucas.

At this point, I was impressed he'd managed to stay single for a whole month.

A fresh wave of embarrassed heat rolled off him, but he swallowed and met my eyes.

"Okay," I said, too quickly, sounding so much like I didn't care that it was beyond obvious that I did. "So?"

I was trying to keep him posted on the evils of the Oracle and a Humdrum kidnapping and what were maybe the beginnings of the end of the world as I knew it. And he was worrying about his obnoxious ex. I glanced past his shoulder and out the window, where drizzly sleet had started to fall.

"I'm only mentioning it because, well, Aubrey might have seen something."

And my attention was back. I frowned at him. "Like what?"

"I don't know," he said. "I wouldn't bring it up, except it was near the Oracle's Fountain, so it might matter. I guess she saw a bunch of teenagers doing some weird dance around a fire in a barrel. The cops broke it up—they aren't supposed to have fires there, you know—but the fire kept burning blue and she said people were doing magic. She called them magic tricks, but she sounded suspicious."

"Why would she be suspicious?" I said. "She's a Humdrum. Humdrums never believe magic is actually happening."

"I'm guessing it wasn't really discreet," Lucas said. "She said something else about how this woman in her neighborhood started doing really accurate tarot card readings or something, plus she said she saw Imogen a while ago and that Imogen's skin was actually glowing."

"Probably fairy dust," I said. "Because *some* people don't know how to show restraint around controlled substances."

Years ago, Imogen had experimented with adding fairy dust to lotion to make it sparkle, but she'd stopped because it gave her too much of a magic high—and too much of a crash afterward. But the Oracle's pet probably didn't need to worry about crashes.

"Have you seen her lately?" Lucas said. "Imogen, I mean?"

"No," I said. "She's stopped coming to school. Teachers said she has mono." I didn't even bother to roll my eyes, the lie

67

was so obvious. Glims didn't get crap like mono. "Her parents said she's prepping for her fancy Glimmering university."

"Oh," Lucas said. He cleared his throat. He didn't want to talk about Imogen. I didn't want to talk about Imogen. And neither of us could get her off our minds. "Anyway." He drummed his hands against his mug. "Aubrey knows something's going on."

"She probably just thinks Portland is weirder than she thought," I said. "Or she's just trying to sound interesting so you'll get back with her. Obviously—"

"She knows something," he said, his voice just sharp enough that I shut my mouth. "She said, 'I think something weird is going on here' and then she asked if I believed in paranormal phenomena."

"Probably thinks it's aliens."

"I think we should be aware," he said. "You said the Oracle is getting more and more obvious about these Humdrum attacks. Don't you think she and her followers might be getting more and more obvious about the Glimmering world, too?"

"She couldn't do that," I said. "She might try to scare the Humdrums away with their own superstitions, but she'd never —"

"How do you know?" he said. "I don't know what all the rules in your world are, Liv, but she's not following them anymore, is she?"

I should have been ready to argue back. His eyes flashed at me and he seemed more than a little worked up. But I couldn't focus on that, because I was too busy turning into a useless puddle.

He'd called me *Liv,* just like he used to when we were kids and just like Imogen used to before she turned into a crazy person. It meant we were the kind of friends who could use nicknames and get into arguments and still be chill with each other at the end of the day. I resisted the urge to reach out and squeeze his hand.

I took a deep breath. "Okay," I said. I tried to collect my stupid twitterpated pieces. "That's a good point."

"I know," he said. "That's why I made it."

He tried to look serious, but a little smile poked at the corner of his mouth.

God, he was cute.

Even if he did have the bad habit of talking about his multiple ex-girlfriends with someone who wished she was his current girlfriend.

This was too complicated.

"Keep an eye on her, then," I said. A second later, I realized I'd given him an order to keep talking to Aubrey. *Rein it in, Feye,* I ordered, and added, "I'm not saying to, like, stalk her or anything. Just if she happens to say anything out of the ordinary, you know."

"Yeah, I know," he said. "I'm not getting back with her, just so you know."

It was my turn to get hot, and I did, brilliantly and completely. I could almost feel my cheeks giving off steam.

Why was it so hard to keep my cool around him? Neither of us had anything to be embarrassed or nervous about. We were just two people having a conversation.

"What about with Imogen?" I said.

Instantly, I wanted to kick myself, but I forced myself to hold still and wait for his answer. We were friends. It had to be okay to at least ask.

He shrugged. "I don't know?" he said. "I mean, I'm not planning on getting back with her, either. But I didn't like the way it ended." He stared into his cocoa, and we both watched his fingers tap against the edge of the mug. "Like… Sorry, I don't really know to explain it without getting all feelings-y on you."

"You can get feelings-y," I said, much too quickly.

He smiled a little, though it wasn't the kind of smile that came from anywhere happy.

"I feel like I didn't get a lot of closure, I guess," he said. "Everything was really sudden."

For the first time since everything had happened, calm settled between us like a pocket of fresh, clean air.

"She broke up with me and I discovered magic exists in almost the same moment," he said. "We'd kind of been fighting, but I didn't expect her to dump me, not then. And then all this." He looked around the room, his dark eyes still drinking everything in. "I feel like I'm running but I can't catch up."

"It must be overwhelming," I said. "Probably more than I realize, huh?"

"Probably," he said. His gaze settled on me. "And then there's you."

And, in a second filled with total panic, I completely lost my powers of eye contact. I stared into my cocoa like someone was paying me to do it.

"What's going on with us?" he said.

I shrugged. It was an impossible question to answer. "We're friends," I said.

"Oh," he said.

The seconds dragged by. I heard a genie on the other side of the room squeal with laughter, but didn't look over to see why.

"Friends isn't a bad thing," I said.

"No, it's good," he said quickly. "I just… I don't know. I thought there was more."

"There was," I said. "I don't know if there is, though. You know?"

It was only a fraction of the truth. I forced myself to look up, and then I couldn't tear my eyes from the way a lock of his dark hair fell down onto his cheekbone.

I pressed my tongue against the back of my front teeth, feeling the smooth curves of their enamel.

I liked him, but I didn't like that I liked him. Aubrey and Imogen had liked him, too, and he'd liked them back. If I got involved the way they had, what would that say about me? And yet, it was impossible not to want to get involved when my stomach leapt every time I looked his way. My thoughts chased each other in circles.

"Sorry," he said. "I'm not good at this kind of thing."

"Could have fooled me," I said, before I could think about the words.

He chuckled, but it was like he was laughing at himself, and not in a nice way. "I know how I must come across," he said. "New girlfriend every two months."

He was like the dude version of Imogen. No wonder they'd hit it off.

"It's not my business," I said. "I'm sorry. I didn't mean, you know."

This was the worst conversation I'd ever had.

I let all my air out in a long, silent sigh, until I was completely empty. My energy fizzled and relaxed. I took several long breaths in and out before I was ready to talk.

"Why do you get into relationships so quickly?" I said.

I forced myself to look at him like this was a normal conversation. And then I waited.

He was silent. I heard him shuffle his feet under the table. He took a deep breath. "I don't know," he said.

I kept waiting.

The bell on the door jingled and a burst of cool air swept in, along with a naiad wearing a Portland State University backpack over her pea coat. Instantly, all my attention was on her. Water creatures were not in my good graces right now. But she didn't have the single-minded energy the Oracle's sprites usually carried with them. Sprites were loyal to the point of being cultish; this naiad's energy was scattered and she instantly started complaining to one of the baristas about her economics class. I kept one eye on her and turned back to Lucas.

"I don't know why," he said. His voice was quiet, his shoulders hunched like he wanted to cave in on himself. "I know it's dumb."

I pressed my fingertips against the hot side of my mug. "It's not dumb," I said.

"Maybe I just take after my mom," he said. "She goes through relationships pretty fast, too."

He was trying to make a joke, but I was a faerie, and I knew full well it wasn't funny. I put my hand on the table, palm up toward him.

"Can I?" I said. Butterflies flew in circles around my stomach. "I'm an empath. Kind of a good one, to be honest. Can I just, like… feel what you mean?"

Some emotion pulsed off of him, something white and sparkling and scared. "You can really do that?" he said.

"Dude," I said. "You would not believe what I can do."

He raised his eyebrows and looked across the room, where a genie was spinning clouds of glittering pink smoke into elaborate sculptures to entertain her friends. I laughed, and he put his hand in mine.

"Go ahead," he said.

It was easy to focus all my attention on his skin against mine. His palm gave off gentle heat, and if I followed the heat I could trace a line through his arm and right to his core, to that weird place that was heart and stomach and sternum all at once, where the strongest emotions took root.

"Think about everyone you've ever dated," I said. "Just kind of remember what it was like to be with them and what it was like when you broke up."

And then I closed my eyes and gave myself over to the feelings.

Buried and insulated in the stillness of our soft breathing, I tumbled headfirst onto a roller coaster. Heat and cold came at me in shifting waves, images of red hair or brown eyes or a ballerina's ankle, tense with the weight of supporting her body as she stretched into a long, perfect line.

With each glimpse of a girl came thrills of excitement or the warmth of trust, broken up by cool gray valleys of sadness and loss. And always, threaded through everything, like the thick string at the center of a pearl necklace, I could feel him.

I stretched my mind and tried to encompass every bit of the Lucas at the center of things. I reached out into cool air and wide spaces, and endless, flat walls of gray stretching out in every direction. Beneath my feet, the ground dropped away to a thousand miles of nothing.

Lucas, at his deepest, most constant core, was the loneliest person I had ever felt.

I squeezed his hand tighter, tethering myself to the warmth of his palm as the vast emptiness stretched out inside of him. Inside, where no one else could see, Lucas felt like nothing at all.

It was too much. I brought my focus back out of him, traveling up out of that cavernous loneliness and into his emotions and memories and muscles and skin until finally, I was back to his palm, then back to mine, and then back inside myself, where the lay of the land was messy and broken but familiar. I opened my eyes to see him staring at me.

I stared back.

"Damn," I breathed.

"That was…" he said, and then he couldn't seem to think of anything that could come next.

"Could you feel all that?" I said. Did he always, or was he numb to it? I'd felt Lucas; I wasn't sure what it was like to *be* Lucas.

He frowned and kept staring at me. "I'm not sure," he said slowly.

Our hands still rested together on the table, palms cupping one another. I noticed, but I didn't pull away.

"Dude?" I said. "I don't want to date you."

His face fell. A wave of the same gray emptiness whooshed off of him, and I shivered. It felt exactly like someone had opened the Pumpkin Spice door again and let the cold in.

"I figured," he said. He forced a smile and looked down at his drink.

I squeezed his hand. "I want to be your friend," I said.

He looked up.

"I really like you," I said. "But if I try to get into a relationship right now, I'm just going to screw it up. And I don't think you need another girlfriend." I watched him, fighting the urge to wrap him in my aura and keep him close. "If we get together, it's going to go great for a little while, and then we're going to start failing to live up to each other's expectations and we're going to break up and it'll suck. If we're friends, though, we never have to break up."

I thought about Imogen and bit my tongue. But whatever I had with Lucas would never be as intense as what I had with Imogen.

Anyway, it was worth trying this friendship thing again. Lucas was worth the risk.

"You idiot," Elle shouted from behind us. I twisted around in my chair in time to see her hit Kyle on top of the head with a dishcloth behind the counter. It made his already unruly hair stand up in little peaks. "That's Star *Trek,* not Star *Wars.*" She grabbed his shirt and pulled him in until their noses were almost touching. "I raised you better than this," she said, in a low, way-too-intense voice.

He cracked up and kissed her, and she melted into him for a second before spinning around to wipe up the counter.

I loved what they had. And someday, if I was really lucky, I'd find it for myself.

In the meantime, I wasn't going to fill in that gap with a lot of halfway attempts. I deserved better than that. So did Lucas.

"I think you just need friends, dude," I said. "Like, real friends. Without expiration dates."

A corner of his mouth quirked. "Why are you calling me 'dude' all of a sudden?" he said.

"Because we're friends, dude. We're bros."

He laughed. I still didn't let go of his hand.

"I think you keep trying to find The One, and then you get really lost when people turn out not to be her," I said. It was the last time I was planning on getting all sappy with him, so I pushed ahead before he could say anything. "And I think it makes you lonely. And I don't want you to be lonely. So, I guess, what I'm saying is, I'm here. And it's not because you're going to bring me flowers or because we're going to live happily ever after. It's just because I think you're cool and I want you in my life."

He smiled, a real one this time that made the corners of his eyes start to crinkle. "I'm okay with that," he said.

"You should be," I said. "Because I'm kind of a badass friend. I bring fairy-dust cookies on your birthday."

I finally let go of him. My hot chocolate had cooled, so I waved my hand over it and watched as steam curled up from the cup. He held out his mug and I did the same for his.

He raised his drink.

"Cheers," he said. "Dude."

CHAPTER SIX

"They're building new fountains," I said, my voice a low, urgent whisper. "I flew Daniel to a friend's birthday party in Oregon City yesterday on a magic carpet and saw them installing a new fountain right down by the river. The entire crew was Glim."

Isabelle pursed her lips and glanced over at Daniel, who'd come to the rose garden with me to get out of the house. He was sitting on a bench down the walkway from us and playing a game on his phone, which I thought wasn't quite dramatic enough an activity to justify the suspicious look on Isabelle's face.

"You've got to chill out," I said.

"There's a war on, or haven't you noticed?"

"It's not a war," I said.

Though if the Oracle kept spreading her reach like this, it might become one sooner rather than later. The fountain in Oregon City was one thing, but I'd heard rumors at school that the Oracle was expanding her personal reach down south as far as Medford, clear down at the bottom of the state. After Oregon, she'd move into the next states, and after that, who knew?

Isabelle groaned and leaned back on our bench. A strand fell out of her loose black braid. "Haidar says I'm too high-strung about all this. He thinks your Faerie Queen is on our side too, by the way."

"I still don't get why you don't," I said.

"I don't trust anyone who can't be bothered to put her boots on the ground," Isabelle said. "While all this has been going on, I haven't heard a peep from our queen. That's not a good sign. But Haidar doesn't agree. And maybe he's right. He's known her for years, you know."

My stomach flipped over every time she mentioned the queen. Amani still hadn't contacted me. I'd told her about the fountain in Oregon City, and all I'd gotten in response was a single-word text: *Thanks.* It wasn't much to go on.

"If they're friends, can't he just, I don't know, call her?" I said.

Restless, she tapped her feet against the pavement beneath us. The ground was dry, though clouds hovered overhead.

"They haven't talked in a long time," she said. She glanced over at me. "They're still on good terms and he still thinks she's worth trusting. It's just, Haidar's past is kind of… complicated. He doesn't talk to other Glims much."

So much for that.

"Lucas thinks some of the Hums are getting suspicious," I said. "His ex-girlfriend saw some Glim kids by the Oracle's Fountain, and they weren't being discreet. Like, at all."

"It wouldn't be the first time," Isabelle said. "The Council had to glamour a bunch of memories last year when sprites burst out of one of the fountains downtown. The Oracle called in a few Council members on special assignment and fed them some story about the sprites' population growing so quickly they outgrew their fountains. Load of crap. She'd let them off the leash too much and they got overexcited."

My ears perked up when she mentioned the Council. At "special assignment," I remembered why: My parents had gotten into a nastier-than-usual argument last year, something about Dad accepting a special assignment from the Oracle and Mom not thinking it was a good idea. I wished now I'd paid more attention to the content of the argument, not just how sick it had made me feel.

It might be worth talking to Mom to talk about it, but I barely saw her these days. She seemed as fed up with our family life as I was.

"What's going on with you guys, anyway?" Isabelle said.

"With who?" I said.

She nudged my foot with hers. "Lucas," she said.

I considered claiming there was nothing there. But Isabelle was a witch, not an idiot.

Instead, I settled for a truth that didn't get anywhere near how I felt. "Nothing's happening," I said. "He dated my Oracle-loving ex-best friend, and the girl before that—the one who saw those kids at the Fountain—is not the nicest person I've ever met. I like Lucas, but he has horrible taste in women. I don't want to be next on the list."

"I respect that," Isabelle said.

"What about you and Haidar?" I said.

Fair was fair. She did mention him a lot.

She snorted. "Yeah, right," she said. "You wouldn't ask if you'd met him. And speak of the devil."

She pointed a toe toward the end of the walkway, where a man with hunched shoulders came toward us like a storm cloud. He was tall, maybe in his thirties, with olive skin and unruly dark hair that went to his shoulders. He could have been handsome, but his grumpy expression killed the possibility. Under his bushy eyebrows, his face practically crackled with annoyance.

"Who's this?" he demanded before he'd even reached us. He glared at me. "Isabelle, I don't pay you to waste time on park benches with high schoolers."

I raised an eyebrow. Nice to meet him, too.

But Isabelle didn't seem perturbed. She didn't even shift on the bench. "This is Olivia," she said. "The godmother, remember? We talked about this."

His scowl didn't change, but his eyes looked slightly less likely to send lightning bolts my way. He grunted. "Who's the boy?"

"That's my brother, Daniel," I said. "He doesn't know about any of this. Don't worry, he can't hear us from here."

"Yes, I can," Daniel said, without looking up from his phone. "And yes, I do."

The air between us froze for a second before I whirled on him.

"*What?*"

He glanced up without moving his head. "It's not like the Oracle problem is a secret," he said. Under his breath, he muttered, "Genius."

I threw out a hand and slammed my energy through any radio waves and electromagnetic fields I could find. The air crackled around his phone and he looked up sharply. "Hey," he said, anger edging his voice.

"These are our allies," Haidar said flatly. "Fantastic."

I glared at him. How did anyone that rude survive adult-hood, let alone become someone's boss? If I was Isabelle, I'd have quit.

"Excuse me," I said. I didn't wait for anyone's permission.

Daniel stared at me as I approached him, his face blank, like nothing I could do or say could possibly impress him. I clenched my fists and resisted the urge to throw every fancy spell I'd ever learned right at his head.

"You want to explain that?" I said, and dropped onto the bench next to him.

"Explain what?" he said.

"Don't be cute," I said.

He rolled his eyes. "Do you seriously think you're the only person who knows the Oracle might cause problems?" he said. "You're not the only one who gets to watch Mom and Dad squawk at each other, you know. Anyway, it's not like she's real discreet."

I leaned in toward him. "What do you know?"

"Same as everyone else," he said. He shrugged. "The Oracle's gotten too big for her britches. Queen Amani told the Council not to accept any more assignments from her."

"Why?"

"Because she's worried the Oracle's going to succumb to peer pressure?" he said.

I frowned, and Daniel rolled his eyes.

"The Oracle and Queen Amani and the Council are all big on us hiding from the Humdrums, right?" he said. "But a bunch of people aren't down with that anymore, so they've been trying to convince the Oracle to reveal us all to the Hums, so we can live in the open and form a new world order or whatever."

I frowned. This was news to me.

Why was this news to me?

"Why would they try to convince the Oracle?" I said. "She doesn't have that kind of authority."

Daniel snorted. "But the Oracle likes attention. Obviously she's not going to give in. But she's definitely giving the idiots more of an audience than Queen Amani would. It makes them hopeful."

Truth had mixed with rumor, but still, Daniel knew way more than I'd thought possible.

"When did Queen Amani tell the Council to stop taking Oracle jobs?" I said.

"Do you ever listen when Dad talks?"

"Does he ever say anything worth listening to?" I said.

"Decent point," Daniel said.

He jabbed a button on his phone. The screen stayed dark.

"Like, months ago," he said. "Queen Amani warned everyone on the Council that the Oracle might be pressured into something. She didn't explain what 'something' meant but Dad sounded like it wasn't good, and it's not hard to figure out from the Oracle parties."

"What the hell is an 'Oracle party'?"

His jaw dropped, just a little too far for me to think he was experiencing any kind of genuine surprise. "Oracle parties," he said. "Where groups of Glims get together and openly perform magic around one of her fountains? To show support for the goal of an openly Glim population? Grassroots politics? Anything ringing a bell?"

It rang more than a few.

How had I gotten so behind the times?

And why had Amani not talked to me about any of this?

I frowned and waited for more information, but he just stared at me with his eyebrows raised.

"Good to know," I finally said. He held up his phone, and I wiggled my fingers in the air to loosen the electrical currents back up. "Thanks," I said.

"Any time," he said. "I could just walk around and point out obvious things that are happening if you want." He took on a dorky voice that made him sound like some hillbilly cartoon character in patched overalls. "The sky is gray today, Olivia! It looks like it might rain! Look, we're surrounded by rose bushes!"

I was never taking him anywhere again.

"Clever," I said. "Real clever."

I stood up and walked away. But his voice stopped me.

"What?" he said. "You don't want to talk about the ring you keep trying to call Queen Amani with?"

I felt myself change colors.

"What do you know about that?" I hissed.

"I saw you," he said. "You were talking to it the other day. You said, 'Hey, Amani, just checking in, I haven't heard anything new but I'm going to be meeting with Isabelle again.' Something like that. Super discreet."

"That doesn't mean it was *Queen* Amani," I said.

"You obviously can't see your face right now," he said.

I was about two seconds away from strangling him. He continued to play on his phone like we were talking about the weather.

"Daniel," I said. He grunted to show he was paying attention. "*Daniel,*" I repeated. "You cannot tell anyone about this."

"Duh," he said. He tapped a few times on the phone screen and then looked up. "So, you going to introduce me to your friends or what?"

CHAPTER SEVEN

"This is Daniel," I said. Above me, the sky remained as flat and gray as my voice.

Isabelle leaned forward on her bench and offered Daniel an encouraging smile.

Haidar just glared. "You're here to help Isabelle save the world," he said finally. "What a relief."

"Don't get smart," Isabelle said. She leaned back onto her bench and folded her arms, which were lost in her oversized moss-green hoodie. "You're still helping me, too."

"I'll have to." Haidar's dark eyes fixed on me, then Daniel. "Otherwise, it's you and two squabbling teenagers against the Oracle and you'll get yourselves killed."

"Naw, you can go," Daniel said. "You'd just spend all your time making smart-ass comments and slowing us down."

I smacked his shoulder.

Haidar barked a laugh. "You'd know about those," he said.

Isabelle groaned. "Haidar, I swear you're the most immature person here and these two are teenagers. Go away."

He turned on me instead.

"So why do you keep trying to absorb my roses?" he demanded.

"Um, what?"

"You," he said. "Keep trying to absorb the magic coming off my roses."

I glanced over my glasses at the nearest bush. Nothing came off it, magic or otherwise.

"I have no idea what you're talking about."

How did Isabelle put up with having him for a boss? Her job must be miserable.

He folded his arms and nodded his chin at me. "Your aura keeps reaching out toward my roses," he said. "Sniffing them like a dog. You don't even know it, do you?"

"Obviously not," I said.

I wished he'd go away and let Isabelle and me get back to "saving the world." Daniel was right: Haidar wasn't going to be any help.

Haidar scowled at me. Isabelle cleared her throat. She jabbed her finger toward the nearest rose bush, her eyebrows raised like he was a total moron.

He coughed and waved one large hand over the bush. It shimmered. A fine glittering layer of what looked like dark pink ice appeared on the branches.

The second I saw it, I felt the pull. Something about the ice drew me; I wanted to touch it, even to taste it.

Haidar grunted. "We keep it glamoured."

"People used to come to the garden to steal rose magic," Isabelle said. She reached out to the bush and ran a finger along the branch. Sparkling pink flakes tumbled lightly to the ground. She held the finger out to me, and I touched the magic.

It felt sweet in a way I couldn't explain, as if the skin on my fingertip had grown tastebuds. I sniffed it and the scent of roses wafted up toward me. That was predictable. The rush of power that followed it was not. The magic entered through my skin and nose. My skin flushed with strength.

No wonder part of me had been reaching toward it.

"That's crazy," Daniel said. He touched the bush without asking and sniffed the magic that came off on his fingers. "Whoa. Do all flowers do this?"

Haidar snorted. "*Do all flowers do this?*" he repeated mockingly.

"No, they don't," Isabelle said, much more gently. "Not even all roses. We cultivate a few special kinds here."

"Spenican," I said, remembering the word from the Imperial College website.

"I wish!" Isabelle said, eyes widening. "No, those take more energy than I can devote to them, though Haidar—"

He coughed. She glanced up and fell silent.

"Haidar what?"

"These are Antique Enraptures," Isabelle said. "They're an older breed, but they give off decent magic."

"Looks like fairy dust," Daniel said. "Once it's rubbed off, anyway."

"Looks like it," Isabelle agreed. "But it's not the same. It's good for you, for one thing."

"No hangovers," Haidar said.

"Enraptures are more for building strength and power over time," Isabelle said. "They make a good rose hip tea. We contract with Moonwort Hospital for this one, actually. They use it in a couple of healing potions."

"Give away all our secrets," Haidar grumbled.

Isabelle continued like he hadn't spoken. "The Allure Miniature Roses over there are a little lighter," she said. She pointed over to some tiny bushes. Like the Enraptures, their branches were frosted with magic, this time palest pink tinged with yellow.

I stared at them, and then I stared beyond them.

The glamour had lifted all around us. The garden, which had been gray-green moments ago, was now alive with colored ice. I'd seen the garden in summer before, when the blooms had been out in full force. We were surrounded by the same colors now, but in a way I'd never seen.

"The Allures are more about charisma," Isabelle said, sounding like a tour guide. "We grow those mostly for the Rose Galas in summer. We drop the flowers in punch bowls and string them on garlands for the festivities. Makes everyone seem much more charming than they really are."

"You've been drugging everyone at the parties," Daniel said, a hint of admiration in his voice. "Nice."

"I've seen those," I said. I could picture them now, tiny pink roses with blushing yellow centers. I'd always been drawn to them at the Galas.

"You like roses," Haidar said.

For the first time, he sounded like a normal person making normal conversation. I eyed him. "Yes," I said.

"Do you work much with plants?" he said.

"I grow some at home," I said. "And I volunteer at a community garden."

He scoffed. "No, I mean do you *work* with plants? Plant magic?"

"Oh," I said. "No."

Because I was an idiot who hadn't realized that was even a thing until recently.

"Haidar's a botanist," Isabelle said. "Not a bad one, at that."

He threw her a death glare.

"I've dedicated my life to the study of magical plants," he growled. "Isabelle likes to refer to it as my 'hobby.' It's a miracle Isabelle still has a job."

Isabelle rolled her eyes at him. Haidar frowned at me, as if I'd disappointed him by existing. I tapped my toes on the pavement. I'd come to talk to Isabelle, not to listen to an insecure wizard defend his job.

"You've never grown magic from plants?" he said.

"No," I said. "I thought you had to be, like, a really good faerie for that. Or wizard or whatever."

"You heard wrong."

I pressed my fingertips together to stop myself from punching him.

"Okay, yippee," I said. I turned back to Isabelle. "We should probably get going."

She pursed her lips and nodded. I felt a sense of effort stretching along her arms and got the feeling she was also trying to not assault her boss. But Daniel was enjoying himself too much to go anywhere.

"Olivia's a terrible faerie," he said.

"Not if she's a good gardener," Haidar said. He stared intently at me, like he was examining a bug under a microscope. "What about breeding? Have you done selective breeding of Glim species? Enchanted Hum plants with Glim qualities?"

"Nope," I said. "I grow herbs on my windowsill. The end."

"Would you like to learn?" Haidar said.

I froze under his intense gaze. The answer rose instantly to my lips: *Yes, but not from you.* But I couldn't say that. I wasn't as rude as him.

"I don't know," I said instead.

"Think about it."

He turned to Daniel. They appraised each other, two sets of sharp dark eyes taking each other in.

"And you like music," Haidar said.

"I'm more of a poet, actually," Daniel said.

I couldn't help but be impressed by how un-ironically he said it. I couldn't claim to be anything. Even when I said, "I'm a faerie godmother," I always tripped over myself right after, adding, "Well, not *really* a godmother. I'm just an intern." But Daniel announced *I'm a poet* like there was nothing to it.

"You're an artist," Haidar said. His face softened just a little. "I have a collection of magical instruments you might be interested in."

"What do you play?" Daniel said.

"Violin, a little," Haidar said. "I don't play well. But my cousin is a great musician. His instruments are rare. I keep them safe when he travels."

Isabelle caught my eye and gestured for me to sit down. I settled back on the bench with her and watched as Daniel and Haidar fell into an easy conversation about instruments and performing. Haidar seemed to relax as he spoke, and for just a brief instant, I caught a glimpse of what he might have looked like when he was young.

"Stories are mixed," Isabelle said softly, like she wanted only me to hear. "Haidar's a perfect example of what I was telling you. No one is all good or all bad."

Her face softened as she watched him.

"We need him," she said. "I know he can be abrasive, but we won't be able to pull this off without his help."

I frowned at her. But her eyes didn't leave his face. Finally, I shrugged.

"If he can help us take the Oracle down a notch or two, I'll put up with whatever I have to," I said.

I reached out a hand toward the nearest rose bush for a dusting of magic. I rubbed it between my fingers and felt the power seep into my skin.

Haidar, Isabelle, or roses—it didn't matter. I'd take all the help I could get.

CHAPTER EIGHT

It was almost embarrassing to serve regular old cranberry-chamomile tea to Elle, but she seemed to be enjoying it. She took a long sip from her mug and leaned back into the couch.

"It's going to be so nice to have a couple days off," she said. "We're closing Christmas Eve and Christmas Day, and I'm shutting down early New Years' Eve. Basically heaven."

"I thought you loved being at Pumpkin Spice," I said.

"Well, yeah, but not all the time," she said. "Sometimes I think I was crazy for wanting to take all that on. Running a business on top of school? One-way ticket to the funny farm."

Despite her words, her face lit up with a smile that was every bit as warm as the tea. She loved her café and she loved running it.

"Speaking of Pumpkin Spice," she said. She set her mug on the coffee table and twisted to face me. Her eyes widened, suddenly eager. "You will not believe what I've been putting up with."

"Is this the Aubrey thing you texted about?"

"She's been hanging around outside the windows," Elle said. "Like, every day for almost a week."

I sipped my tea and turned this over in my mind. It shouldn't be possible. Aubrey was a Humdrum through and through; she shouldn't be able to see the café was there.

"Maybe she's been visiting the buildings on either side?" I said.

"Unless she's secretly working at the Lebanese restaurant but never goes in, probably not," Elle said. "Or maybe she's looking at apartments? The real estate office is the only thing on that side, but they're basically never open. Sign says 'Open by Appointment' but I don't think anyone makes appointments."

"But she shouldn't know Pumpkin Spice is there," I said, as if Elle hadn't put the Humdrum repellent onto the building herself. It was a tight enchantment; I'd tested it thoroughly and hadn't been able to sense a single crack. It had definitely fooled Lucas.

"Are we sure she's Humdrum?"

"Positive," I said. I'd studied Aubrey enough times over my glasses. Nothing surrounded her except a constant air of superiority.

"It's weird."

"Maybe she remembers from when it was there before?" I said. "A lot of people went there before we went Glim."

"Yeah, she used to come by all the time," Elle said. "She loved the place. But the glamour takes care of that. I've got a whole memory charm layered over the thing. Humdrums show up and get a vague idea that we moved and the real estate business took over the spot. It looks so boring that no one remembers it was there in the first place."

"Then I have no idea."

She picked her tea back up. "She's been taking photos," Elle said. "Right at what *should* be the dividing line between the two other buildings."

"Maybe she followed you back from the Saturday Market," I said.

Elle frowned. "She has come to our stall a couple times."

"But she still wouldn't be able to see the café," I said.

Elle pulled her phone out and started tapping on it. A few swipes later, she held the screen out to me. The words *PursuitOfVerity* were smashed together in the search bar above a list of results.

"This is Aubrey," she said. "Kyle set up an alert for Pumpkin Spice mentions on the Humdrum side of the internet. These started coming up when a couple of her posts mentioned the Pumpkin Spice stall. She goes to a lot of effort to stay anonymous, but it's not hard to put the pieces together."

A string of results marched down the page in black and blue letters.

"Pick one," Elle said. "They're all her. If she were to start getting ideas about the Glimmering world, do you realize how many people she could tell by hitting a couple of buttons?"

Aubrey—username PursuitOfVerity—wasn't a hard person to find. She was on Facebook, Twitter, Instagram, Tumblr, and had her own website. I clicked the Facebook link. Here, she was named Verity Pursuit. I surveyed her page. She had way more friends than any person could juggle. I was pretty sure she had more followers online than I actually knew in real life. Twitter showed the same thing, and so did the sites after that.

Every profile picture was identical. In each, her face was hidden by a giant black bar, like she was being censored on the news or something. I recognized her red lioness hair.

Her posts ran the gamut from the pretentious to the cliché. Comments about probably-obscure bands followed mirror selfies, and she seemed to spend a lot of time talking about where people could find "real" Indian food or see "real" films in Portland.

"Ew," Elle said, reaching over my shoulder to point at a link to Aubrey's blog. She sounded disgusted. "I read that one. She's claiming that no one in America really *understands* miso soup, because *she* tried it in Japan and it's *so* different there."

"Gross."

I kept scrolling. It was strangely transfixing. In Aubrey's world, she was a very important person.

The scary part was, she might be right. Anyone with that many followers had at least some influence. If Aubrey was getting suspicious about the Glimmering world, she'd be able to share her thoughts with thousands of people. It would only take a couple of status updates that would take ten seconds to write and even less time to read.

"Let's hope she doesn't get a picture," I said.

Elle propped her feet up against the edge of the coffee table. I hoped Dad wouldn't come home any time soon. He hated when people "disrespected" furniture.

I put my feet up, too.

"She's one of those self-obsessed regulars who came a lot right before we went Glim. The posts Kyle found said we have *real* coffee. She comes by our Saturday Market stall almost every week asking when we're going to find a new place."

"What do you tell her?"

"I say I have to focus on school and I'm running the business out of my house for now," Elle said. "But she's not buying it. And she seems convinced the café's in the same spot it was in before, which shouldn't be possible, but maybe I'm a terrible witch. Whatever it is, she's not about to let any annoying spells keep her away. Which is flattering, but—"

"But totally awful," I said.

"The Pumpkin crowd isn't really helping convince her the world is as it seems, either," Elle said. "The enchantments lock Glims out if Hums are watching, obviously, but you can only have so many faeries hanging around outside a real estate office before things start looking weird."

"The Council would never be able to do damage control," I said. "If she actually got a photo, I mean."

"People would think it was faked," Elle said. "Wouldn't they?"

I frowned and kept scrolling down the page.

"Yeah, probably. But we've had internet fiascos before. You can only make so many people look like morons or con artists before people notice a pattern. Aubrey's one person. But if other people jump on the bandwagon with her?"

Normally I'd have brushed this off and told Elle to stop worrying.

But things had changed. The Oracle had started rewarding people who did horrible things to Humdrums a while ago. Now, people were holding Oracle parties to advocate for the right to live openly as Glims, and I wasn't about to assume they were looking for a peaceful coexistence. This was not a good time for a narcissistic Hum like Aubrey to start trying to expose the city's best Glim café.

"This could blow up really big," I said. "You know my dad's on the Council, right?"

"Yeah?"

"The Council members have been kind of disagreeing with each other lately," I said.

It was an oversimplification, but I couldn't tell Elle everything that was going on. Unless Elle came to me with information the way Isabelle had, I needed to keep her at a safe distance.

"Basically, some of them have different ideas about how the Glim and Hum worlds should be connected. Or not connected. Or whatever."

"I've heard people say that," Elle said. "Which, whatever. I don't get what's wrong with the way it is now. We're way progressive when it comes to social issues."

I lifted my hands. I was helpless to explain. The only real answer was *Because the Oracle is a nincompoop*, which wasn't going to cut it.

"People are greedy, I guess," I said. "It's not enough to be Glim; the rest of the world has to know about it. Maybe the rest of the world even has to admit we're superior. Glims talk like that sometimes, when they don't think they'll get in trouble for it. If the Council members don't get on the same page with each other, it's going to be a nightmare trying to assign Erasers to clean up the mess."

"Hold it," Elle said, raising her hand. "Erasers."

Elle had taken to our world so easily that it was hard to remember she hadn't always been one of us.

"Erasers are from the Office of Cross-Cultural Relations," I said. "They work under direction of the Council. Erasers glamour the memories of Hums who shouldn't have been exposed to our world. They'd be in charge of crisis control if Aubrey did manage to actually get some, I don't know, evidence. And then the Inkers do the opposite—they make sure that important Hums know everything they need to know to work with the Glim world. Like, when a new governor is appointed, the Inks introduce them to our world and then enchant them so they remember all the details they need to remember in order to keep things running."

"Those sound like horrible jobs," Elle said.

"Says the barista."

She pointed at me. "Don't knock it," she said. "Baristas probably know as much as the Council. Aubrey isn't the only thing I wanted to talk to you about."

This couldn't be good.

"I've heard a little about people wanting to change how we relate to the Humdrums," Elle said. "Mostly, people seem to think that we should let the Humdrums know about us, which is… I don't know, I don't think I have an opinion on that yet. But it's also happening the other way around."

"What is?"

"Like, the Humdrums want to know about the Glims. Have you heard of Huntsmen?"

Something about the word sent a chill down my spine. It was the same feeling I got whenever I thought about the Oracle, a sort of intuitive sense that something horrible and super stressful was about to land squarely on my shoulders.

"Like, people who go hunting?" I said. If only I could be so lucky.

"I wish," Elle said. "You could just give them a season every year and be done with it. No, Huntsmen are, like, magic-hunters. Kyle found some stuff online, where groups of these people get together and talk about where they've seen 'magic' lately. Some Hums are starting to get suspicious. And I don't know why."

"Oracle parties," I said.

"What?"

"It's a thing Glims do when they're trying to advocate for blowing up our world all over the Hums," I said. "They go perform magic—"

"In front of one of the Oracle's fountains," Elle interrupted. "I didn't realize that's what they were called."

"They're screwing a lot of things up," I said. "The Council's cracking down hard."

"Good luck with that," Elle muttered. "It's going to get beyond the Council soon. These magic hunters are all Humdrums who've noticed weird stuff going on. And they've started talking to each other—thanks, internet—and they're actually organizing. They're like ghost hunters, except instead of ghosts, they're trying to catch us."

"I haven't heard about them," I said.

"It's not a major thing," Elle said. "There are a couple of small groups here and there, not anything you'd take seriously. The kind of people who go Glim hunting are the kind of people who go Bigfoot hunting. But I catch rumors. You wouldn't believe how much stuff I overhear at Pumpkin."

"I'm glad you do," I said. "Keep an ear out. I don't want to blow this out of proportion or anything, but…"

I trailed off and swirled my tea around my mug. It had cooled, but I didn't bother to re-heat it.

"Something's happening," Elle said. She looked at me, waiting for me to look back and tell her the truth.

The truth was too much, and too complicated. But I nodded.

"Just let me know if you hear anything else," I said. "It could be important."

CHAPTER NINE

Christmas music blared from the gold bells Mom had strung over the kitchen entryway. These were all classic Christmas songs, sung by crooners who sounded like they were trying to seduce us while we worked on dinner. The whole house smelled like spruce branches. For the first time in months, I was happy to be home.

Dad being on his third glass of mulled wine probably had something to do with it. He sat in his office, drinking and doing only he knew what. Mom, Daniel, and I were in the kitchen, up to our elbows in the ingredients for Christmas Eve dinner. Mom twirled her wand with some extra flair over the pan I was working on, and a thin stream of fragrant butter poured from its tip and into the mashed potatoes.

"And a happy new year!" she sang, directly into my ear.

The doorbell rang. A moment later, without anyone having answered it, Mrs. Dann walked in, a giant poinsettia tucked in her curly hair and a cellophane-wrapped loaf of lemon poppy-seed bread in her hand.

Mom hugged her. I smiled and waved. Imogen might be the stupidest person alive, but I still loved her family.

"This is for you," Mrs. Dann said. She tossed the loaf my way. It hovered gently in the air and settled like a feather into my outstretched hand. "Poppy seeds for—"

"For good dreams," I finished with her. Mrs. Dann's poppy-seed bread was a tradition, one that stretched back to the first Christmas after our families had met.

My mom asked how the Danns were doing, and Mrs. Dann asked how we were doing, and I tuned them out while I finished the potatoes and got started on the baked yams. I wasn't nearly as good at cooking enchantments as Mom was, and it took all my focus to heat and soften the yams in their glass dish without turning them into mush.

"Olivia." Mrs. Dann's voice broke into my thoughts. I looked up.

"Sorry?"

"I have a box of your mom's stuff in the car," she said. "Would you come get it before I go?"

I blew on the tip of my wand to cool it and stuck it in my hair.

We went out to the car together. The wind was cold and strong tonight. There was no snow—Portland wasn't big on the white stuff—but it still felt like the holidays. Dazzling Christmas lights covered the old houses on our street, half the buildings competing for the most spectacular flashing displays and the other half trying to prove how understated they were with their wreaths and simple white lights. Behind me, a single white strand of lights lined the edge of our roof.

Mrs. Dann opened the back of her silver minivan. A box was there, loaded with Mom's old silver tea set and a few vases.

"We used these for the school fundraiser months ago and they've been sitting in my entryway ever since," Mrs. Dann said. "I'm happy they're going home!"

"I hadn't even noticed they were gone," I said.

"Well, how often do you use heirlooms in real life?" Mrs. Dann said. She started to lean over and pick up the box, then stopped. She looked at me.

I felt it coming before she spoke.

"How are you and Imogen?" she said, her voice hesitant.

A chilly breeze crept down the back of my neck. I wished I'd put on a jacket. "We're not really talking," I said.

"I gathered that much," she said. "I haven't seen you around lately. But, well, can I ask why? I know she misses you."

A tiny seedling of hope sprouted inside me.

"Did she say that?"

"No," Mrs. Dann said. The seedling drooped. "But I know she does."

I folded my arms, but more against the cold than against her questions. I didn't want to talk about Imogen, but Mrs. Dann had a way of making even prying questions feel natural. She was such a mom that nothing seemed like a secret from her.

"I promise, that's not the case," I said. "She's really upset with me."

"That's too bad," Mrs. Dann said. She eyed me, opened her mouth, and then closed it again.

"We're going off to college soon anyway," I said. "We'll find new friends."

My throat closed up. She patted my arm.

"You know she's been busy, right?" Mrs. Dann said. She tilted her head. I felt her energy reaching out toward me, trying to intuit what I hadn't said.

"Yeah," I said. "She's working with the Oracle."

It wasn't a secret. Everyone at Wishes Fulfilled knew that Imogen Dann had been chosen as the Oracle's protégé. Some people whispered she'd be the Oracle's intern until she left for Institut Glänzen; others thought the Oracle might be training her for even greater things. She'd stopped Proctoring at the Department of Tests & Quests, at any rate.

"I hope you aren't…" Mrs. Dann trailed off and pursed her lips.

"Jealous?" I said.

I could feel the question hovering around her. I wished I could reassure her, but the truth was worse than anything she could be imagining.

"No, I'm not jealous," I said. "I'm happy for her. I hope she finds everything she's ever dreamed of."

I just hoped her dreams weren't about destroying the world Queen Amani worked so hard to protect, and ruining the lives of who knew how many Hums in the process.

"I don't really want to talk about it," I said. "It's Christmas Eve."

"Of course," Mrs. Dann said immediately. "I'm so sorry, honey. Enjoy the evening."

She handed me the box. It was heavier than it looked, but I didn't reach for my wand. It felt nice to be doing something.

"Merry Christmas," she said.

I wished I knew what to do with the sympathy in her eyes.

"You too," I said.

I propped the box against my hip as Mrs. Dann walked around to the driver's seat. As she was about to climb in, a dark blue car pulled up to the curb. It was older, and the sight of it made me smile before I'd realized it.

Lucas climbed out, wrapped in a black coat and blue scarf. I nodded at him.

Mrs. Dann's aura seemed to jerk in surprise. By the time I looked over, her face was smooth and pleasant.

"Lucas!" she said brightly. "What a surprise."

"Mrs. Dann," he said. "How are you?"

Of course. They knew each other from that whole Imogen-stealing-the-guy-I-liked thing. I plastered on a smile and tried to pretend it wasn't awkward.

She said something about everyone being well, then wished us both another cheery "Merry Christmas!" before climbing into the van. I watched her pull out and drive away.

"Get the door for me?" I said.

He was already halfway up the front steps. I edged sideways through the door, careful to not jam my fingers between the box and the doorframe, and carried it into the kitchen. I sent a quick mental image of Lucas ahead.

They got the hint. Mom and Daniel both had their wands hidden by the time we made it into the kitchen. I put the box on the kitchen table. The house felt weirdly quiet. The bells, triggered by the Humdrum shield that covered our property, had stopped playing music before Lucas entered the house.

"Oh, hello, Lucas!" Mom said. She was a shade too enthusiastic. "How are you? It's so nice to see you again!"

"Hi, Mrs. Feye," he said. "Merry Christmas."

"You too. What on earth are you doing here tonight?" She tucked a stray strand of dark hair behind her ear. "Oh, no, I'm sorry. I'm making assumptions. Do you celebrate Christmas?"

"Yeah," he said. He smiled, and Mom relaxed a little. She always got flustered around my Humdrum friends. "My mom's a nurse," Lucas explained. "She's working tonight. We're going to celebrate in a couple days."

"You'll have to stay to dinner here," Mom said.

"That's okay," Lucas said. "I don't want to intrude."

"Nonsense," Mom said.

She glanced at Daniel, who was standing behind the counter with a bowl of whipped cream and nothing to mix it with.

"I think we have things taken care of here," she said. "Olivia, did you finish the potatoes?"

"And got halfway through the yams," I said. "But I think I burned them."

"That's perfectly fine," she said. She dusted her hands off on her apron, which was patterned with tiny dancing gingerbread men. "I can finish up here, if you two want to go hang out."

In other words, it was time to get the Humdrum out of there.

Lucas followed me out of the kitchen, past my dad's open office door, and upstairs. Dad didn't glance up from the book he was reading. I wondered how he'd react when he learned

Mom had invited a Hum for dinner, then decided he was too mellow with wine to care.

I led Lucas to my room. Imogen wasn't allowed to have guys alone with her in her bedroom, but that kind of rule had never come up at the Feye house. There had never been a reason.

"Have a seat," I said. Lucas took the chair by my desk. I sat on the bed.

The plants on my windowsill seemed to be waiting, counting the seconds until one of us spoke. I'd insulated them from the window drafts with a small shielding spell, and their green leaves seemed out of place on such a cold day.

"Sorry your mom had to work," I said.

He shrugged. "I'm used to it. She works a lot of holidays. Everyone else has little kids at home."

"And you're a big kid who doesn't mind celebrating Christmas late."

He grinned. "Everything goes on sale the day after Christmas."

"Mercenary reasons!"

"Basically," he said. "But listen, I actually have something to tell you." He glanced at the door. I'd left it cracked. He lowered his voice. "I ran into Imogen at the hospital."

I leaned forward. My heartbeat seemed to trip over itself. "Is she okay?"

"Yeah, yeah, she's fine," he said quickly. "Sorry, she's not there for herself. She was bringing presents to sick kids."

That didn't seem like the Imogen I'd known the last few months. I felt my eyebrows crinkle into a question.

"She's doing a service project for something called the Rose Galas," Lucas said.

"Oh," I said. "I forgot about that."

He shrugged. I tried to explain.

"They're parties," I said. "Every June, around the time the Humdrums celebrate the annual Rose Festival, the Glimmering world has a celebration, too. They're called the Rose Galas, and it's a series of events that happen throughout the week. It's one of the only times we can really share our world with Humdrum relatives."

"And friends?" he said.

It hadn't occurred to me before now. I grinned back at him. "Yeah, and friends," I said. "Anyone important to us who knows about our world. You're definitely coming with me next year. After I come up with a story about why you know about us, anyway."

It was too easy to lose track of the conversation while I was busy grinning at him.

"At every Gala, a bunch of Glim teenagers are part of what's called the Rose Court," I said. "There's a whole process to apply—you have to submit an essay and plan service projects and stuff. And the rule is that your service project has to serve the world you're not part of. Hum kids serve Glims, and Glims serve Hums."

"Which is why Imogen was at the hospital," Lucas said.

"It's a nice tradition," I said. "It's one of things I think we got right."

"I like it," Lucas said. "Imogen must have really impressed them if she's going to be the Empress."

I frowned. "She can't be the Empress," I said.

He shrugged. "That's what she said."

"You must have heard wrong," I said. "The Rose Empress is always a Humdrum. It's a gesture of respect."

Lucas frowned. He got a tiny dimple on one side of his chin when he frowned. I'd never really noticed it before.

"She definitely said Empress. She said she's a lady-in-waiting now, but that will change in… May?"

"That's when they announce the court," I said. "But that's against all the rules."

But then, Imogen had stopped following the rules. Especially when it came to the Humdrums.

"I hate the Oracle," I said. My voice was soft, and the words felt like they were inviting doom down on my head. But our house was safe. There was no clear water sitting around, and even if there had been, I'd covered my room with a dozen enchantments.

I could be honest here.

And I could be honest with Lucas.

"I wish I knew more about her," he said. He jostled his knee, bouncing the heel of his shoe up and down on my carpet. "I feel like I got sucked into all this stuff, but I'm clueless."

"It's a lot to learn," I said. "I wish I could help, but I don't know much more than you do. The Oracle is a mystery even to us. Queen Amani knows more than the rest, but…"

I trailed off. Lucas scooted his chair a few inches closer to the bed, so he could almost reach out and kick my foot if he'd wanted.

"She hasn't talked to you much lately, has she?"

I shook my head. "I don't know why," I said. "She's probably just busy."

"She should be talking to you, though," Lucas said.

There was nothing to say in response. She *should* be talking to me. There was too much I didn't know and wished I could learn from her. But she was the queen. All I could do was send her updates and hope they were useful.

"This isn't about the Galas, I know that much."

Somehow, it was easier to talk about even Imogen and the Oracle than Amani's silence.

"Imogen wanted to be on the court for the scholarship money, but she's thinking about more than scholarships now."

"She's going to be the next Oracle, isn't she?" Lucas said.

The words made the pit of my stomach crawl. That was the truth I'd been trying to avoid. But there was no way around it: Imogen would be the Oracle's successor. And Queen Amani had probably stopped talking to me because I didn't want to be hers.

"Pretty stupid, huh?" I said.

My phone beeped in my pocket. I reached for it automatically, my body ready for an escape from this line of conversation.

Elle: Aubrey's back. Saw her when I went by to grab my extra house keys.

Elle: P.S. Merry Christmas. You'd think she'd have somewhere to be.

I sent her back a quick *Thanks, Merry Christmas!,* then clicked off the screen. This was my holiday, and I was going to enjoy it come hell or high water or Imogen or Aubrey or the Oracle or Amani or anyone else who wanted to get in the way of my peace of mind.

I stood up. "Dinner's probably almost done," I said. "You sure you can keep pretending to be a regular Humdrum clear through dinner?"

"It's cool, I can play stupid," he said.

"That's not what I meant."

"I know," he said. He smiled, a look that was almost rueful. "It's easy to get jealous of your life, you know?"

"No," I said. "I seriously, seriously don't. Come on, I can smell pumpkin pie."

"Last one downstairs is a Christmas turkey."

"Nice try," I said. "We have ham."

He rolled his eyes at me, then darted past me. I flung myself out the door and raced him down the stairs.

CHAPTER TEN

Music pulsed dully beyond the edges of the silencing bubble and shielding field that surrounded Isabelle and me. It was hard to believe Imogen had practically had to beg me to come to Gilt last year. I'd been here so many times since then that it felt almost homey.

"She was selected as Rose Empress," Isabelle confirmed. "I heard it from a friend on the Rose Galas committee."

Isabelle was so dressed up for New Year's Eve that I barely recognized her. That was good; maybe it'd be a little harder for the Oracle to realize she and I had met up again.

The official story—one I'd mentioned loudly in public a few times when talking to Lucas or anyone at Wishes Fulfilled —was that Isabelle was a hedge witch who'd agreed to mentor me in my gardening pursuits. But I wasn't dumb enough to think that would throw the Oracle off for long, or even at all.

Isabelle ran silver fingernails through her curling, glitter-dusted hair. "It hasn't been announced yet, obviously, but it's happened," she said. "Everyone on the committee agreed."

"How?" I said. "It's hugely offensive for us to just take that role. Rose Empress is for the Humdrums. Period."

"Guess," Isabelle said. She took a sip of her drink—pomegranate soda and black dragon tears, with not a drop of clear liquid in sight.

"Yay, Oracle," I said flatly.

"The Oracle sent a sprite to speak with the committee," Isabelle said. "The sprite told them Imogen was particularly qualified and was expected to be a 'great leader of the Glimmering world,' and that the Oracle strongly recommended she be given the honor this year."

"The Oracle's a moron," I said.

Isabelle glanced nervously around us but didn't say anything.

My phone buzzed. I didn't even have to look to know it was from Lucas.

Lucas: A girl wearing an enormous silver top hat just fell into the punch bowl. The six-inch heels might have had something to do with it.

I laughed and showed the text to Isabelle. Since Lucas couldn't come to Gilt, and since I'd agreed to "chaperone" Daniel here this evening, Lucas had gone to a New Year's party with some friends from school. He'd been texting me updates all night.

Lucas, I was discovering, was a major-league people watcher.

Olivia: A genie lit her hair on fire a couple minutes ago. Not sure if it was an accident.

I hit Send and turned back to Isabelle.

"Is anyone on the committee suspicious?"

"My friend was," Isabelle said. "But he's already got issues with the Oracle."

"Which friend?" I said. "How many people know about this? I get that people are having Oracle parties and I get that the Council is freaking out, but I feel like we're trying to keep secrets that just aren't secret."

I had tried to be discreet. Even so, Daniel and Elle had already known half of what I tried to hide from them.

Isabelle waved. "Geb's unusual," she said. "And by that, I mean he's kind of paranoid. He's a gnome. You know how they are when they come to the surface."

I paused with my glass of pomegranate fizz halfway to my lips.

"You're friends with a gnome?"

She laughed. "Oh, yeah," she said. "I do a lot of work with the soil."

"Yeah, but a gnome?"

No one was friends with gnomes. They lived in tunnels under the city, and they were super not into talking to surface-dwellers. Once in a while you'd hear of a sorcerer collaborating with one, and they were always represented on major councils and committees, but that was strictly business.

I set the glass down and accidentally bumped it against my small plate of appetizers.

"His name is Geb," she said. "I met him a few years ago when I was doing landscaping. We were on this huge project for this ultra-rich Glim prince's garden, and Geb had been contracted to bring in boulders and river rock for the place. I think he did a gravel Zen garden, too." She frowned. "That might have been the leprechaun they brought over from Ireland, actually. I don't remember."

My phone buzzed again.

Lucas: Luis Peralta does the best Yoda impression I've ever heard. File that info away. May come in handy someday.

"So, besides paranoid Geb," I said.

"Besides paranoid Geb, some people know. The kind of people who tend to stay politically active know. The rest of the world is just continuing life as usual behind their safe picket fences."

"I wouldn't have known if Imogen and the Oracle hadn't sucked me into it," I said.

Amani had pulled me in first, of course, but Isabelle still didn't know the depth of my relationship with the queen.

Assuming there was any depth left, seeing as how she'd stopped talking to me.

"I used to be one of those picket-fence people," I said. "I was clueless about our world."

Isabelle tapped her glass with a pointed silver nail. "Glad you got your head in the game," she said.

I looked out across the floor to where Daniel stood, shaking his head in time to the music. His friend Devyn was way more into it, swaying her body and shaking her dreadlocks around whenever the beat got intense.

"It doesn't feel like a game," I said.

My phone buzzed twice in rapid succession.

Lucas: Some guy just tried to sell me weed. I'm 99% sure it was oregano.

Lucas: I'm 95% sure he doesn't know it's oregano.

Someday, I would spend New Year's Eve at a boring Humdrum party. It was going to be awesome.

Olivia: How do YOU know the difference between weed and oregano?

The music changed to a rapid electronic beat. I watched a couple of younger faeries start jumping up and down. Sparks flew from their fingertips into the air.

Lucas: Um, I cook. Dude.

I couldn't keep myself from smiling. Life felt less like it was falling apart when I had a friend in my corner.

"I did some more research on those magic hunters you mentioned," Isabelle said.

"What'd you find out?"

"They're for real," she said. "Not many of them, but the ones that are out there seem dedicated."

"Obviously," I said. When she frowned, I added, "The Humdrums who'd join in on magic-hunting are the ones who are already keeping one eye out for UFOs."

"Turns out people like to make documentaries about folks who look for UFOs," Isabelle said.

I picked up a cracker slathered in salmon spread. "They're trying to document Glims?" I said. A knot tensed in my stomach. "That's a headache waiting to happen."

"Not the Glims," Isabelle said. "The Huntsmen. Some wannabe filmmaker from California is in town, and he's been interviewing them."

The knot loosened.

"Good," I said.

"Better than one of them trying to target us," Isabelle said. "Still not good."

Lucas: Makayla Whatsername from AP English just ate three raw eggs on a dare.

"At this point, I'll take whatever I can get," I said.

Around us, a countdown started. Isabelle raised her drink as the numbers wound down to zero.

"Happy New Year," she said.

I clinked my glass against hers.

"I hope," I muttered, but my words were drowned out as the room burst into cheers around us.

CHAPTER ELEVEN

The door slammed open. Daniel and I winced and stared at each other from our separate armchairs. Our homework, strewn across the coffee table, seemed to ripple in anticipation of Dad's anger.

"That lousy, rotten, Humdrum *rat*," he bellowed from the foyer. "Marigold? Marigold, damn it!"

It would be worse if he had to keep calling her.

"Mom's at the garden store," I shouted across the house. "We ran out of dragon manure."

"What in Morgaine's name do we need with dragon manure?" He swept into the living room like a storm front.

"She's repotting the fire lilies," I said. "She always does that in January."

"God *damn*," he said. He slammed his coat down on the back of the sofa.

Daniel seemed to shrink into his chair.

"Everything okay?" I said.

"No, everything is not okay," Dad said. "Damn that Humdrum *louse*."

I'd never heard Dad call anyone a "louse" before. I'd never heard *anyone* call anyone a "louse" before. It didn't seem like the kind of insult people used in real life.

He stormed across the room, then stormed back, pacing like a lion that might spring on Daniel or me at any moment.

"Goddamn social media," Dad said. "What's wrong with passing notes like kids did in my generation?"

I wanted to point out that the Glim-kid version of "passing notes" was basically the same as texting, only on slips of paper instead of phone screens. Instead, I bit my tongue, then asked, "What happened with social media?"

Daniel widened his eyes at me. He didn't even need to throw an emotion my way. The message was clearly, *Do you want to get yourself killed?*

Dad let out a long sigh and stopped pacing long enough to hit the back of the sofa with the palm of his hand. "It's nothing we can't clean up," he said. "Just another half-wit Humdrum hiding behind a computer and trying to reveal our world.

Not that she's any good at hiding. This one was easy enough to track down."

Definitely a girl, then. My stomach flipped over and sank.

"Problem is, she's got more than a little bit of influence, and this isn't the best time to have Humdrums skulking around the edges of Glim establishments."

"What establishments?" I said.

"Titania knows," Dad said. Talking seemed to deflate him; his voice became milder and slower the more he spoke. "There's a Humdrum girl, you see, and she has a lot of, what do you call them, *stalkers* on social media."

"Followers," I said quietly. He carried on without acknowledging me.

"For some reason—maybe she has a Glim friend or family member who hasn't been careful enough—she thinks she knows something about people who can do magic. Humdrums usually write off people who believe in magic as crazy, but this girl has started talking at the wrong time. You know how busy the Council is."

He shot Daniel and me stern looks to make sure we understood how stressful and important his job was. We both nodded.

"Normally, we'd catch this sort of thing before anyone saw it, but this time, *this* time she posted her nonsense almost a day before we found out. We've been overloaded with other things," he added, like we were about to accuse him of negligence. "Normally, people would think she'd lost her marbles. They'd think she was doing it for the attention. But people are getting less and less careful about hiding our world from the Humdrums."

He glared at Daniel and me, like we had something to do with it.

"People are getting *political* about it," he said. His nose crinkled in distaste. "And there are Humdrums who are getting interested. There are *Huntsmen.*"

He drummed against the back of the sofa some more.

"Magic hunters," he said, like the words tasted bad. "Bunch of goddamn conspiracy theorists thinking they're going to uncover everything we hold dear. They call themselves Huntsmen because they claim they're going to chase away the 'big bad wolf' that's 'plaguing our city.' Mother of Ptolemy."

The word echoed around my head: *Huntsmen.* It was the same one Elle had used. The Huntsman was an Archetype we ran into occasionally at Wishes Fulfilled. He usually played a heroic role in our Stories, but this seemed like bad news.

"At least they got the fairy tale and Archetype thing right," I said.

Again, Daniel shot me a *Shut up now* look. But again, Dad didn't seem to care.

"Bunch of thugs," he said. "Some people can't leave well enough alone."

"But the Council will take care of it, right?" I said.

My fingers itched for my phone. I had to know.

"Yes, the Council will handle it," Dad said. But I caught a faint wave of uncertainty from him. It was a shifting thing that was hard to pin down, like a smell I couldn't quite identify.

Daniel shifted in his chair, tensing his body as if for protection.

"The Council isn't in great shape, is it?" he said.

Dad looked at Daniel, and Daniel froze, like he was waiting for the hammer to fall. But Dad's frown just etched itself deeper into its face.

"No, it's not," he said. "We're not in great shape at all." He ran a hand through his thick hair. "Just hope Queen Amani is able to get things sorted out," he said, but in a lowered voice, as though he was ordering himself around instead of us. "We all need to just hope Her Majesty…"

And then he trailed off. Something about her name took his thoughts elsewhere. I watched as his face grew distant, even tired.

"Has she named an heir yet?" Daniel said.

Dad looked up, startled, like he'd forgotten we were in the room. "An heir?" he said. "No." A line appeared on his forehead that hadn't been there a moment earlier. It was the curse of all faeries: Everything we felt showed up on our faces, sooner or later. "No, she hasn't chosen an heir. I doubt she's had time to try."

He took a deep breath and let it out. The last of the swearing and fighting spirit he'd had when he came through the door seemed to leak out of him.

"I'm going to go work in my office for a while," he said. "Tell your mother I'd like to talk to her when she gets home."

"Sure," Daniel said.

"You got it," I said.

We waited until he was out of the room. Then Daniel openly gaped at me and whispered, "What was that?"

I grabbed my phone.

A few taps and swipes, and PursuitOfVerity's account was up. My gaze ran down the small screen, devouring the words.

You think you're safe, Aubrey's latest post said. *But how can you be safe when you don't know who the enemy is? We all live in a #DarkForest.*

A few hours before that, she'd posted, *They live among us. We can't see the forest for the trees, if you know what I mean. #DarkForest #Huntsmen*

And prior to that, *We're in the #DarkForest. No one knows who surrounds us. Only the #Huntsmen can find them. Only the #Huntsmen can see.*

"What the hell is this?" I muttered. I crossed the room and sat on the floor next to Daniel, so we could talk without our voices carrying to Dad's office. I showed him the texts.

He scrolled down.

"'A bunch of my posts got deleted,'" he read in a low voice. "'They're trying to hide me in a hashtag-Dark Forest. None of us are safe.' Okay, she's crazy."

"I think we're the forest?" I said.

"I think we're the trees," Daniel said. "And I think she's trying way too hard to make these hashtags a thing."

I kept reading. All the posts were cryptic. Then, as I watched, a notification popped up on the screen. She'd posted again. I scrolled up.

A bunch of you let me know my old posts disappeared. They're trying to silence me, she said. If a tree falls in a forest and there's no one to hear, does it make a sound? Read more at my blog. WE WILL NOT BE SILENCED. #DarkForest #Huntsmen #ChopThemDown #Timber

They were just tiny black words on a screen, but they creeped me out.

Chop them down?

I clicked the link to her blog. And there was a post, under a banner of—

"A dark forest," Daniel said dryly. "So insight. Much clever. Wow."

The photo, of looming pine trees under a dark sky, had the words *Follow the #Huntsmen* across it in big white letters.

The post was below.

You've noticed funny things around Portland, it said. *I know you have. You know you have. Let's not lie to each other.*

We have to talk about this.

You want to think they're urban legends.

You want to think that person you know is just unusual. You know who I mean. The one who gives you goosebumps, who makes you feel like something is off, who makes you look over your shoulder just in case.

You want to think the strange things that happen around you are coincidence.

But what if I told you there was more?

What if I told you magic was real?

"What if I stopped trying to scandalize the world with crappy rhetorical questions?" Daniel muttered.

There are people all around you who have powers you can only imagine. There are witches in the world, practitioners of the occult.

They are strong.

They are dangerous.

I know this, because I've been watching them.

A coffee shop I used to visit just disappeared.

That's right.

Gone.

Poof.

People tried to claim it had never been there. The owner, a girl I speak to regularly, insists the business has become a quiet operation selling coffee beans at the Saturday Market. (The stall is Pumpkin Spice. Ask to talk to Elle. Maybe with enough pressure we can get her to tell us the TRUTH.)

I cringed and made a mental note to warn Elle.

I know better than to believe her stories.

People keep going to the café. They're hard to catch, hard to see. But they walk right into a wall where the building used to be, and they disappear.

Why do I care?

Because I'm not the only one to have noticed.

Have you seen strange people around? Have you seen hints of things the way they shouldn't be? Have you felt as if you are in danger when someone different walks by?

Look closer.

You think you're in a city. You are wrong.

We are all in a dark forest, and the trees are closing in.

Join the fight. Become a Huntsman.

The last three lines were underlined. Just beneath them, a notice said, in large, bold letters, *I WILL KEEP POSTING*

THIS EVERY DAY. THEY WILL NOT SILENCE ME.
-VERITY

Aubrey was so, so much more unhinged than I had ever thought possible.

I clicked on the link at the end of her post. It led to a sketchy-looking forum with a black background and stark white letters. And if Aubrey's article had been weird, it was nothing compared to the stuff here.

Daniel was scrolling on his own phone now.

"This guy claims to have seen a hobbit running across the Walmart parking lot," he said. "A hobbit. Like we're in Middle Earth."

"This one saw an Oracle party," I said. "He was with a group of people, and it looks like he's the only one who didn't have a meeting with an Eraser. He remembers. None of his friends do."

"This is a whole community," Daniel said. "This is freaky."

"Isabelle told me about these guys," I said. I scanned down an all-caps post from someone who claimed an elf girl had cheated on him. It ended with the sentence *NEVER TRUST A DARKTREE.* "Some guy's in Portland filming a documentary on them."

Daniel sat up. "Seriously? Does Dad know?"

"Yeah, because I totally run to Dad with all my secret Isabelle meetings," I said

"How'd you meet her anyway?" he said.

I bit the inside of my cheek. *I was turned into a newt!,* said one of the forum headlines.

"It's kind of a long story."

"Too bad. I'd love to hear it except I'm super interested in this history homework." He picked up the history book he'd abandoned on his lap and dropped it on the floor. I threw out a hand and muffled the thump it made before Dad could hear.

"You really want to know?"

He nodded. For once, he didn't seem like he was being sarcastic. I twisted so I could rest my elbow against his chair and look up at him.

"This needs to be kept secret."

"Obviously."

"No, I mean, like, *secret,*" I said. "You can't tell anyone. Not Devyn, not anyone."

He held out his pinkie. I raised my eyebrow, but he pushed the finger toward me.

I hooked his pinkie with mine. An instant later, the rush of magic flowed between us, sealing his promise not to tell.

"Thanks," I said.

He waved me off. "So?" he said.

I let out a long breath. The words fought against leaving my lips, but I forced them out.

"Queen Amani asked me to be her heir," I said.

I waited for the usual Daniel response—a shrug, or an eye roll, or an "I know."

Instead, his mouth dropped open.

"What?" he whispered.

"Yeah."

"No, seriously, *what?*"

"Seriously, Queen Amani asked me to be her heir. I still have no clue why. She saw me in a divination and somehow thought that was a good enough reason."

"She's braver than I am," Daniel said.

"Well, obviously. She's the Faerie Queen. So I said no, obviously, and—"

"You said *what?*"

"This isn't going to work if I have to repeat everything seventeen times," I said.

Inside, though, I felt instantly warm and like somehow, suddenly, I wasn't alone. It was such a relief to tell, and such a relief to feel like my own shock and confusion had been justified.

It was crazy. The whole thing, from start to finish, was nuts.

And Daniel got it.

"I said no," I said again. "And then, a while later, Imogen started going out with a guy I like."

"Lucas," Daniel said.

"It doesn't matter."

"No, it's, like, very obviously Lucas," Daniel said. "Go on."

"Whatever," I said. "So Imogen and I kind of got in a fight, and by the time I was finally ready to make up with her, she didn't want anything to do with me. And later, come to find out, it's because the Oracle told her that the Faerie Queen had picked me."

"You didn't tell Imogen about the queen?"

His face was a condemnation. The old, familiar heavy feeling in my stomach reminded me that it was still there.

"I know, I suck," I said. "I didn't think I was supposed to. It was stupid. Anyway, the Oracle told Imogen. And Imogen was super upset, and she... I don't know."

It was hard to explain what had happened that night. I still couldn't wrap my mind—or my heart—around it.

"She chose the Oracle," I said, finally. "I'm like ninety percent sure the Oracle had enchanted her. She went into the Fountain, and I've barely seen her since. And the Oracle was creepy about it. And then Isabelle showed up because the Oracle screwed her over, too."

"And now you're trying to topple the second most powerful figure in the universe," Daniel said.

He didn't bother to hide the admiration in his voice. It was stupid to be so flattered by my little brother's attention, but the warm feeling settled inside like it was there to stay a while.

"Liv?" Daniel said. "That's badass."

"It kind of is," I said.

"I mean, you're going to die," he said. "You're absolutely, totally going to die. Or at least you're going to get cursed or something. But good for you."

"Um, thanks?" I said.

My phone buzzed. It was just a text from Mom, saying she'd be home in ten minutes and to turn the oven on to preheat. But I must have hit the Back button, because the screen with Aubrey's blog on it had reloaded. A new, short post was there.

The week after Portland's Rose Festival, a witch will perform a terrible spell, it said. *The magic-users don't want us here. This is REAL MAGIC. The spell will terrorize and even kill anyone THEY don't think "belongs."*

The trees are closing in.

The Huntsmen are all that can save us now.

Grab an ax. Join the fight.

Daniel let out a low whistle. "Yikes," he said. "She's like a serial killer. And she's on a witch hunt. Literally."

The hundreds of posts in the forum flitted through my mind. They'd all talked about witches and ghosts and aliens, mixing up things that belonged to our world and things that belonged only to their imaginations into one frenzied mess.

"She's just a girl looking for drama and a way to feel special," I said. "The trouble is, she's not alone."

CHAPTER TWELVE

"I overheard some Hums talking about the Huntsmen on my way to work," I whispered. Behind the walls of my cubicle, I could hear the voices of the other godmothers, raised and talking fast. "I tagged them with a spell and sent some Erasers after them as soon as I got into work. I'll let you know if I hear anything else of interest. I hope you're doing okay."

I paused, trying to decide if I should say more. But what else could I say? I didn't even know if Amani was listening anymore. I shoved the silver ring back beneath my shirt. The chain dug against my neck and I considered taking the whole thing off and dropping it in the garbage. Instead, I pushed away from my desk and stepped out of my cubicle.

"Mirror her back and let her know we're going to have to put off her ball for a couple weeks," Aster said to her assistant, a new intern named Megan who looked terrified by everything that was happening. She nodded, glanced at me with her big brown eyes, and disappeared into her cubicle.

I went over to the water cooler, pulled my wand out of my hair, and waved a couple tight spirals over my palm. A silver cup formed in my hand with a tiny copper leaf garland twining its way around the base. I filled the cup. I'd thrown about twenty enchantments on the cooler water to keep the Oracle out, but even so, there was no telling how many eyes or allies she had in Wishes Fulfilled.

I wished I could warn the others. But I couldn't, not without bringing Amani into it or outing myself as being way too involved. Even so, it was impossible to avoid the gossip: The Oracle had been approached by a group of activists who wanted to see the Glimmering world come into the open. The Queen had told the Council to stop accepting assignments from the Oracle until further notice. The local Glim news station had tried to interview a Fountain sprite and been met only with a terse "No comment."

Around here, everyone thought the gossip was only gossip. The Oracle was still in charge. She still approved our trickiest cases and dispensed the coins that rewarded us for the Stories we resolved. I didn't know what my coworkers thought privately, but none of us were foolish enough to say anything against her. Especially not with Lorinda sweeping around, constantly ranting about "Our poor Oracle, being harassed by these agitators!"

"It looks like a few of us are getting moved off our cases," Aster said. I jumped; I hadn't heard her come up beside me. She was a tall, lanky faerie with blond hair, thin lips, and the kind of good skin that suggested—accurately—that she was an outdoorsy kind of person who went jogging for fun. "Have you heard anything from Tabitha?"

"I've barely seen Tabitha," I said. "She's been locked up with Lorinda all morning."

"That's not surprising," Aster said. "Sounds like entire teams of us are being reassigned to keep an eye on this PursuitOfVerity person."

"Better you than me," I said.

"You might get assigned," Aster said.

I shook my head and took a drink. The water felt cool all the way down.

"Lorinda said I'm too big a liability," I said. "I know PursuitOfVerity."

Suspicion narrowed Aster's eyes. "You're friends?"

"Not in a thousand years," I said. "She's awful. But she knows who I am, and she's seen me at the Pumpkin Spice stall."

"That's too bad," Aster said. "We could have used an inside person."

"I don't know why we can't just wipe her memory," I said.

Maybelle, another younger godmother with curling brown hair and a pleasant face, sidled up to us under pretense of getting a drink.

"She's got enchantments on her," Maybelle said.

I turned to frown at her, but Aster nodded.

"Lorinda mentioned it this morning before you got in," Aster said. "She's got at least one Glim on her side. Probably more."

"Verity's goals dovetail nicely with all those people who have been pressuring the Oracle," Maybelle said. "They all want the Glim world exposed, just for different reasons."

"I don't know what good they think will come out of it," Aster said. Her voice rose. "The Glims want us exposed because they want be in charge, and the Hums want us exposed so they can get rid of us. Ugh, people are awful."

She shook her hands like she was trying to fling the stupidity of humanity and Glimkind off of her, then stalked back to her desk.

Maybelle offered me an encouraging smile, then took her drink back to her cubicle. Within seconds, one of the godfathers, Curtis, had stopped by to distract her into another round of gossip and speculation.

I refilled my water and took it back to my cubicle.

A memo was on my desk, written on my notepad. I watched as the final silver letters wrote themselves and Lorinda's name appeared on the bottom with a flourish.

Aster, Seth, Tabitha, and Olivia, please come to my office at 11, the note said.

It was 10:45. I refreshed my browser. The computer screen flashed, bringing up new articles, blog posts, tweets, campaigns, and videos. I had a news alert set to anything tagged *#Dark-Forest* or *#Huntsmen,* and the new posts had been coming in thick and fast all morning.

There was no reason it should have gone viral this quickly. Even I, who knew it was all true, thought Aubrey came across as a conspiracy theorist—so why were the Humdrums listening to her?

Fringe Group Claims Kidnapped Toddler Victim of Witches, a headline read. The toddler still hadn't been found, though the rumor mill churned with claims that the little girl's aunt, a muse who sympathized with the groups pressuring the Oracle, had taken her from her Humdrum father to fully immerse her in the Glimmering world.

The aunt had to be a powerful muse, though. No one should be able to hide a Humdrum toddler from the legions of skilled Glims looking for her.

Unless, of course, the aunt had a powerful friend.

I could practically feel the Oracle watching us through the windows. Her Fountain across the street sat far too close for my comfort.

A chatty Humdrum news article claimed *So-Called "Magic Hunters" Are Keeping Portland Weird,* and a popular blog on the JinxNet featured *Our Panelists Sound Off on #DarkForest.* I skimmed through the article. Most of the panelists hated the hashtag—no surprise there. A few people in favor of exposing us to the Humdrums suggested fighting back with *#EnchantedForest,* a hashtag meant to show that the Glim world was delightful and not scary at all.

It was stupid, all of it.

The Council could do nothing against a barrage like this. They could only glamour so many memories in a day, and the internet was stronger than all of us.

Portland was full of Glims, but the internet wasn't confined to Portland. It wasn't confined to the other cities with large Glim populations, either. The internet was for everyone, everywhere, all the time, and our magic couldn't keep up. Even hacking into Aubrey's account and glamouring or deleting her posts had stopped working. Sometime in the last few days, someone had thrown some seriously good electronic magic up to protect her pages.

The memo on my desk suddenly caught fire, the lilac flames letting me know I was late.

Lorinda's office walls were a rich shade of purple over mahogany wainscoting. Photos of her posing with satisfied clients dotted the walls, each in a flower-laden silver frame. The newest photo was of a Cinderella archetype who'd just married into actual English aristocracy. She waved from her new manor in the engagement portrait. The Cinderella looked almost as pleased as Lorinda had the day the case closed.

Aster was already there, sitting in one of the amethyst-colored chairs. I settled next to her. The silver clock on Lorinda's desk ticked the seconds by, each click of the second hand a sharp break in the silence.

"Lorinda went to the bathroom," Aster said. "She'll be back in a minute."

"Oh," I said.

The clock kept ticking.

Tabitha and Seth came in next. Tabitha waved Seth to take the last open seat. She leaned against the wall, skeletal in a black fringed shawl, and swiped her long-nailed thumb back and forth on her phone. Seth drew his knees together, bounced them, and then held onto them to keep himself still.

I liked Seth. He was a tall, awkward-looking guy with sandy hair and long fingers. He'd been working at Wishes Fulfilled a little longer than I had, but we'd never had more than a couple of conversations. I'd heard gossip that before becoming a godparent, he'd been an Eraser.

Lorinda bustled in. Her suit was mint green today. It clashed horribly with the walls.

Tabitha closed the door behind her.

"Are you all aware of the situation?" Lorinda said, looking at each of us in turn.

It was impossible not to be. We nodded.

Lorinda sat down behind the desk and leaned toward us, resting her elbows on a messy pile of papers on the polished desk surface. "Then you're aware we at Godparenting Services are working with the Office of Cross-Cultural Relations and the Department of Tests & Quests to keep surveillance teams on Ms. Aubrey Weston twenty-four/seven."

"Surveillance teams consist of two staff members," Tabitha said. "Four-hour shifts, to keep everyone sharp."

"We haven't been able to do much," Lorinda said. "Some of our teams have been able to use charms to distract Miss Weston, keeping her from her online vendetta, but she clearly has some powerful magical aid and a great deal of motivation to stick to her distasteful task." Lorinda's nose wrinkled. "We have our best web witches on the case, but hacking into her accounts and deleting her posts clearly isn't a sustainable solution."

Aster raised a hand. "I'm sorry to interrupt," she said. "But I'm a little lost. Can't we just let this play out? This has escalated quickly and I'm not sure why everyone's taking it so seriously at this point. She's just another lunatic on the internet—and that describes half the internet."

Seth shook his head and opened his mouth, but Lorinda replied first.

"She's gaining traction faster than any of us could have anticipated," Lorinda said. "We haven't seen a political movement like the one surrounding the Oracle take off so quickly in a long time. Miss Weston seems to be stoking the Humdrum side of that fire. Due to these *deeply* misguided Glim activists, many Humdrums are more suspicious of our presence than any of us would like, and they're inclined to follow her. There are *blogs*."

"They're getting onboard with this Huntsmen thing," Tabitha said. "She's got people following her online. They've nicknamed her 'Queen of the Forest.'" Her jaw hardened.

So did mine. That was one of Queen Amani's many titles.

"There's nothing humans like more than joining a mob," Aster said. The contempt practically dripped off her voice.

"She's crazy," I said.

All eyes turned on me.

"I know her," I said. I glanced around, aware of their eyes on me. "In case anyone hadn't heard, I'm friends with her ex, so we've met a couple of times. She's crazy. She likes... I don't know how to explain it."

I glanced around. No one read my mind. I pressed on.

"Aubrey likes to be special," I said. "If this makes her feel like she knows something no one else does, she's not going to let it go. She likes making people follow her and share her opinions."

I remembered, with painful clarity, what it had been like to go prom dress shopping with her. Every comment had been calculated to let me know that she was gorgeous and I was a tasteless idiot with big hips who should buy only the dress she finally approved.

I made a mental note to kick Lucas for ever going out with her.

I still hadn't told him about any of this. There hadn't been time. I mentally made another note to catch him up.

"All the more reason we need to address this problem now, before it gets completely out of control," Lorinda said. She clucked her tongue. "If I'd told myself a year ago that I'd be expending all this effort over a Humdrum teenager, I'd never have believed myself."

"Have you asked the Oracle for help?" Seth said.

Lorinda waved a hand. "She has her own problems," she said. She pursed her lips and shifted in her seat.

Lorinda loved the Oracle. She thought they had a "special relationship."

If only she knew.

I wished Amani would hurry up and tell people already. Even if she wouldn't or couldn't do that, I wished she'd hurry up and at least talk to me. I didn't mind keeping secrets, but I *did* mind not knowing what was going on.

"We're going to try to handle this on our own first," Lorinda said. "We are, of course, working closely with the Grand Council of Magical Beings. Olivia's father is overseeing our work."

She gave me a significant, deferential nod. I resisted the urge to throw her the world's most sarcastic double thumbs-up.

"And the Council's given us a job," Tabitha said.

"In addition to our surveillance work," Lorinda said. "We learned this morning that a documentary filmmaker will be interviewing Miss Weston."

I wished she'd stop calling her *Miss Weston.* A more appropriate name, like *that idiot,* would have been plenty.

"The interview takes place this evening," Lorinda said. "I'm sending all three of you to her house before the filmmaker arrives."

"I thought Olivia couldn't work with Aubrey," Aster said. She glanced over at me.

"Not until now, no," Lorinda said. She clasped her hands together on the desk. "But the time has come for more direct measures than simple surveillance, and Olivia is perhaps the best one to get the three of you in the door."

And then she laid out the plan. Aster, Seth, and I would go to Aubrey's house. We'd knock on her door, me visible and Aster and Seth glamoured so that she couldn't see them.

"The enchantments on her property are strong," Lorinda explained. "However, we believe they're conventional."

"Meaning we can get in if we're invited," Aster said.

Lorinda tapped her nose.

"Once inside, you, Olivia, will talk Aubrey into taking you to her room, or somewhere else with some privacy. You'll cast a spell to keep her family and any friends away so Aster and Seth can get to work. Seth—"

"I'll Erase," Seth said.

"Not all her memories," Tabitha said. "Just enough that she can't quite connect the pieces."

"Aster will provide security," Lorinda said.

I glanced over at Aster. "Security" wasn't the first word that came to mind when I looked at her, but I knew better than to judge by appearances. Aster was a hell of a faerie.

"The Glims who are helping her will probably be close by," Seth said.

Aster leaned back in her seat. "I can handle her."

"We don't think any of them are actually with her right now," Tabitha said. "Whoever they are, whatever help they provide is in the form of enchanting the property and keeping her posts online."

Seth cut in. "You still don't know who they are?"

"We have a few names," Lorinda said. "But not nearly enough."

Once Seth had done his work, he and Aster would switch places. Together, while I stood guard and alerted them to trouble, Aster would enchant Aubrey, planting new memories and loading her with jinxes that would make her seem completely off her rocker when the filmmaker came by.

"And then he'll broadcast the message that Aubrey can't be trusted," Lorinda finished. She smiled, though the expression looked stretched. "In the end, he and Miss Weston will do all our work for us."

CHAPTER THIRTEEN

I hated traveling by pixie dust.

It wasn't like flying on a carpet. The pixie dust acted like helium, lifting my body into the air but giving me only about half the control I wanted.

The rooftop garden over Wishes Fulfilled seemed to sway beneath me. Overgrown branches tangled together. They were brown and damp in the light January rain, jumbled in a way that made my stomach shift. I looked up, but that only made the dizzy feeling worse.

Aster pulled her wand out of her inside jacket pocket.

"Try this," she said.

She hovered gracefully a few inches above me, as relaxed in the air as if she'd been floating in a pool. A green fleece beanie held down her pale hair. She pointed the wand to her left. A stream of bubbles shot from its tip, and she drifted to the right.

"Bubbles?" I said. "Seriously?"

My wand had been holding my messy bun together on the back of my head. I tapped its handle, shot some magic into my hair so it would stay, and pulled my wand out.

"Bubbles are gentle," Aster said. "You could try straight air but I don't think you'd like it."

"I'll take your word for it," I said.

I focused my energy on where my fingers met the handle of my wand. The smooth silver seemed to pulse beneath my fingertips, and a stream of small bubbles blew from the tip. I drifted a few inches to the right.

"We need to get moving," Seth said. He floated up alongside us like it was nothing.

"Cool your jets," Aster said. She bumped his shoulder with hers. "Olivia, just follow behind us, okay? If you need help, holler."

"Thanks," I said. I shot a stream of bubbles toward the ground and floated a few more inches up.

A few feet later, the Glimmering roads shimmered into view. The traffic here was shielded from Hums and Glims alike by powerful enchantments. But above the glamour line, three thin rainbow roads were fully visible, stacked on top of each other like a triple-decker bridge.

Rush hour was over, and the usual mad crush of carpets and carriages had slowed to just a few vehicles. We merged onto the lowest road, which was reserved for pixie dust, enchanted bicycles, and other modes of faster-than-walking but slower-than-driving transportation. Above my head, a golden carriage being drawn by two white horses clopped past us.

I shot a jet of bubbles behind me and pulsed forward.

"Try to stay on the road," Aster said, as the next jet took me way too far to the left. I wouldn't fall down into Humdrum traffic—which was always a big risk on these roads, second only to being run over by a Glim on the wrong level—but I tried to straighten anyway.

After a while, it started to make sense. Shoot bubbles, pulse forward, and shoot again. Soon I was skimming along with Aster and Seth. The sun had just set behind the gray wall of clouds, and I watched as the lights of the city twinkled on below us. The rainbows gave off their own faint light as their colors stretched into the distance.

A large frog in a tricorn hat passed on my left, riding a penny-farthing bicycle that was much too big for him. I tried not to stare.

I spent the entire journey mentally rehearsing what I was going to say. I didn't have long. Aubrey lived in an artsy district not too far from downtown. When we were still a few blocks away, Seth caught my eye and shone a laser light down onto the roof of a dark green Victorian home. From the rainbow, its most prominent features were the russet-colored shingles and the weather vane that topped a turret.

Seth surveyed the neighborhood and nodded that the coast was clear. Anyone stepping off the rainbow was protected by a glamour, of course, but it was better to be careful. Aster had calculated the amount of pixie dust exactly, and I felt the last bits wear off the moment my foot touched the ground.

It was impossible to overstate how much I wanted to be somewhere else. Filing papers and even taking on actual cases at Wishes Fulfilled was one thing. Sneaking into my least favorite person's house in order to mess with her brain was something else entirely.

But what choice did I have? We had to get in, and my connection with Aubrey was the easiest way. She seemed capable of doing more damage than I would have thought possible. I might not be crazy about the Glimmering world, but I did care about some of the people in it, and I wanted them to stay safe and hidden.

Landscaped flower beds marched around the front porch. A small white dog sat on the top step, watching the neighborhood while sheltered from the light sprinkling rain.

Aster and Seth followed me up the walkway to the house, their invisibility glamours securely in place. The dog jumped up. Its tail began wagging wildly.

My stomach flipped over.

How had I gotten here?

It seemed like I'd done nothing but ask myself that question for a year. The dog sniffed around Aster's ankles as I rang the doorbell.

I felt the family inside before anyone came to the door. A mom, appearance-conscious and annoyed; a dad, good at concentrating but not good at seeing what went on around him; the nastiness that was Aubrey; and two boys, probably teenagers, who mostly wanted to be left alone. And then footsteps, and the sound of a muffled voice.

Aubrey's mom opened the door. She shared Aubrey's same halo of auburn hair and big eyes. Her makeup was polished, her eyebrows perfectly plucked, and she wore a bead-studded green blouse and large gold-faced watch. I smiled at her and wished I'd thought to put on a glamour that would make me come across as even halfway put-together.

"Hi," I said, forcing confidence into my voice. "Is Aubrey home?"

The woman smiled, and I had no idea whether it was genuine or not. "She is," she said. "Who can I tell her is calling?"

"My name's Olivia," I said.

She waited, like she expected more details, but I pressed my lips together. She brushed her hands on her jeans and opened the door wider.

"Come in and I'll go fetch her," she said with another big, unclear smile.

I shuffled inside, with Aster and Seth close behind. The dog scooted in, too. The tag on its collar jingled as it stepped inside. Aubrey's mom gave it a critical look, as if it should have wiped its paws first, but didn't say anything.

The foyer was gorgeous, with original details carefully restored. I studied the pattern of the rug while Aubrey's mom jogged up the intricately carved wooden stairs. Aster and Seth stood motionless beside me. Their invisibility glamour would prevent anyone from hearing them move or speak, too, but I got the feeling they didn't want to push their luck.

It was easy to get absorbed in the architecture, and I was almost surprised when I heard footsteps and looked up to see Aubrey coming down the stairs.

The second she registered that it was me, her gaze intensified like she was trying to light me on fire. Her smile was much too big.

"Hi," she said, too enthusiastic. Everything about her was too much. "Wow, what a surprise."

"Sorry to just show up like this," I said.

"No, no, that's totally okay." She ran a hand through her hair, fluffing it into an even bigger cloud. "How are you doing? What's up?"

The lie sprang up easily. "I wanted to talk to you about Lucas," I said. "Could we maybe go somewhere private?"

She kept staring and smiling. She didn't know whether to believe me. On the one hand, Lucas was the only thing we had in common, and I had no doubt she'd be thrilled at the opportunity to reiterate how much *happier* she was dating college guys. On the other, she knew. I could feel her certainty that I was one of them, and that I was here about dark forests and Huntsmen and everything else she'd conjured up. She'd seen me at the Pumpkin Spice stall before, and the timing was too convenient.

A weird feeling tingled up my spine, a sense that we were being watched.

"Sure," she said slowly. "Yeah. Come on up to my room. I don't have long. A, um, friend is dropping by."

I followed her up the stairs with Aster and Seth right behind. My feet sank into the emerald plush runner carpet that snaked up them. Her house smelled old, like polished wood and dusty curtains and orange peel potpourri. A family portrait smiled down at me, in which Aubrey's normally wild hair had been swept into a French twist.

Aubrey paused at the top of the stairs.

"He's not still dating Imogen, is he?" she asked. "I thought they broke up."

It was impossible how much to describe I didn't want to actually have this conversation with my coworkers present.

"They did," I said. "But I think they're going to get back together. She's been texting him and I think he might go for it. Except I don't know if it's a good idea."

She eyed me up and down. The gaze was just long enough to make sure that I knew she was judging me. Even though I also knew she was a horrible person who had no right to judge me, I still felt abruptly self-conscious about my scuffed tennis shoes and faded shirt. I resisted the urge to fold my arms across my chest.

"He's my ex," she said.

"I know," I said.

"So why are you talking to me?" she said. "Lucas is not part of my life anymore."

She pushed a door open. It led to a dark green-walled room at the front of the house, and I could only assume it was hers. An actual four-poster bed stood against one wall, its majestic shape not completely softened by its green-and-gold brocade canopy.

"Nice room," I said.

"Furniture's antique," she said offhandedly. "It's been with the house for, like, decades."

Of course it had.

I stepped further into the room to make sure Seth and Aster could get in behind me. I heard the small tap of an elbow hitting the old wooden door and instantly put my hand on the door to shut it. Aubrey's eyebrows drew together, but she didn't say anything.

Once the door was closed, I turned to face her.

The hair on the back of my neck prickled.

It was back, the feeling of being watched by someone who wasn't here. It was stronger this time. I felt goosebumps rise on my arms under my jacket.

There was no clear water in this room. The Oracle shouldn't be able to see us.

I felt a hand on my shoulder. Aster leaned down and said softly in my ear, "I feel it too."

I couldn't respond, so I sent her a wave of gratitude. She squeezed my shoulder.

"I came to talk to you because I think Lucas still has feelings for you," I said. Silently, I hoped I was telling a lie. I had never followed up with him on that conversation where he'd said she wanted to get back together. I hadn't been able to bring myself to ask.

Aubrey's eyebrows went up.

Aster and Seth crept around me. I had to keep her talking while they worked on her memories.

"I think Imogen was just a rebound, you know?" I said.

"Well, obviously," Aubrey said.

She *obviously* thought I was an idiot.

I felt the same about her, but she didn't need to know that right this second.

Aster stalked to the window to keep guard. Seth pulled out his wand.

"I've been talking to both of them, and Imogen really cares about him," I lied.

Aubrey's eyes narrowed. "I thought you and Imogen weren't talking. You know, after she freaked out at you at her sister's wedding."

I wanted to take whichever high school numbskulls were running the rumor mill and poke them in the eye with my wand.

"We made up," I said, forcing a sickly sweet smile onto my face. "She was just having a hard couple of weeks, but we're totally over it."

"That's good, I guess," Aubrey said.

"Anyway," I said, pointedly. "Imogen wanting to get back with Lucas would be great, you know, if he really cared about her back. But I don't think he does, and I don't want her to get involved with him if it's just going to end badly. And I was wondering, I mean, has he been talking to you or anything?"

She laughed, not in a nice way.

"Um, no," she said. "That ship has sailed. I have moved on. I have moved so on."

"Curse it," Aster hissed. She put her hands on the window frame and leaned in so closely her nose almost touched the antique glass. "Guys, we have a visitor."

Seth's forehead tensed in concentration. "Filmmaker?" he said.

"No," Aster said. "No, I have no idea who this is. But he doesn't look like he was invited. Olivia, I need this window open."

I didn't want to ask Aubrey to open it. She was already suspicious, and if anything went wrong and Aster's glamour was compromised, things were going to go downhill quickly. But there were other rooms in the house.

"Sorry to change the topic," I said. "But, um, can I use your bathroom?"

She judged me harder. This time, I didn't care.

"Sure," she said, like this was the most inconvenient thing anyone had ever asked her. She walked to the door and held it open. "Two doors down that way," she said, pointing down the hall away from the stairs.

We were in luck. It was at the front of the house, too. I made a beeline for it. Aster and Seth darted to follow.

Once inside the elegant bathroom, I threw up a sound bubble.

"What's going on?" I said.

Aster was already tugging the window open. The wood creaked in protest.

"Pssst," she said. She stuck her head out. Thankfully, the house was too old to have window screens. After a second of staring intently to the left, she waved her wand vaguely at herself. The glamour that had kept her and Seth concealed fizzled and faded. "You," she hissed. "Yes, *you.*"

I moved in next to her. Seth hovered behind us, his wand out and pointed at the door.

On the side of the house, clinging like a lizard, was a teenage faerie. A fire faerie, judging by his aura. Over my glasses, I could see flames licking up the top of his head, mixed in with his unruly white-blond hair. His skin looked hot and sparks jumped out of his fingertips every few seconds, like his long, skinny fingers were wires with shorts in them.

"You can see me?" he said.

Aster gave him a look that could freeze a bonfire.

"Obviously," she said flatly.

His face fell.

"Who are you?" he said.

"How about you tell first, since you're the one attempting a break-in?" Aster said.

"This is PursuitOfVerity's house, right?" he said. Panic flitted across his features. "I double-checked."

"Not what I asked," Aster said.

I ducked under Aster's arm. "Yes, this is her house," I said. "Who are you?"

"My name's Aidan," he said. "I'm here to deal with her."

I stared at him.

So did Aster. Across the bathroom, Seth snorted.

"As authorized by whom, exactly?" Aster said.

He crept along the side of the house, fingers clinging to the siding. Over my glasses, I could see the small white swirls of magic that glowed at each fingertip and made him stick like a gecko.

"I live in the neighborhood," he said.

Aster let out a hissing noise that I wasn't sure was voluntary. "So you're just, what, going to murder her?"

"No!" he said. His thin face widened in horror. "I'm not going to kill her. I'm just going to incapacitate her and turn her over to the Faerie Queen."

"Oh, Titania," Aster said, not bothering to keep her voice down.

Aidan crept over some more. He was right outside Aubrey's window now.

We needed to wrap this up.

"Aidan?" I said. "We're here for the same reason. The Grand Council on Magical Beings sent us. We've got things under control here."

"I need to see this through," Aidan said. "This is my chance to be a Hero."

My entire body cringed.

"Maybe you can be a Hero a different day," I said. "Maybe on something that's less, I don't know, really high stakes. Can you just let us do this, please?"

His skin flushed, not pink, but red—a deep, orangey red that made him look like he was about to explode. I lowered my glasses down the bridge of my nose. The flames licking around his head had engulfed his entire body, making him look like a human bonfire.

"It's okay, Aidan," I said. "I know you were hoping this was going to turn out."

I stretched my energy toward him, trying to get a sense for what he was feeling and how I could redirect those emotions.

But Aster was having none of it.

"Get off this house, now," she ordered. "We're here on official business. You're obstructing us. Do we need to call law enforcement?"

The flames intensified.

"Aster," I muttered.

"No, this is ridiculous," she said. "We don't need a teenager around here screwing things up. No offense," she added. "I don't mind having *you* around. But *you* know what you're doing."

"Then let me handle it," I said.

"We can't stay in here all evening," Seth said. "Documentary guy arrives any second."

I stretched a hand out toward Aidan. "Why don't you come in and we can talk?" I said. "Maybe we can find a way for you to help us."

The fire around him settled as though it had been blown into submission by a strong breeze. Aidan's sparking blue eyes met mine through the lingering flames. He nodded, just barely, and swung out a hand to move toward us. With every inch, the tension in my spine relaxed.

"Almost there," I said under my breath. I could practically feel Aubrey in the next room, more suspicious and annoyed with every second I stayed in the bathroom.

"Come on," Aster muttered.

Aidan's fingers were close enough that I could almost touch them. Behind me, Aster's patience snapped.

She turned away from the window. Under her breath, she muttered, "Seth, deal with him. He is not staying to help."

It wasn't far enough under her breath. A hot wave of panic engulfed me, so strongly that I had to close my eyes against the emotion and hold onto the windowsill for balance. An instant later, I sprang back into action.

"She didn't mean it," I said, reaching out toward him. "I promise, I won't let them—"

Aidan yelped as though he'd been burned. A flaming ball of fire formed in his palm almost too quickly to see, and then it flew toward us. I screamed and ducked as the ball roared through the window and over my head. I pointed my wand at it in one reflexive move. The ball fizzled into nothing an instant before it hit the closed bathroom door.

"What is wrong with you?" I shouted at Aster. The ball of silence around us shimmered; the magic that had held the fire-ball together had cracked it.

Seth spun around both of us and shot a spell out the window at Aidan. The kid shouted, but I could feel that he hadn't been hurt.

"I don't—"

I threw out a hand. The silence solidified around us, stifling Aster's words before they could go on. Seth shot another spell out the window before I hissed at him to stop.

A muffled sound came from the hall. Then, Aubrey's voice.

"Are you okay in there?" she said.

The skepticism dripped off her voice.

We all held still, each trembling hand or fluttering eyelash seeming like an enormous gesture. I felt as though people could hear our breathing for miles.

"I'm fine," I said, in a strained voice. "I'll be a minute. Sorry. Ate some bad Mexican food."

Nothing. Then, sounding thoroughly grossed-out, she said, "O-*kay*, then."

Her footsteps receded.

No more fireballs had come whizzing over my head, and I let myself relax. Behind me, I could still feel Aidan, tense and ready to jump from spark to inferno.

And then, with no warning, his energy shifted again. This time, it was as though all those flames had been frozen.

Seth and Aster looked at each other, then at me. We threw ourselves toward the window.

Aidan clung, absolutely still, onto the side of the building. His wide blue eyes were fixed on a figure below. At the end of Aubrey's walkway, a man with an overgrown beard stood. He caught my eye and a slow smile crept across his face. In his hands, pointed directly at us, was a camera phone.

Aster swore. In a split second of frantic wand-waving, she glamoured Aidan into invisibility, threw the same glamour over Seth and herself, and removed the sound bubble.

I didn't need to be told.

We tumbled into the hallway, me holding onto my stomach and Seth and Aster tense behind me. I didn't know about Aidan. I didn't care.

I stopped in Aubrey's doorway.

"Sorry," I said. "I think I'm sick."

Behind me, Seth conjured up a gurgling noise aimed in my general direction. Aubrey's nose crinkled.

"Food poisoning, maybe," I said. "I think your friend is here. Can we talk about Lucas later? Sorry to bother you."

"I'll walk you out," she said, like she wanted to make sure I made it.

The door opened onto the man, still staring at the end of the walkway. He'd put his phone down, but his eyes were fixed on the house like he expected a miracle.

"Bye," I said.

The white dog had followed us to the door. It looked up at Seth and wagged its tail. A shiver ran down my spine, but no sign of magic rose off its fur. I was just on edge, and everything screamed *danger!*

I brushed past the dog and hurried down the walkway, shaking my hair around my face so the man couldn't get a close look.

"Hi," Aubrey said, brightly. "My friend was just leaving. Come on in."

I felt his eyes on me until I'd reached the next house and heard the door shut behind them.

CHAPTER FOURTEEN

"I've never seen anything like this," Kyle said. He tapped the edge of the newspaper spread in front of us. The typed letters jumbled and rearranged themselves magically across the page, forming a new story that sounded exhaustingly like the ones before.

Two days had passed since the filmmaker had uploaded his video to the internet and thrown Portland into chaos, after which my mom had called my school and told them I would be out for a few weeks for "personal reasons." Two hours had passed since Lucas and I had come to Pumpkin Spice to talk things over, and the enormity of our situation still hadn't sunk in. The café was closed as a defense against the Huntsmen, but Elle had let us in through the back door.

"A cruise ship on the river was tagged with a bunch of Huntsmen slogans," Kyle said. His eyes were trained on the paper, devouring one horrible news story after another. "And another group had an Oracle party right outside your work. They're calling for a full reveal of the Glimmering world so we can have 'the peace of openness.'"

I shrank in on myself and tried to press my body as hard as I could into the back of the chair that supported me.

"I don't want to hear any more," I said.

Lucas pushed a plate of cookies toward me. I shook my head. I couldn't stand the thought of eating.

I'd spent the entire day being grilled by everyone from Lorinda to the local Glim law enforcement to the Overseer of Interspecies Cooperation himself. Every time, I'd told them the same thing: the truth. I'd been there on a work assignment. It had been approved by the Council. We'd done the best we could. As far as I knew, the video that had landed online was the only one that had been taken, and it had been on the internet within minutes of our leaving the property. Due to luck and blurring as the phone's camera had tried to focus, Aidan was the only one whose face had been clearly captured. He was in official Glim custody, and I promised to keep myself glamoured when I went out in public for the next few weeks, just in case.

At the end of the interrogation, they were all satisfied—even my dad.

And I was exhausted.

"You know what was nice?" I said. I gently kicked Elle's foot under the table with mine. "When the biggest headache I had was trying to get you to prom."

She laughed, but her face was full of sympathy.

I took a deep breath and let it all out, trying to attach as much of my stress to the air as I could. But there was more. There was always more.

"It's weird that it's blown up this quickly," Kyle said. "This thing's gone viral overnight. Even the skeptics who think it's a hoax are talking about it."

"Not that weird," Elle said. "There's always been tension between the Glim and Hum worlds. That's what you told me, anyway."

"Not like this," he said. "There's always been tension, yeah, but people have never been bloodthirsty about it."

He tapped the newspaper again. The words jumbled and re-formed. Upside-down, I read the words, *MISSING TOD-DLER FOUND; KIDNAPPER ARRESTED.*

I dropped my hand down onto the paper, preventing him from refreshing the page again. I leaned over, trying to make out the small upside-down print. He handed the newspaper over to me.

My eyes raced down the page. *Toddler was reported missing… Rumors circulated that the kidnapping was a domestic affair… With the recent Hum tensions…* And then, there it was, new information.

The child was found in the custody of her aunt, Ms. Ruby Barnes, a muse who has long been vocal about her wishes for a visible Glimmering society. The muse was arrested by a special task force ordered by Her Majesty, Queen Amani Zarina.

"This kind of behavior is unacceptable," said Queen Amani, speaking at a press conference this morning. "Glimmers have a right to hold and express their own beliefs, but when that expression turns into the violation of others' rights or safety, the law must step in."

Barnes will be held in custody until the date of the next Faerie Court, at which point she will face judgment.

I summarized the article for the rest of the table. Elle visibly relaxed. Kyle nodded, like he wasn't that surprised. Lucas hung onto every word. I could practically see his thoughts racing, trying to absorb the details: *Muses exist, the queen is Amani Zarina, there's something called a Faerie Court.*

The news was good. The toddler was safe. Queen Amani was protecting us all, as she always had.

But I knew, deep in the pit of my stomach, that this had been nothing. In just the past day, law enforcement had broken up three Oracle parties. More people than I could count had been sent to prison, and I'd heard rumors that more than a few had been transported to the Glimmering hospital.

It was only a matter of time before someone got killed.

A man walked by outside the front windows. He stopped and stared resolutely inside, but his eyes were glassy and unseeing.

Elle's gaze followed mine.

"Ignore him," Elle said. "I get one every few hours. They never see anything."

"The thing is," I said slowly. I bit my lip and pressed my fingertips against the newspaper. "The thing is, I wouldn't be so upset normally. But Kyle's right. This is spreading really quickly. And maybe there's a reason for that. Maybe we do need to re-examine the way our worlds intersect. You all know how I feel about the Hums. I might even be in favor of all of this, except—"

"Except the movement's being led by thugs?" Kyle said.

I shook my head.

"Lots of movements have thugs in them," I said. "As leaders or members."

My thoughts flitted back to my history classes. Every revolution or social change had involved some rabble-rousers. They'd had to, or no one would have listened.

"This is different," I said. "Because I know who they're appealing to. Maybe the goal is good, and we should integrate our societies. And maybe it's going to take some pretty serious activism to make it happen. But not through the Oracle. They're petitioning her, and they're starting to call for her to take on the role of queen, and that's the worst thing that could happen."

"I don't know," Kyle said. "The Oracle definitely shouldn't replace the queen, but she wouldn't be the worst. She's a good leader."

I swallowed. It was hard to remember sometimes that not everyone knew what I knew. Under the table, Lucas reached for my hand and gave it a squeeze.

"I need to tell you something," I said. "And it can't leave this room. It can't leave this table."

Elle leaned forward. Her brown eyes lit up with interest. Kyle frowned, but he leaned in, too. Lucas nodded at me, giving me the courage to go forward.

I took a huge breath.

"The Oracle isn't being harassed by all these people," I said. "She's done a good job of making it look like she is, but she's a puppet master. She's pulling the strings in the background, and no one can see it."

Kyle kept frowning. Elle pursed her lips.

"I had an experience with her late last year," I said, talking too fast. "She's not trying to mix the Glim and Hum worlds so we can all have peace and eat s'mores and sing Kumbaya. She wants a war."

"A big one," Lucas said.

Elle whirled to stare at him. "You know about this?"

"I was there," Lucas said. "Last year. I wasn't as involved as Olivia was, but I saw enough."

"I learned about it from my last case," I said. "You remember Lily?"

And then, as the pumpkin-shaped clock on the wall ticked the seconds by, I told them what I knew: that the Oracle had been paying people to prank the Humdrums, that the Oracle believed Glims were superior, that she said a war was coming, that she'd asked me to join her, and that I'd said no. I fought past the lump in my throat to tell them that Imogen had made her choice and left Lucas and me behind to step into the Fountain. I told them that I'd been working with some friends to keep an eye on the Oracle's activities for months before Aubrey had blown everything out of the water. And then I told them my latest theory, that perhaps all these Humdrums were able to believe so quickly because her sprites were enchanting them to.

"It all has to be connected," I said. "And the sprites have been everywhere lately."

The only thing I left out was my connection to Queen Amani. That secret was one I wanted to keep for myself.

Kyle let out a low whistle.

"Now we're trying to figure out what to do next," I said. "One of my friends has been watching the Oracle for longer than I have, but this has thrown all our work out the window."

I hadn't dared meet with Isabelle since the video had been released, but she'd found a way to communicate anyway. This morning, I'd woken up to find a single enormous leaf growing in one of my window boxes. On it, in pale green ink, she'd written, *Our approach needs to be more direct now. I heard you were involved, so you lie low. H. & I will find a way to expose her to the masses. Destroy this leaf.*

It hadn't been encouraging.

What would "exposing her to the masses" do, anyway? Half of the Glims *wanted* the Oracle to reveal us to the world, and half of the Humdrums weren't even going to be surprised to learn we existed.

But the scary part, the part that made my spine prickle, was the possibility that these people might want something Kelda hadn't yet offered aloud: a conflict.

I could imagine a successful, slow integration of our worlds, overseen by the Faerie Queen and rational Humdrum leaders. But I could imagine a quick integration even more vividly, and I knew it would mean nothing short of a war. Too many Glims in this city were itching for change, and Humdrums were terrible at avoiding wars at the best of times.

Not everyone would be support a conflict, of course, but would that even matter? Those of us who wanted to keep the peace weren't half as organized as the people throwing Oracle parties.

I took a long drink of tea and focused on the heat as it rushed down my throat.

I just wanted to go to a Hum university already and be done with all this.

Not that I could. If our world was exposed, there wouldn't be a Hum world to escape to.

Kyle tapped the paper again while it lay in front of me. I caught the phrase *RELIGIOUS GROUPS SPEAK OUT AGAINST WITCHCRAFT* next to *SKEPTICS ORGANI-ZATION WARNS WORLD NOT TO BE DECEIVED.* I handed it back to him.

"This is beyond—" Elle started. Then she froze, staring down at the table.

Our mugs had started rattling on their pumpkin coasters like we were in an earthquake. The flavored-syrup bottles behind the counter tinkled and clicked together. A candle holder on the next table toppled over.

Before I had time to react, the shaking stopped. A voice cut through the café, smooth, clipped, and familiar. I couldn't tell where the voice came from, only that it seemed to pervade every inch of the space.

The greater Portland area is in a state of general emergency, Queen Amani's voice said. *All Glimmers within the region are advised to remain in their homes where possible. All Glimmers associated with the so-called Dark Forest movement are hereby ordered to cease and desist immediately. A special session of the Faerie Court will be held starting at eight o'clock tomorrow morning. Glimmers are advised to bring their complaints and petitions to the Waterfall Palace then.*

Her voice faded, leaving behind an echoing silence.

I looked over at Lucas. He looked as shocked as the rest of us, which meant he'd been able to hear it even despite his Humdrum-ness. The Oracle really had thrown him headfirst into this world.

Elle stood up and went to the other table. She straightened the candle holder that had fallen and surveyed the café for damage. The Humdrum man still stood outside, oblivious to what had just happened.

"That's... good?" Lucas said, looking around.

"That's good," I said. "The queen doesn't make announcements like that very often. It means she's taking a stand and every Glim in the area knows it."

Kyle opened his mouth, but he was cut off by another booming voice. This one said *Listen carefully,* and seemed to come from the back of the building. Elle ran toward the kitchen. A second later, she returned. She held a glass of clear water at arm's length and looked at it like the thing was about to explode.

I'd thrown blocking spells over all the clear water I'd seen since entering Pumpkin Spice. It was habit by now. But I'd completely forgotten to wrap a spell around the faucet in the kitchen in the back of the café.

I unite my voice with Queen Amani's, the Oracle's voice boomed. *We must cease this violence immediately. My sprites are stationed in fountains across the city. As of this moment, they are under instructions to maintain order. They will punish wrongdoers. Those who obey our laws need have no fear.*

Her voice faded. The water sat still, as if it hadn't just played host to the thundering voice of the only faerie who could make my blood run cold.

I pulled out my wand and shot a blocking spell at the glass. The water fizzed white for an instant so brief it could have been my imagination, and then settled.

"What was that?" Elle said.

"She can see through water," I said. "Any clear water."

Elle's eyes widened and she looked around the room. I waved my hand to catch her attention.

"This room's fine," I said, but I could hear my voice shaking. "I've been enchanting as I go. I forgot about the faucet."

"I notice she didn't define who *wrongdoers* are," Lucas said.

Kyle tapped the paper again. A stream of new headlines spilled across the page: *HUMDRUM GOVERNOR AD-VISES SKEPTICISM AS CONSPIRACY THEORIES OVERTAKE POPULAR MEDIA.*

I hoped people would listen. At this point, their skepticism might be the only thing that could save us.

CHAPTER FIFTEEN

I held my fingers inches from the rose stem and felt the air grow soft and hot between us. The magic siphoned into my fingers, smooth and sweet and sparkling. With my glasses propped on top of my head, the crystalline pink shone clearly in the late afternoon sunlight. When the magic was reduced to a thin pink dusting, I mentally clipped off the flow and gave myself a moment to absorb it.

"That looks great," Isabelle said. "Thanks for your help, by the way. Pruning these babies takes me weeks working alone."

She blew an air kiss toward one of the "babies," a healthy long-stemmed rose bush almost as tall as I was.

"I love it," I said. "Thanks for letting me keep the magic, seriously."

"There's plenty to spare," she said.

She smiled. For the first time in days, the air around us was calm, and we both felt it. I took a deep breath and let it out, savoring the chilly fresh air and peace.

Maybe it was the energy of the plants making me feel better, or maybe it was just that Glims had stopped attacking Hums, which meant Hums were starting to think the whole video-Huntsmen-Dark-Forest thing was just some social meme that had run its course. Below the garden, the city gleamed in the sunlight.

Down the row of bushes, Lucas and Daniel sat on a bench warmed by the sun, both playing games on their phones. They seemed to be enjoying ignoring each other. Once in a while I'd hear one of them shout, "Take that!" or "Got it!"

I had a feeling Daniel had only come in hopes of seeing Haidar again. But Lucas was the real surprise.

The Oracle had used him. She'd roped him into our world just to bring the tension between Imogen and me to its boiling point. I kept waiting for him to throw up his hands and say it was too much, but instead, he seemed to be getting comfortable. He liked my world. And even though I'd always been glad he was a Hum, I was also glad he was here.

My ears starting ringing, like I'd been listening to music too loudly. I frowned and plugged one of my ears, trying to get the annoying whistle to go away. But Isabelle touched my arm and shook her head.

She leaned toward the bush she'd been pruning. After a moment, she reached in and touched one stem that looked like all the others. Instantly, a bud appeared. In mere seconds, it swelled and burst into a fragrant pink bloom. She crooked a finger toward me and we both leaned in.

There's been an attack, Haidar's terse voice said. *Clear the garden of Glims and secure yourselves. I'll be there in a moment.*

Nausea pooled in the pit of my stomach. I'd been deluding myself to think this peace was going to last.

Isabelle stood up. A strand of her dark hair fell out of its braid. "Get your brother and your friend," she said. "I'll sweep the rest of the garden."

I ran. Daniel and Lucas hadn't heard a thing, and I had to say Daniel's name twice to get him to look up. When he saw my face, he shut off his game. Lucas was already standing and next to me.

"Is everything okay?" he said. He looked down at me, and his eyes were too intense. He knew it wasn't.

"I don't know," I said. Panic flooded me. "Daniel, get out your wand, just in case."

He pulled his collapsible wooden wand out of his pocket and assembled it with a wave of his hand. Lucas watched in fascination, and then Daniel and I stood back-to-back with Lucas alert next to us.

"What's going on?" Daniel said over his shoulder.

"Another attack," I said. "I don't know any details."

The garden was nearly abandoned this time of year, but the sunshine had brought out a few visitors. Down the hill from us, I could see Isabelle walking down the rows, trying to determine who was Glim. She couldn't see magic like I could; my gift was a unique one, even for a faerie. I sent a nudge of energy to her, and she looked up.

I pointed. Not too far from her, a single Glim in a long black coat took pictures of the dead-looking roses with a fancy camera. A staticky, sparking aura crackled around her. Isabelle strode toward her. I saw them talking for a moment, and then the woman tucked her camera into her coat and walked quickly out of the garden.

"Where's Isabelle?" a voice demanded.

I jumped. Haidar stood next to us.

"I thought you were keeping a lookout," I hissed to Daniel.

"He literally just popped out of thin air," Daniel said.

"She's down there," Lucas said. He pointed to where Isabelle's green hoodie and dark hair blended in with the scenery.

A final scan of the garden told me that the remaining visitors were Humdrums. I sent Isabelle another jolt of energy and waved her up.

Haidar watched her ascend the hill. His eyebrows drew together, making his already dark eyes seem shadowed. His gaze fixed on her and kept track of her every move as she came toward us.

"Some Glims attacked a group of Huntsmen," Haidar said without waiting to be asked.

The ridiculous term rolled off his tongue like he'd been using it forever. I had a sudden flood of instinct that he'd been watching all this more closely and for longer than any of us.

"Three of the Humdrums were wounded, and at least one Glim is in the hospital. They haven't caught anyone."

"So much for sprites punishing the wrongdoers," Lucas said.

Haidar stared at him for a brief second, like he couldn't place him and then couldn't be bothered to try anymore.

"The Humdrum community is panicking," Haidar said. "Just yesterday, only a small group of Humdrums was following this. It was something they only saw if they paid attention. Today, everyone will notice."

An unexpected twinge of empathy rose up in me for my dad. Judging by how sick this made me feel, I figured he was going to have a nervous breakdown.

"This is—" Isabelle said.

This was the first attack, the Oracle's voice boomed.

I flinched. The sound rose up from all around the garden. The water inside the garden was protected and stayed silent, but in the city on every side, her voice echoed and rang out from fountains, ponds, creeks—even the river.

My intelligence reports indicate there will be more, she said. All Glims are hereby ordered to return to their homes. Each home will observe a full lockdown until further notice. You have two hours to comply. Any Glimmers out on the street after that time will be considered allies of the Dark Forest movement and will be taken into custody. Protect yourselves.

"She doesn't want to protect anyone," I started, but Daniel elbowed me. I shut up and listened. My breath sounded almost loud enough to drown Kelda's voice out.

But she'd stopped talking. The omnipresent voice was gone, replaced by the pounding of my heart.

"Her intelligence has nothing to do with it," I whispered. "She's behind this."

"We know," Isabelle said. She put a warm hand on my arm.

"She's lying!" I said.

"What are you going to do about it?" Isabelle said. "She can lie as much as she wants. We don't have enough evidence."

"Meanwhile, she's just given her Dark Forest allies permission to roam freely, and ensured everyone else will stay in their homes where they can't defend the Hums," Haidar said. His jaw tightened into a hard line.

Lucas tensed beside me. "Defend them from what?"

"What do you think?" Isabelle said. She caught sight of his face and winced. "I'm so sorry. I didn't mean it like that," she said. "I'm stressed right now."

Lucas' face was pale. I wrapped one arm around him.

"It's okay," I said. "We'll protect your mom."

"It's not just my mom," he said. His voice was low but steady. "Everyone I know besides you guys are Humdrums. Everyone."

"She's not going to kill everyone," Haidar said. His dark eyes skimmed the skyline that spread out ahead of us. "She's going to scare as many out of the city as she can. Less messy, and they'll spread the word to stay away. She's after a stronghold."

"But she will kill the people who don't leave," Lucas said.

"Or she'll just try to control them," Isabelle said. "That's what I'd do. Create a police state, make the Humdrums keep their heads down, and claim that we've created a fully open, integrated society."

"Doesn't anyone get it?" Daniel said. "We shouldn't be integrated."

"I don't know," I said. "If anyone besides the Oracle was leading the charge, I might think it was a good idea."

"You hate Humdrums," Daniel said. "You don't want them to know about us, because then they'd know you're Glim and it'd be so embarrassing."

"I don't hate—"

"We don't have time to argue the point," Haidar cut in. He stared out toward the city, and I followed his gaze.

Rising up from the sparkling gray, an undulating silver-blue mist began to rise from between the buildings like water seeping through cracks.

"Is that a spell?" Lucas said, squinting at the mist. His shoulders felt so tight I expected them to snap like a rubber band.

"They're sprites," Isabelle said.

We were too far to see details, but she was right. The blue was thickest near fountains. Specks of blue began to fly toward us.

The earth began to shake.

Stay in your homes, Queen Amani's voice boomed. *You will be informed as we have more information.* And then, more silence.

Below us in the garden, the Humdrum visitors continued to walk between the bushes like nothing was wrong, like they hadn't felt the earth shaking and weren't about to be descended upon by swarms of vengeful, blindly loyal water sprites.

"We have to protect them," I said.

"They're safe as long as they stay in the garden," Isabelle said. "I'll warn them. Haidar, get these kids to safety."

"I'll help you," I said.

"Go," she said. She and Haidar looked at one another, and a conversation seemed to pass between them. "We need to make a plan and we'll need help from all of you, but you need to be safe first."

Haidar stalked to the bottom of the garden. We followed, walking so quickly the sloping ground jolted my knees with each step. At the bottom of the hill, native plants and trees grew wild and thick outside the landscaped edges of the rose garden. A casual hiking path wound through the trees and further down the hill.

Haidar led us off the path and under the branches of a giant magnolia tree, its branches bare for the winter. We crashed through the underbrush. Further in, under another magnolia tree, Haidar stopped. Around us, the woods seemed to breathe. I could barely see the rose garden through all the entwined branches and clusters of dead leaves that never seemed to fall.

I felt Lucas' heartbeat racing like a frightened rabbit's. I reached out and took his hand. He held on so tight it felt like my knuckles were about to crush each other.

Haidar pressed both his palms against the trunk of the magnolia tree. A tiny shadow nestled between ridges of bark grew and shifted. In a moment, it was large enough to put a hand through; in another moment, a child might have fit. Seconds later, it was big enough for even Haidar.

"This leads straight to my house," Haidar said. He stepped back from the tree. "You all go in first and I'll close the way behind us."

"We're not going home?" Daniel said.

"I can't get you there fast enough," he said.

For the first time, Haidar seemed flustered, like he didn't have everything figured out. His face had an urgent, over-whelmed look to it, and it made me dislike him a little less.

"I'll go first," I said.

He nodded at me. I pulled my hand out of Lucas' grip.

Twigs crunched under my feet as I stepped toward the hole. I couldn't see more than an inch in. The darkness was absolute and looked ready to swallow me whole.

I took a deep breath and stepped in.

Warmth surrounded me instantly. It was black, but it was the coziest blackness I'd ever experienced. I wanted to sit on the leaf-strewn floor and take a nap. A tiny speck of light shone in the distance. I walked toward it, feeling springy ground beneath my feet. The smells of soil and moss filled the darkness.

Sooner than I expected, I stumbled out of the darkness and into a garden dazzling with light glinting off leaves. Cool air washed over me.

A moment later, Lucas stepped out of the magnolia tree be-hind me. This tree was a mirror image of the one in the rose garden, but its branches were heavy with enormous pale pink blooms.

Worried as Lucas was, even he was distracted by the archway of wisteria, the elegantly gnarled cherry tree, and the stand of fierce orange tiger lilies. None of these plants should be flowering this time of year, but the garden seemed to be ready to explode with blossoms. Lucas stared around, trying to take everything in.

Daniel came next, and Haidar followed him. The magnolia tree closed up with a crackling rustle.

I heard a distant scream. The blood drained back out of Lucas' face.

Haidar led us across the garden, down a gravel path laced with what looked like unpolished precious gems. I didn't have time to stop and check. He flew through the garden like a predator on the scent of prey.

If the garden had been impressive, it was only a prelude to the house. I'd thought the homes in my neighborhood were pretentious. This cluster of stone towers was only one step below a castle, and then only if I turned my head and squinted. Haidar threw open an arched wooden door with a heavy brass latch and slammed it shut behind us.

It took a moment for my eyes to adjust to the darkness. The musty smell of abandoned space flooded my senses. We stood in a sparse stone room heavy with dust and filled with shelves of old pots and bags of soil. It clearly wasn't a part of the house that got much use. Haidar led us out, into a wallpapered hallway that led straight up a flight of stone stairs.

"Don't touch anything," Haidar warned.

CHAPTER SIXTEEN

We followed him up the steps. I shoved my hands in my pockets to resist the urge to touch the tapestries and wallpaper we walked by.

Haidar's home was absurd. I hadn't thought people lived in houses like this anymore. It had the quiet feel of a museum, paired with the opulence of a palace and the heady smell of a garden.

"My family had some influence a long time ago," Haidar said. He waved a hand around, gesturing at and dismissing his enormous manor in the same movement.

After a few turns, we reached a large, spacious hall glittering with gold and crimson wallpaper. The deep red carpets beneath our feet muffled our footsteps to near-silence, and underneath them, peeking out at the edges, I saw a polished floor of dark, warm mahogany. Through doorways, I glimpsed majestic rooms: a dark blue parlor, a study with an enormous glistening desk, a library with bookshelves stretching to the ceiling. Between each door, a small table stood, and on each table was an enormous bouquet of roses.

Haidar strode forward as though he was going to take us through the giant front door, which was inlaid with a stained glass rose. But then he turned off to his left and led us into a parlor at the very front of the house.

"Sit," he ordered.

I made sure Lucas took the spot next to me. The floral brocade sofas felt stiff and unused. A bronze statue of a lion glared at us from the mantelpiece.

Haidar went to the bay window at the front of the room and tugged up one of the sashes. From outside, a series of voices and cries floated over his immaculate lawn. Haidar scowled and leaned against the window, muttering. Beyond the lawn, a sturdy brick wall circled his property. I didn't need to look over my glasses to know the thing would be thick with charms.

"She'll be okay," Daniel said.

Haidar grunted.

I put an arm around Lucas' shoulders and pulled him close. Normally, this kind of touch would have freaked me out and made me start overthinking everything.

Right now, though, my friend needed a hug.

A moment later, he shifted away from me and stood. "I'm going to call my mom," he said.

I nodded. Haidar ignored him, which was as close to permission as we'd get.

Lucas went into the hallway. I watched him pace back and forth on the carpet in front of the door with his phone pressed to his ear. I tried not to listen to his conversation, but he was close, and the house was silent, and I could feel the way his heart skittered like a hummingbird's.

"Mom?" he said, after waiting too long for her to pick up. "Mom, I need you to call me as soon as you get this. It's important. I love you. Just call me, okay?"

He came back into the room, face still white, and continued to pace.

After what felt like hours—hours pierced by the occasional scream from somewhere far away—I heard steps in the hall. Haidar jerked away from the window as Isabelle appeared in the doorway.

"They're all safe," she said.

He didn't care. He crossed the room in two strides and wrapped her in his arms.

The room warmed with the electricity of the touch. I felt myself flush with the intensity of it, and Daniel rolled his eyes.

Lucas, who didn't have faerie sensitivity and was busy wearing a hole in the carpet, didn't notice.

"The Humdrums agreed to stay in the garden," Isabelle said, pulling away from Haidar. He looked down at her with single-minded intensity. "I made sure they had enough food to get through the day and conjured up a few tents, but we'll need to go back tomorrow and check on them."

"Will that keep them safe?" Lucas asked. He forced himself to look up at her.

"They'll be okay," she said. "The garden is one of the safest places they can be. But your mom's going to be okay, too. I have a friend who works at the hospital. She's another witch, and she agreed to find your mom and keep an eye on her. That's what took me so long. I was talking to her to make sure your mom had protection."

Lucas swallowed. "Thanks," he said. A muscle in his jaw twitched. I held out a hand, and he sat back down next to me. His shoulders hunched and he twisted his hands together between his knees. His face was like milk beneath his dark hair.

"You said tomorrow," I said. "Do you think this is going to go on all night?"

Isabelle and Haidar exchanged glances.

"I think it's going to go longer than tonight," Isabelle said. "It's a mess out there. The scariest part is, the Humdrums still don't know what's going on. Humdrums can't see sprites in their water form," she added, for Lucas' benefit.

"When a sprite knocks them down, they'll think they've tripped on a crack in the pavement," I said.

"When their car turns into oncoming traffic, everyone will blame it on texting while driving," Haidar said. His mouth hardened into a grim line.

"That's the worst," Daniel said. "It's one thing to have someone attacking you. But the Oracle's trying to make everyone think they've gone crazy. That's brutal."

"She's gaslighting the whole city," Lucas said softly.

"What's that?" I said.

He frowned. "It's a kind of mental abuse," he said. "It's when someone insists that something didn't happen, even though you know it did, until you start to doubt your own memory. Or like when someone treats you horribly and then blames you for being 'too sensitive.'"

"Sounds like our dad," Daniel said.

"That sucks, man," Lucas said. He kept fiddling with his hands. "My mom used to talk about it all the time. She had this friend, and this woman was always criticizing my mom. Lots of passive-aggressive crap, like, 'Should you *really* be eating that, with your figure?' And then when my mom asked her to stop making personal comments, she somehow turned it around and made it look like my mom was the one being critical. Mom said it was a 'toxic friendship' and that if I was in a situation that made me doubt my own sanity, I should get out." He laughed. There was no warmth behind it. "Guess I should have listened before all this happened."

I put my arm back around him. This time, he leaned in.

Isabelle sat across from us on the other sofa. Haidar remained standing where he could see out the window. A long driveway led from the brick wall to the house. On either side of the gate, two enormous marble lions stood guard. As I watched, one of them tensed its stone haunches and pulled back its ears.

Isabelle tugged at the ribbon that held her disheveled braid together. She ran her fingers through her hair and massaged her scalp. From behind her, Haidar watched, a glint of something in his eye that had nothing to do with the day's chaos.

"You guys are stuck here until the lockdown's lifted," Isabelle said. "We should all get comfortable."

I glanced around the ornate room. This was not the kind of place where people *got comfortable.*

"I thought we were going to expose the Oracle," I said.

"That was before Queen Amani ordered everyone to stay in their homes," Haidar said.

"Odd, that Queen Amani and the Oracle are asking for the same thing," Isabelle said.

I tensed. But I didn't have to say anything.

"We will obey the queen," Haidar growled.

Isabelle pursed her lips. She didn't like it one bit, but she didn't argue.

"You guys should call your mom," she said. "There's a magic mirror in the study if you want some privacy. She'd probably like to see that you're okay."

Haidar's eyes jumped to me immediately, but he didn't order me to stay out of his office. I nodded and stood.

"You can take this one," Daniel said, before I'd even asked. "Mom's going to be freaking out."

"With good reason," Isabelle said. But Daniel didn't seem inclined to chat. He leaned back in his chair and pulled out his phone.

The study felt even more private than the rest of the house. Papers sat on the heavy wooden desk. I wanted to know everything about Haidar and this house, but I resisted the urge to peek. I had a feeling he watched everything that went on in this building, and I had enough to worry about without him freaking out that I'd looked at his stuff.

An oval mirror in an elaborate gold frame hung on the wall behind the desk. I stood in front of it. A stray leaf fragment was tangled in my messy hair, and I had dirt on my nose that hadn't been there this morning. I combed my hair with my fingers and tried to clean up my face, then tapped the tip of my wand to the edge of the frame.

The image of my own face shimmered. Colors swirled on its surface as I waited for someone to answer. If no one answered at the house, the reflection would shift to the pocket mirror Mom kept in her purse. When the image resolved, though, Mom stood in our living room.

"Olivia!" Her face was as pale as Lucas', and her auburn ponytail was a disheveled mess. Her roots showed through dark at her scalp, just enough that I could tell she hadn't done her weekly touch-up charm. "Where are you?" she demanded. "Are you okay? Why haven't you been answering my calls?"

"I'm fine," I said, loudly enough to cut over her frantic voice.

I pulled out my phone and checked the notifications.

"No missed calls," I said.

"They've probably jammed the cell towers," Mom said. "Why did it take you so long to mirror?"

"We were busy finding a safe place," I said. I took a deep breath and ordered myself to not get irritated. She was just scared, like everyone else in the entire city. "We're with my friend Isabelle. You know, the one who's been teaching me about gardening?"

I could see her fighting to regain composure. She pressed her lips together. "Is Daniel with you?"

"Yes," I said. "He's fine. We're at Isabelle's boss's house. He's Glim, too, and we're really well protected here. It was safer than trying to come home."

"Okay," she said. She ran a hand through her hair, tugging even more of it loose from the ponytail. "Your dad is downtown. He's trying to deal with… all this."

"I figured," I said.

She closed her eyes and rubbed the spot between her eyebrows. It was harder to get empathetic impressions through a mirror than with a live person, but I still felt the tension radiating from her.

"Are you safe?" I said.

"Yes," she said. She pursed her lips. "Your father won't be home for a few days, but I'll be all right alone. I always am."

"There's probably a lot of work to do," I said.

"Isn't there always?" she said.

She let out another long sigh. It didn't sound like it helped.

"I'm sorry," she said. "Your father and I just had another enormous fight, just when we should have been coming together. But I suppose we should all be used to that by now."

I studied her face. There were fine lines there I'd never noticed before. And under them, she didn't look like my mom. She looked like a *person*.

"He's not going to change," I said. "You know that, right?"

She touched her fingertip between her eyebrows again.

"I can't get my divination to work," she said. "I've been trying all afternoon, looking for the two of you and trying to get a sense for what's going to happen next. I'm not getting anything."

"You're probably overwhelmed," I said. "Try to relax. We're all stuck where we are for a few days, so make some popcorn and put on a movie."

She laughed. "Right," she said.

"I should probably go," I said. "I'm borrowing Isabelle's friend's mirror for this."

"Stay safe," she said. The lines on her forehead creased. "Keep Daniel with you."

"We're all going to be okay, Mom," I said. "I promise."

Off in the distance, I heard another scream.

It was a promise I had no right to make.

CHAPTER SEVENTEEN

I'd expected sleep to be impossible, but before I knew it, I was opening my eyes in one of Haidar's lush guest bedrooms. Everything in the room seemed to dance with busy floral patterns. The down-filled comforter blossomed with images of white grandiflora blooms over a pale green background, and the wallpaper crawled with elaborate bouquets of roses and daisies.

The sound of a violin running up and down the scales floated into my room. I listened as the sound faded. Somewhere down on the first floor, it was replaced with Haidar's low, rumbling voice.

I slid out of bed. The mattress was so high up I'd needed to use a tiny flight of carpeted stairs last night to get onto it. A fresh set of clothes sat on a chair in front of a mirrored vanity table. Isabelle must have enchanted them in last night. I replaced the old-fashioned cream nightgown I'd borrowed with the soft jeans and pale pink T-shirt, then put my hoodie on over that.

The smell of breakfast greeted me on the landing. Daniel, Lucas, and I had slept on the second floor. The stairs kept going up, though, and I wondered how many rooms could possibly be in this mansion, and what Haidar did with them all. Across the hall, the door to Lucas and Daniel's aggressively blue bedroom stood ajar. No one was inside.

I followed the smell of food downstairs. Isabelle had insisted on sleeping on the couch in the parlor to keep guard "just in case." Now, she sat in another room across the entrance hall with a book in one hand and fork in the other. A platter of bacon, eggs, and pancakes sat in front of her. Across the table, on the other side of an enormous arrangement of white and purple lilacs, Lucas sat picking at a plate of Belgian waffles and staring at his phone.

I pulled out the chair next to him. He looked up, startled. When he saw me, his shoulders seemed to relax.

"Morning," I said. I wasn't willing yet to call it a *good* one.

"Morning," he said. "You sleep okay?"

"Like a rock," I said. "One of those rocks that passes out when it's stressed, you know."

"Darn rocks and their escapist coping tactics," he said. He forced a tiny smile.

I wished I could bottle the smile and store it as a talisman. The willpower it took for him to arrange his face like that sent prickles of empathy up my arms.

"Have you heard from your mom?" I said.

"She called late last night," he said. "I tried to explain what was going on, but she kind of already knew."

Isabelle's eyes darted up from her book.

"Not about magic," Lucas added. Isabelle looked back down. "She just knows the Huntsmen conspiracy theorists are getting violent. Another Hum got hurt last night; looked like a bullet wound. Sounds like a lot of the people at the hospital think it's a surge in gun violence."

"May as well be," I muttered.

"I told her I was safe and she said she was staying away from anywhere that looked like trouble," he said. "She called school and told them I'd be out for a few days. Isabelle said they're still keeping an eye on her."

"Two eyes," Isabelle said, without looking up from her book. "My friend's watching her, and Queen Amani stationed security around the hospital."

"That's good," I said.

"Probably political pressure," Isabelle said. She turned a page.

EMMA SAVANT

I wished I could talk to Amani. Isabelle didn't trust her, but even now, after such a long silence, I had to believe my queen was on the right side of this conflict. Last time we'd spoken about the Oracle, it had all seemed so personal to her. She *had* to be spending all her energy trying to solve the problem.

Lucas reached out and picked up a small rectangle of creamy paper up off the table.

"Here," he said, handing it to me. "Breakfast. Just tell the flowers your order."

I glanced at the bouquet. The lilacs did seem alert, in their own way, like maybe they'd just been cut that morning.

My eyes took in the paper. It was covered in silver calligraphy.

"Crepes with lingonberry butter," I said. "Side of eggs, over easy, with black pepper."

The flowers shook themselves, as though I'd said something funny and they were laughing at the joke.

A moment later, the food shimmered into being in front of me.

"You told me to order from the flowers like a pro," I said. I nudged Lucas with my knee. "We'll make a Glim out of you yet."

I wanted to see his smile again, but his face stayed tight and pale.

"You and your mom are really close, huh?" I said.

He swallowed and nodded. His gaze seemed to bore into the strawberries on the waffles in front of him.

He was beyond any comfort I could give.

Instead of continuing my sad attempt to make him feel better, I turned to my breakfast. The crepes were perfect and the lingonberry butter was even better. I wondered what kind of magic created the food. Did Haidar have servants? Were the flowers contributing their magic? Did lilacs have an innate ability to enchant food into being? What other plants gave off magic besides roses, and why hadn't I known about roses in the first place? And could any of these flowers be used to solve this stupid Oracle situation?

After a few bites, Lucas' quiet voice broke into my thoughts.

"This will all be fine if she's okay," he said. "I'm sorry. I just worry about her. I mean, not just now. I worry about her all the time, and so now, it's just worry on top of worry and it's kind of messing with me."

I took a deep breath and resisted the urge to reach out for his hand.

"She's lucky to have you," I said. "Most guys your age can't stand their moms."

"I guess I must seem pretty lame right now."

"You seem really sweet, actually," I said. I wished Isabelle wasn't in the room listening. Throwing up a sound bubble would be rude, but I didn't want her listening in on this conversation. I lowered my voice. "It's cool that you and your mom care about each other so much."

"It's just, I'm all she has," he said. He pushed a strawberry around his plate. It was like he was talking to the food instead of me; his eyes stayed trained on the plate. "I have my dad, too, but we don't live together. And I know he can take care of himself. But Mom, she needs people."

"Dude, your mom's a nurse," I said. "I'll bet she's amazing in an emergency."

Finally, a smile. It was tiny, but it was real.

"Yeah, she's good in a crisis," he said. "Way better than I am. Obviously."

"You're doing great," I said.

Violin music screeched through the room, a high-pitched stream of frantic notes. I heard Daniel burst into laughter as the violin faded.

"Volume down, please!" Isabelle shouted over the top of her book.

Wherever they were, Haidar and Daniel clearly weren't letting this Oracle business get them down.

"They've been at that all morning," Lucas said.

Isabelle sat her book down on the table, pages splayed and facing downward. "Haidar has an enormous collection of enchanted antique instruments," she said. "And he's finally found someone who can appreciate them." She speared a link of sausage with her knife.

"Daniel doesn't play," I said. "I don't think so, anyway."

"He wants to work violin into his next poetry performance," Lucas said. I stared at him and he shrugged. "That's what he said."

"I hope he learns what the strings are for first," I said.

Another string of high notes screeched after one another. Wherever they were, it was way too close for auditory comfort.

"Haidar," Isabelle shouted. "Some people are trying to enjoy their morning."

The violin squawked at her in response.

Isabelle scowled across the table, like Lucas and I had something to do with it. Then she let out a big sigh.

"I am sleep-deprived," she said. "And I hate everything."

"You're welcome to go nap in my room if you want," I said.

"Or one of the six other bedrooms," she said. "No, I don't have time. Thanks, though."

She picked her book back up, tore a sprig of lilac from the bouquet, and stuck it between the pages. She slammed the book shut with a thump.

"Do you want the news?"

I shifted in my seat. "Yes, please," I said.

"Since none of us are going to be able to read in peace, I'll be happy to tell you all about it," she said. She cast a dirty look toward the door.

"I'm guessing everyone's still on lockdown," I said.

"Obviously," she said. "We're stuck where we are for now. What's new is that the Oracle has also forced Council members into lockdown. Originally they were still roaming the city under Queen Amani's protection, but I guess her protection isn't enough against the Oracle's sprites."

She leaned back in her chair and lifted a glass of orange juice. She examined it for a moment. "The Oracle has started using her little supporters to start circulating the idea that we'll all be better off with new leadership. Queen Amani clearly can't restore the peace, they say, so why not let the Oracle take a stab at it?"

"You think the queen and the Oracle are on the same side anyway, so why does it matter?" I said.

Isabelle's eyes darkened, and she shot me a sharp look across the table. The intensity of the expression was ruined by a tiny speck of fried egg white stuck to the corner of her mouth.

"Meanwhile, the Humdrums are obviously aware something's going on," she said, like I hadn't spoken. "It would be impossible for them to stay ignorant."

"They don't know what's actually happening, though," Lucas said. His voice sounded a little stronger. Maybe he needed to be talking instead of just dwelling on what might happen. He held up his phone. "Half the people I follow online think it's gang wars. The other half are older people who think these are the consequences of legalizing marijuana."

The corner of his mouth quirked. I felt the tiniest bit of amusement rise off him like steam.

"Oh, dear mother of cannabis," Isabelle muttered. She picked the speck of egg off her lips and wiped it on a napkin. "I guess that's still better than the ones who think aliens have taken over. Half the conspiracy theorists think UFOs must have landed; the other half thinks government brainwashing has made everyone go mad."

"Wow," I said.

Lucas snorted. "What do you expect them to think?" he said. When Isabelle and I both looked at him, he raised his eyebrows. "What? They're supposed to know it's fairy tale characters? How is that any saner than UFOs?"

I opened my mouth to respond, then looked to Isabelle.

She pursed her lips and pointed a fork at him.

"Kid has a point."

Lucas propped his wrists against the edge of the table and leaned toward Isabelle.

"What's your deal with Queen Amani?" he said.

He looked at her intently, either oblivious or indifferent to the sudden spark in her eyes.

She picked her book back up, but it seemed like a prop, something to keep her from looking as serious as she felt.

"She let the situation go too far," Isabelle said.

"That's it?" Lucas said. "Come on. If she was a Humdrum political leader no one would even be surprised."

"Our politics aren't like yours," she said. "We don't just let things spiral out of control. Our government doesn't take long paid vacations when there's trouble or make decisions based on the interests of whoever will do them favors later. Our queens handle things."

"But you don't think Amani's handling things," I said.

"All I know is what I see: that the Oracle thinks she can get away with a coup, that Queen Amani has done next to nothing to stop her, and that they keep giving the same orders," Isabelle said. "Maybe Amani's on the Oracle's side. Maybe she's not. But if she's not, and she's still letting all this happen, she's a terrible queen."

Lucas frowned. I could feel him turning this over in his mind. I wanted to spring to the queen's defense, but the words wouldn't come.

Things were out of control. Amani and Kelda were giving the same orders. And Humdrums were suffering for it.

Things were getting worse, not better.

Haidar coughed loudly in the doorway. I jumped and looked up. I hadn't heard or felt him come in. How long had he been standing there?

"You," he said. It took me a second to determine that his black eyes were, in fact, turned on me and not Lucas. His dark hair was pulled back into a ponytail, but the rest of his face still seemed raw and untamed.

"Yeah?"

"Out here," he said. "Now."

CHAPTER EIGHTEEN

He didn't wait for an answer, just turned and walked across the entrance hall and into the parlor. I raised my eyebrows at Lucas, then got up, abandoning Amani and my breakfast all in one go.

Once I was in the parlor, Haidar closed the door behind us.

I spun on him.

"What is Isabelle's problem?" I said. "You trust Amani, don't you?"

"I do," he said.

"Then what's her deal?" Sudden heat rose up in me. "She says you know the queen," I snapped. "Don't take this the wrong way, but you don't seem like the kind of guy who just goes around trusting people. If you think Amani's on the right side of all this, don't you think Isabelle should, I don't know, *listen?*"

"Listening has never been Isabelle's first reaction to anything except roses," Haidar said.

Underneath the gruff words, an undercurrent of affection ran strong and clear.

They deserved each other.

"We have no evidence Queen Amani wants any of this," I said. "Yes, maybe she hasn't handled it perfectly. But—"

I didn't know what else to say. *But Amani is my friend, and she's as worried about this as any of us.* But I couldn't say that. I didn't even know if it was true anymore.

"Isabelle has to make up her own mind about things," Haidar said. "It doesn't matter how much evidence is staring her in the face or who disagrees with her. Isabelle doesn't believe anything until she thinks believing it was her idea."

"Real healthy way to go through life," I muttered.

Haidar snorted. "Yes, you're much more level-headed than that," he said.

His sarcasm was so thick I could practically chew on it.

"What do you want?" I said.

A small sense of guilt nudged at me. I could almost hear my mom hissing in my ear about politeness and gracious manners. I looked over his shoulder and out onto the sloping lawn. The sky hung heavy with pearly clouds.

"Thanks for letting us stay here," I said.

"I couldn't let you get carried off by sprites," he said. "Amani would kill me."

I inhaled sharply. He watched me too closely, and there was a faint amusement behind his words, a *gotcha* waiting to happen. I schooled my face to keep it neutral.

"I don't think Queen Amani is worried about my safety," I said.

"I think Amani is *extremely* worried about your safety," Haidar said. "And your allegiance. I think she's spent a lot of energy worrying about those things lately, maybe even enough to demand I take you to my house instead of yours when the Oracle attacked."

I folded my arms.

"You should see your face," he said. "You and Isabelle ought to have a contest to see who can give me the dirtiest look. You might win."

"She talked to you?"

"Isabelle?" he said. "No, but I know she'd enjoy an evil eye contest. She's competitive like that."

Good Titania. He was worse than Daniel.

I tightened my mouth and kept trying to nail him with a death glare. Finally, he sat down, his back to the bay window. Even on the formal floral sofa, he seemed wild.

"Your brother is gifted with considerable music magic," he said, voice suddenly light.

"Don't change the subject."

"Have a seat and maybe we'll talk," he said.

I sat down across from him, folded my arms, and leaned back. I wanted to put my feet on the coffee table, but that seemed like it might be going too far.

"You don't like me," he said.

I narrowed my eyes, as if squinting might somehow help me see him better.

"I don't get you," I said.

At least I felt like I could be honest with him. He didn't seem like he'd get offended over much.

"You keep stuff to yourself," I said. "It's not a bad thing, but honestly, I don't have the mental energy to deal with it."

He nodded, expressionless.

"I get you," he said.

I couldn't help laughing. "Somehow, I seriously doubt that," I said.

"Isabelle tells me you're planning on going to a Humdrum school to study biology," he said. "Maybe you'll get to learn about selective breeding and plant evolution. What about genealogy? Are you interested in that?"

I stared at him. The world was crashing around our ears, so he thought it was a good time for a conversation about my interests and college plans? I glanced at the door.

"Do you know what genealogy is?" he said, in a flatter voice, when I didn't answer.

"Dead people," I said, even more flatly. "Family trees."

"Family history," he said. "The study of all the ancestors who made you who you are today."

"No," I said. "Not really interested."

"It was a rhetorical question," he said. "You could only be this apathetic if you'd never studied up."

Behind him, just outside the bay window, a bluebird fluttered from one bush to another.

I sighed. I was stuck here. I may as well play along. Better this than try to talk Isabelle into thinking Queen Amani wasn't the worst ruler ever.

"What am I missing out on?" I said. "Tell me all about it. I literally have all day."

"Do you know why Queen Amani is as powerful as she is?" he said.

Every time he said her name, something uncomfortable prickled down my arms. I rubbed one of my biceps, trying to calm the tingles. The soft inside of my hoodie pressed fuzzy on my skin.

I knew our queen was powerful. The legends said her magic made the rain fall and the grass grow. But why?

My mind drifted back to the day I'd first met her in the Waterfall Palace. I'd been practically vibrating with nerves, and so had she. She'd explained her power to me, at least a little bit. *We need people to believe in us,* she'd said. *So much of my magic comes from them.*

"People believe in her," I said slowly. I kept a close eye on Haidar, watching for a sign that I was too far off track or, worse, that I'd said too much. "She's powerful because every Glim in our world sends her a little of their magic just by believing in her, and she doesn't want to let them down."

"Now, how could you know that?" he said. He folded his arms, mirroring my posture, and leaned back into the stiff couch.

"I think you already know the answer to that," I said.

He didn't contradict me.

"She's interested in you," he said. "Amani is. Kelda too, but especially Amani."

"Kelda," I said.

"The Oracle," he said.

"I know that," I said. "I didn't think *you* knew that."

"Says the girl who doesn't even know why she matters in all this," he said.

He was enjoying gloating. I stayed silent. I could wait him out.

He crossed his legs, propping one ankle up on his other knee, and clasped his hands behind his head. "You had a great-great-something-grandmother, I don't know how many greats, who was around when Portland was a new city," he said.

I kept waiting.

"Her name was Fianna McDermott," he said. "She was an Irish immigrant and a descendant of the Fair Folk."

Haidar watched me closely, but my Ireland connection wasn't news. Most of the faeries in this region were descended from Celtic ancestors.

"Fianna had a strong will," he said. "She knew what she wanted and didn't let things get in her way."

"Let me guess," I said. "This was my dad's side of the family."

He tilted his head and examined me.

"No," he said, sounding almost confused. "Your mother's. You don't give your mother much credit, do you?"

I shrugged. It wasn't a question I could answer.

My mom was a powerful faerie. Her divination gifts were nothing to sneeze at, and I suspected she was the only person who could have kept a handle on her enchanted ring. The ring, an elegant piece with quartz carved into the shape of a rose, was an heirloom loaded with more charms than I could keep track of. Normally, too many enchantments on one object made the Glim using it go a little crazy. I'd seen that firsthand when Elle had joined our world. But Mom had been wielding that thing as long as I'd been alive like it was nothing.

She'd also been hiding behind my dad for as long as I'd been alive. At some point, she'd traded in her apparently awesome powers for a life as Dad's arm candy. Until these last few years, when they'd started fighting all the time, she'd let him walk all over her.

She still did, sometimes. Sure, she'd started taking divination jobs lately, and she'd dyed her hair and started speaking up more. Even with all that, it was still clear that everything she did was in opposition to him, or in defiance of him. None of it felt like it was really about *her*. And anyone who could build her entire life around Reginald Feye probably didn't deserve much credit.

But I didn't want to go into any of that with Haidar.

"Mom doesn't talk about her family much," I said instead. "But Dad's always blathering on about the Feye family name. I assumed anything special would come through him."

"That's because he's full of himself," Haidar said. "He knows your bloodlines on both sides are old and important, but he doesn't understand the power in that."

"And you do."

He seemed to expand even more, stretching his elbows off to the sides like he planned to fill the whole couch.

"Fianna McDermott was the only person in Glimmering history to turn down the job of faerie queen," he said.

Time seemed to suspend for a moment. I felt my heartbeat stop, and the silence of the room seemed to flood in and fill all the empty spaces between my fingers and ribs.

Lucas' muffled voice floated in from across the hall.

Then I landed softly back in reality. The seconds began ticking by again, uniform and relentless.

"What do you know about me?" I said.

I pressed my knees together and clasped my hands around them. Haidar looked at me like he could see everything in my head. Silently, I threw up a wall like Amani had taught me, a silver one with vines glimmering at its edges. The corner of his mouth tightened, though I couldn't read what it meant.

"I've known Queen Amani for years," he said. "Kelda, too. She and I aren't on good terms. I offended a favorite sprite of hers a few years ago and she took it personally."

"What did you do?"

"None of your business," he said.

I folded my arms.

"Amani and I always got on well, though," he said. "We went to the same Glimmering homeschool co-op as teenagers and hit it off. We stopped spending much time together after she was named Queen Phoebe's heir, but we've stayed friends."

I couldn't imagine Amani and Haidar hanging out. Amani was friendly and casual. Haidar seemed to get a kick out of being as rude and intimidating as possible. The only thing they had in common was the hugeness of their houses.

"A couple of years ago, she started telling me about visions she'd been getting," Haidar said. "She kept seeing this girl in her divinations."

"Me."

"Come on, now, you're going to spoil the ending," Haidar said.

I cut my eyes at him. "You'll survive," I said.

"She insisted this girl was going to save our world."

The hair on the back of my neck prickled.

"Amani was excited when she met you," he said. "She said it was pure luck, that you seemed to fall out of the sky. And then she asked you to be her heir, and you said no."

Haidar started laughing, a low chuckle in the back of his throat. His stormy face relaxed for a moment.

"Who does that?" he said.

I didn't see how any of this was funny. He waited for me to join in on his amusement. The best I could manage was a tepid smile. Finally, he shook his head.

"She respected your decision," he said. He rubbed his chin, stroking the five o' clock shadow that seemed to perpetually grace his face. "She wasn't thrilled, but she admired that you had the guts to say no. She thought that was her message: that she had to have the courage to say no to the people in her life who were asking too much of her."

He gave me a significant look, staring at me like this was my one chance to prove I wasn't a complete moron.

"People like Kelda," I said.

He leaned back, satisfied.

"But you kept showing up in her pool, and Amani saying no to Kelda wasn't making the difference she'd hoped. The Oracle wanted change, and she wanted it right that second. Amani was on board, to an extent. She understands that altering the structure of our world is something that would need to happen slowly, but she agreed with Kelda's goal of an integrated Glim-Hum society. But then Kelda started taking it too far, and Amani realized she wasn't after an integrated society. She was after one where Glims ran the show. Well, Amani's too much of a Humdrum-lover for that."

Imogen used to call me a Humdrum-lover all the time. It was nice to have company, even if Amani and I weren't really connected anymore.

"So she asked you again, and you kept saying no, and all this messy business with the Oracle just kept getting worse."

"Did she know it was Kelda?" I said. "For sure, I mean?"

"Of course she did," Haidar said.

The tiny bubble of confidence that had been sitting inside me for months popped. Amani had hinted that she'd known who was causing problems with the Humdrums, but she'd always acted like she wasn't sure, like it *could* have been anybody. Haidar saw the look on my face, and his expression softened.

"Don't take it personally," he said. "She was trying to keep you safe."

"That worked," I said under my breath.

"Give her a break," he said. "You wanted to be kept out of this, so she tried to keep you out of it. And for all you know, that's killing the Glimmering world. You were supposed to save the world, after all."

"Divinations don't always show the truth," I said. "There's never just one path."

"You sure showed up in a lot of them, though," he said. "And you're still showing up, and Amani doesn't know what to do about it. You're Fianna's descendent. You can sustain belief in yourself in a way that most faeries can't. Why do you think you've been able to resist your dad's pressure all these years?"

I frowned, and he waved a dismissive hand.

"Daniel told me all about your dad and how you and he don't always get along," he said. "I happen to know from Queen Amani that your father used influencing spells on you at one point, trying to get you to attend the same university he did. And you didn't even notice. You just kept your head down and kept plugging along in the hopes of going to some tedious Humdrum university. Why? That's a lot of pressure. Why were you so stubborn?"

I made a mental note to never speak to my father again.

"I want to study plants, and I don't want to be in the Glimmering world," I said. "I'm not good at being a faerie. Why bother? There's a rich world out there, even if none of you can see it."

He slammed his palm down onto the stiff brocade seat beside him. "Right there," he said. He pointed at me. "That's it, right there. You're stubborn, Olivia. You believe in yourself, not in what people tell you or what you're 'supposed' to think."

"So?" I said. "What does that have to do with anything?"

"A choice like Fianna's leaves a powerful magical residue," Haidar said. His eyes practically burned with black fire. I couldn't help staring at him, even as I wanted to run away and leave this conversation behind. "That choice has been with your family for generations, and it found a home in you."

So none of my choices were my own? Everything I was and wanted to be was just the leftovers from some decision a great-great-grandma I'd never heard of had made over a hundred years ago?

I could never escape. Everything I ever did or thought all came back to my stupid heritage. I was a Glimmer. I was a faerie. I was a Feye.

I was incredibly, unbearably stuck.

"I still don't get the point of all this," I snapped.

I stood up and stalked to the door, but I couldn't make myself open it. This conversation was stupid and everything I didn't want to hear, but I couldn't leave it unfinished.

"What does any of it have to do with me?" I said. "Why are you telling me this?"

Haidar leaned forward. He put his elbows on his knees and seemed to be trying to pin me down with his stare.

"You're fated to be an exceptionally strong faerie," he said. "The kind of faerie who can turn tides."

A barking laugh jumped out of my throat before I realized it was there.

"Why do you think Amani and the Oracle noticed you?" he said. "Where do you think their power comes from? Belief, Olivia. They're powerful because everyone in our world believes they are. But you? You don't need that. You don't need other people's approval. You just march in and do what you want, and if they don't like it, too bad. You haven't even noticed. Do you know how rare that is?"

I stalked to stand behind the couch I'd been sitting on. I leaned over it, bracing my hands across its stiff back.

"I don't need other people, so the queen and the Oracle are both after me?" I said. "I'm just some power source?"

"You've got something other faeries don't," he said.

He stood up and crossed the room. Only the sofa shielded me from the potency that radiated from him.

"You have a gift, Olivia." He leaned in toward me until I could smell his woodsy deodorant. "Your gift is that you just don't give a damn."

CHAPTER NINETEEN

Isabelle knelt on the damp lawn in front of Haidar's mansion. In front of her sat a rose bush. Like everything else on Haidar's property, the plant was blooming out of season. Enormous red roses hung heavy from their stems, nodding their heads as Isabelle listened and relayed the news.

"She's using spells and curses and sprites and whatever else she can to get people to leave the city. She's trying to force the Hums out entirely. It's not working as fast as she'd like, but it is working. People are leaving; some of them don't even know why."

She scowled in concentration and leaned in until one of her ears was nearly touching a blossom. A light rain had been fading in and out all day; now, a single drop landed on her cheek and rolled down it like a tear.

"The Oracle has sent a few sprites to get the same things going in Vancouver, but she's still got most of her attention on Portland. She wants to turn it into a Glimmering stronghold. It will eventually serve as the base for a war designed to take over the Pacific northwest, and from there she'll spread out."

It was what we had assumed, but hearing our fears confirmed chilled me.

"The Glims are starting to wake up to the truth," she said. "She's not being as discreet as she was and her sprites are openly roaming the streets in their corporeal forms. The activists who were 'petitioning' her are calling it a victory. Proof that she listens to her people or some crap like that. Everyone else is getting nervous. This being the work of some small disgruntled groups is one thing, but they're realizing it's coming from the Oracle, and that scares them."

"Which only makes her stronger," Haidar said. He turned toward Lucas, as though what he said next was for his benefit, but I knew better. The words were for me. "Belief is a powerful energy. The leaders of our world feed on it to survive. Someone like the Oracle requires a lot of belief to stay powerful, and fear is just another way of believing."

"The more people get nervous about her, the stronger she'll be," Lucas said.

His jaw was clenched. Whatever was going on inside his head, he seemed to have decided to deal with it. His body was strung tight with anxiety, but his eyes and mind were sharp and ready to take in everything.

"She's going to need a lot of fear to get what she wants," I said.

"She'll need to get the belief of a powerful faerie on her side," Haidar said.

He didn't look at me. He didn't have to.

"That, or she'll kill any Glims strong enough to dismiss her," he said. "Anyone who keeps or strengthens an allegiance to Queen Amani will be especially dangerous to her."

Isabelle rolled her eyes but didn't contradict him.

I'd be on Kelda's chopping block, and doubly so. I wasn't going to support her, and I wasn't going to let my fear of her leak out. I bit my tongue and tried to create a shield inside my own body, something that would keep all my emotions locked deep inside.

Before I got very far, though, a horrible thought struck me.

"My dad," I said. "He works with Amani. He's one of her biggest fans. He's going to support her. Loudly, knowing him."

"Mom, too," Daniel said. He kept his voice dry and neutral, but I felt the tiny surge of worry that spun through him. His face seemed even paler than usual, though it may have only been the gray afternoon light.

My parents were usually on my last nerve, Dad especially. But I still wanted to keep them alive.

Isabelle leaned back on her heels. Whatever news the rose had caught, she'd listened to it all.

"She's going to destroy this city," she said. "And there's nothing new from Queen Amani, and nothing useful from the Council. Apparently they're having a 'strategy meeting.' Fat lot of good that'll do."

"We have to get people to stop believing in her and being scared of her," I said. "She can't do this."

"Look around," Isabelle said. "She already is doing this."

She looked at Haidar. Something passed between them. She frowned and looked back at the rose, like maybe it held the answers.

There had to be a way to stop this. The Hum world was too valuable to lose. So much of what made the city great came from the Hums and their culture. Besides that, they didn't deserve to be frightened and bullied out like this. No one deserved that.

My phone buzzed. My heart pounded. Everything threatened bad news. Daniel watched me as I read it.

Dad: It appears the Oracle has been swayed by these rabble-rousers more than we had hoped. Your mother tells me you're somewhere safe, so do not leave. Queen Amani has asked that we continue to shelter. The Council is working on a plan.

Dad never texted me. Things must be serious.

Olivia: Okay. Good luck.

He might be a jerk, but at least Dad was on the right side of all this. That counted for something.

But it wouldn't save him.

Queen Amani wanted us to stay sheltered. It made sense, and of course it was only right to obey the Faerie Queen.

It wasn't smart, though. Staying in Haidar's mansion might protect us, but it wouldn't protect the Humdrums, and what good was our temporary safety? Kelda would take over in the end, and I didn't plan on spending the rest of my life in hiding.

"I've got to go somewhere," I said suddenly. "Haidar, do you have a car I can borrow?"

Everyone turned to look at me. Lucas' face got even tighter.

"What the devil makes you think I'd let you take one of my cars?" he said.

"I've got to go," I said. "It's important."

"You're on lockdown," he said.

I looked at him, waiting for his eyes to connect with mine. "Apparently," I said, stressing each word, "I don't give a damn. There's a faerie I need to talk to. Can I take your car?"

He looked back at me, calculations and guesses ticking up behind his shadowed eyes.

"Everyone, sit tight," he said. "Olivia has somewhere to be."

CHAPTER TWENTY

Haidar led me up the stairs.

"This isn't the garage," I said.

"You're not taking my car," he said over his shoulder. Ahead of me, he lumbered up the steps like a hulking animal. "Kelda's sprites are swarming the freeways. But I can do you one better."

He led me past the bedrooms where Lucas, Daniel, and I had been staying, then up another flight of stairs. At the top of that one, he turned and went through a door. I felt instantly uncomfortable when I followed him in.

The four-poster bed and forest green wallpaper were as pretentious as the rest of the house, but this room was strewn with stray papers and dirty clothes he hadn't bothered to put in a hamper. An old remote-control quadcopter sat on a shelf, one of its propellers broken. A flat-screen TV was mounted on the wall across from his bed.

I picked my way over a wadded-up T-shirt and followed Haidar across the room. On his nightstand, I caught a glimpse of a sketch: Isabelle's face, her eyes luminous and her hair blowing across her face in the breeze. He saw me looking and snapped his fingers.

"This way, nosy," he said. He disappeared into a closet.

But it wasn't a closet. The moment I walked in, the racks of clothes and shoes shimmered and disappeared. In front of me, in the otherwise empty space, sat a tall wooden dresser. It looked ancient and worn, but ordinary. A faint trace of magic rose from it, a quiet thing like the smell of aging fabric.

Haidar opened the second drawer down. Inside was a shallow tray, fitted with dozens of tiny square compartments. Inside each square of polished wood sat a ring. Dozens of them winked up at me, each slightly different from the last.

"You'll want this one," Haidar said.

He pulled out a wide silver ring carved with undulating ripples that wove around the band. He pressed it in my palm.

"Put this on," he said. "Turn it three times clockwise. You'll find yourself at the entrance to the Waterfall Palace."

I closed my hand around the ring. The other bands glinted at me, each one promising something completely different.

"Where do all these go?" I said.

Haidar shut the drawer.

"Farthest one will take you to Egypt," he said. "But you might have a headache when you get there. That one won't hurt you. Probably not, anyway. To get back here, turn it three times counter-clockwise. You'll land back in the closet. Don't go poking around my room."

"Wouldn't dream of it," I said. I lifted the ring to examine it more closely. "You sure she'll be there?"

"This is your adventure, not mine," he said. "If she's not there, come back. I'm not heading into the forest to look for you."

"Thanks," I said.

He looked down at me, searching my face like he was trying to figure out whether to say something. He seemed to decide against it. He gave me a brisk nod, then backed out of the closet and shut the door.

The ring slid onto my finger like it had been made for me. I took a deep breath and turned it once.

This had better work.

I turned it again, then a third time. The moment it nestled back into place against my skin, the closet began to close in around me. The closet darkened and turned to blackness.

An instant later, with the whooshing sound of wind filling a vacuum, the world rushed back in on me, thick and heavy with trees. Cool air and the smell of moss and decomposing pine needles rose up around me. The thundering rush of hundreds of gallons of water filled my ears, and a gentle spray of mist kissed my face.

Directly ahead, a mossy rock face glistened in the gray afternoon light. Not far away, a handful of Humdrums stood on the bridge over Multnomah Falls. One of them raised a camera to her face and took a shot of the waterfall plunging from hundreds of feet above our heads. None of them had noticed me. None of them would.

I pulled my wand out of my hair. The bun it had been holding together fell apart, and my always-frazzled curls fell around my shoulders. I pressed the wand's tip gently to the rock face and wrote my name: *Olivia Feye.*

Moss grew along the lines I drew, following my wand like green paint.

The last time I had been here, I had been invited right in, through the rock face and straight into Amani's palace built into the hill.

Now I had to wait.

I felt something examining me. It might have been the rock wall. It might have been the trees. I couldn't tell. I stood up straighter. Behind me, a Humdrum woman shepherded three young children along the path that led down the hillside and to the viewing platform at the bottom of the falls. They didn't notice me—the glamour in the cliff made sure of that.

"I don't have an appointment," I said in a low voice.

Whatever presence was there seemed to consider this. Then, from inside my own head, a soft voice whispered *Proceed.*

I pressed my hand to the rock. It felt wet and alive beneath my palm as it gave way and allowed me to step through. Chunks of earth fell around me in a soft cascade, but they were gone the moment I stepped into Queen Amani's entrance hall.

The room was still the most beautiful I had ever seen, a dozen textures in shades of silver. In front of me, a glittering waterfall fell from the ceiling into a silver and blue tiled pool. Behind it, a curtain of hanging crystals illuminated the room.

There wasn't time to admire. I glanced around the room, taking in the four silver doors that led out. I knew which one I'd taken last time. I didn't know which one would lead me to Amani now. The white moth that had been my guide before was gone. The hall felt empty.

Underneath my shirt, the silver ring Amani had given me hung heavy and still. I hadn't used it in a while. I pulled it out from under my shirt, and the chain it hung from radiated warmth from my skin. I put the delicate ring on my smallest finger, where it glittered next to the thick one that had brought me here.

"Queen Amani," I said. My voice echoed around the silver room as though it were being reflected back to me by all the polished surfaces. The enchanted mirror set into the ring stayed clear, showing my own tiny face back at me.

I waited.

"Queen Amani," I said. I raised my voice. "I need to talk to you. Are you here? I need your help."

Nothing. The ring stayed clear. Within the mirror, I saw my eyebrows push together and my mouth tighten into a hard line.

"*Amani*," I said.

The farthest silver door on my left swung open. I looked down, expecting her face, but the ring stayed clear and silent.

The moment I stepped through the door, it swung shut behind me. I felt a frisson of magic and turned in time to see the edges of the door glow white. I didn't have to test the spell to know I'd been locked in.

The last time I'd been here, I'd been led to a hallway covered in pictures of Oregon. That hall had been tidy and proper, the photographs meant to highlight the region's beauty for the benefit of visiting dignitaries.

This corridor was something else entirely. Here, I felt as though I really was walking through a tunnel in the cliff face that surrounded Multnomah Falls. Roughly carved rock stretched up above my head, disappearing into shadows above.

The air smelled of damp earth, and cool air hung heavily around me and clung to my skin.

No lights lit the way. Instead, tiny glittering particles sparkled in the stone walls like shards of starlight. They cast a pale, eerie glow in the tunnel, barely enough to let me know that the ground beneath my feet was smooth and polished.

My wand was still in my hand. Creating a light wouldn't be hard. But I clenched my fingers around the wand's handle and held it still. Something about this corridor felt heavy and old. This wasn't a place for my magic.

Above me, something rustled. I looked up. It was impossible to make out anything clearly, but it seemed as though a white patch of something grew on the rock, maybe a lichen or another fungus. I mentally ran through my Oregon plants field guide, but no plants I knew rustled and shifted like that.

Then, as I watched, a tiny piece of white detached. It fluttered down and flapped its wings until it found a new spot on the side of the tunnel. As if called, a string of more papery moths followed it. They flitted together in a loose, quivering cloud and landed on the wall. I stepped to the side to give them room as they lazily beat their wings in place and settled in.

After what felt like minutes of silent walking, I reached the end of the tunnel. A silver door gleamed faintly in the glittering light. It had no handle, but when I pressed my hand against it, the door dissolved into mist.

What lay behind it was not a room.

It wasn't anything, as far as I could tell. Below, above, and off to every side, I was met only with swirling white fog.

The fog was deadly silent.

This looked like the inside of a cloud, or like the mist churning at the bottom of Multnomah Falls magnified a hundred times over. I bent down and waved my hand, trying to find a floor, but there was none.

Only the slightest shadows between curls of mist broke up the relentless whiteness. I felt my eyes focus and refocus as they tried to make sense of the senseless nothing that seethed before me.

Step through, said Amani's voice in my head.

I looked down. There was nothing below me. If I stepped over this doorway, I could land anywhere.

Or maybe I wouldn't land at all.

I stepped.

The ground materialized beneath me. I couldn't see it, but I felt it, firm and flat beneath my shoe.

Tension that I hadn't noticed building in my arms and between my eyes rushed away with a tingle. I let out the breath I'd been holding and walked deeper in. On the third step, something shifted. The air in the room grew warmer, and the fog seemed to shift. A moment later, I could make out shapes and colors. In another breath, the mist was gone.

"Olivia," Amani breathed.

CHAPTER TWENTY-ONE

Her appearance sent a chill down my spine.

"Are you okay?" I said.

Her face seemed thinner than usual, and the glazed exhaustion behind her eyes was impossible to miss or to hide. Her always-luminous skin seemed flat now. Everything about her seemed tired, from her limp hair to her mouth, set in a thin line.

But she smiled and beckoned me forward into the strangest room I'd ever seen.

A round moon so big I couldn't have wrapped my arms around it hung above us in the center of the circular room, rotating as if suspended from an invisible string. As I watched, it shifted from a sliver to a crescent, then from crescent to gibbous. Once it waxed full, it began melting, back to gibbous and then to a tiny sliver before growing again.

My eyes scanned the space. The room was broken into concentric circles, each one lower than the last, like steps in an amphitheater.

The outermost circle, the one that met the deep blue walls, was a slender gold flowerbed filled with dark soil. The scent of cedar rose into the air. From the soil grew pale mushrooms that ringed the room like sentinels. Behind them, on the walls, seven-pointed gold stars glittered in the luminous light of the moon.

In the next circle, half a foot down, the white mist that had filled the room hovered over a floor of silver tiles. The mist seemed contained, locked into the shape of a ring. Below that, a pool circled the room like a moat. The water inside it shone with vivid aqua light. Inside that, down another half-foot, tongues of orange fire licked up from a bed of blue crystals.

And there, in the heart of the room, surrounded by flames, Amani knelt on a silver floor engraved with a seven-pointed star.

She reached out a hand to me.

"It's okay," she said. "Come on down."

The stairs that led from the doorway were the only way in or out. I walked down the gleaming black steps, careful to place my feet in the center of each step so I wouldn't risk touching anything I shouldn't. On either side, I felt the magic creeping out toward me. In the corners of my vision, past the edges of my glasses, magic swirled thick and gold.

The center of the floor was bigger than I'd expected. I knelt across from Amani. The heat from the fires warmed my skin and lit hers up with a faint orange glow.

"I'm glad you're in one piece," she said.

"Someone was watching out for me."

Her face relaxed. "Haidar," she said. "I asked him to keep an eye on you as soon as you started going to the Rose Garden."

"You knew I was going," I said.

I couldn't stop it from sounding like a question. The Faerie Queen knew everything; it was well within her power to find out what I'd been doing. I just hadn't thought she'd cared.

She put a hand on my knee. Her skin burned through the fabric of my jeans.

"I'm so glad you've been pursuing your plants," she said.

I searched her face. This wasn't the time to be talking about my career goals. And anyway, the roses had been the least of it.

"The Oracle," I said.

A shadow passed over her face.

"She's strong," Amani said. "Does she know you're here?"

"I don't think so," I said. "I came straight from Haidar's house."

Amani's shoulders relaxed. She shifted from her knees to a cross-legged position and allowed herself to slouch.

She was wearing yoga pants, I noticed, and a sequined purple tank top. They both looked completely wrong in this room.

"Good," she breathed. "I've gone to so much trouble to make her think we were no longer associated." She gestured vaguely at me.

"I thought you just didn't want my help anymore," I said.

"I hope she thinks so, too," Amani said. "She's been collecting her strength for months, but even I had no idea how far she was willing to go." She stretched her arms out in front of her, like she was warming up before exercising. "Of course, I've always had a blind spot when it comes to Kelda."

She pressed her lips tight together and sighed sharply out through her nose. I recognized her expression. It was pure annoyance, directed entirely inward. It was impossible to be sure, but I had a feeling I wore that face a lot.

Amani snapped a hair tie on her wrist a few times. Despite the exhaustion that hung from her body, her movements were quick and restless. She put her hair up in a ponytail. Her normally wild curls seemed as tired and frazzled as the rest of her.

Suddenly, Amani's face changed. Her jaw grew tight and her eyes flashed. On instinct, I pushed myself back and away from her.

I was just in time.

She whipped both hands up between us. They sliced through the air, exactly where my face had been a moment earlier. Her eyes focused on something far in the distance, and I knew she couldn't see me anymore.

She rolled up to a crouch, then sprang to her feet and slammed both hands forward.

A blinding ball of gold fire shot out of her hands. It crashed against the blue walls. Around the impact, the gold stars on the walls burned hot and white. They seemed to diffuse the fire and absorb it into themselves. Around us, the ring of flames flared up. Amani's face shone gold in the light.

A tremor ran through me.

Her eyes blazed with a power I'd never seen in the face of a living being. Beneath her pale brown skin and mossy green eyes, Amani was a swirling inferno of magic and rage.

Our legends said the power of the Faerie Queen made the sea storm and the crops grow. When she was glad, our world floated on the power of her smile. When she was angry, we all paid the price.

Someone was paying the price now.

She threw out a hand. A bolt of blue lightning crackled from her fingertips, tracing a sparking line of electricity up to the sky. The moon crackled with the heat. She threw out another hand, and I crouched low to the floor to avoid the worst of a gust of wind so icy it made my hair freeze. The ring of fog spun like an out-of-control carousel around us, causing the flames on the lowest ring to flicker.

Then, as suddenly as it had started, everything stopped. Amani deflated. She crumpled to the ground and pressed her palms against the engraved silver floor.

When she looked up, she was just Amani again: a tired woman in yoga pants who looked like she could use a hug.

"What the hell was that?" I said. The icicles that had formed around my hair clinked gently by my ears.

She reached out toward me and touched a lock of my frozen hair. A moment later, it was soft and warm and dry again.

"Are you okay?"

"I moved in time," I said.

She pressed her hands flat to the floor again. "This is my studio."

I looked up, from the ring of fire to the glowing pool to the fog to the mushrooms, each layer like a stair leading up to the white door. Above us, the moon silently melted from full to waning.

"You're the only person who's ever been in here," she said. "Apart from Queen Phoebe, of course."

"Why?" I said. "What do you do here?"

A "studio" implied that this might be where she practiced her magic. But whatever had just happened, that hadn't been practicing.

"I fight off Kelda's sprites, lately," Amani said. "I can't get to her and she won't talk to me. We could fix this if she would just have a conversation like a normal adult."

"I don't think the Oracle is a normal adult," I said.

Amani scoffed. "You got that right," she said. She winced. "Sorry, hold on."

She doubled over and pressed her forehead to the cool silver floor. I watched her back rise and fall several times as she took deep, calming breaths.

My stomach turned over. This wasn't right. Nothing about this was right.

I held a hand out. Hesitantly, unsure whether this was okay or allowed or even safe, I touched her back.

"Amani," I said. "Are you okay?"

Beneath my hand, her skin trembled with another breath. She let it out in a heavy gust, and as she knelt there with her face to the floor, I felt my hand begin to tingle.

She breathed again, and this time, the air shuddered into her lungs. Beneath my fingertips, her energy began to pull from mine. I felt it, like a tiny breeze had formed just under my hand, as my strength and magic flowed from me into the tiny bumps of her spine.

Her breathing steadied. The next inhale was clean and easy. She moaned softly and sat up. I let my hand fall back into my lap.

Her eyes fluttered open and her gaze met mine.

"Thank you," she said. "That helps more than I can explain."

But she didn't have to explain. I could see it. Her skin, which had been flat and dry a moment before, had regained a tiny bit of its usual glow. Her shoulders drew back taller, and the crease between her eyes had softened.

"What are you doing in here?" I said.

"I can't be everywhere at once," she said. "Sometimes things happen quickly, and I need to be able to respond. Other times, I need to meet with other Glimmering leaders around the world, and we can't be in the same place at the same time. That's when I use this room. Duck," she added, suddenly sharp.

Again, she leapt to her feet. She held out a hand and thrust it out directly in front of her. Mist poured from her palm and surrounded us like fog rolling in off the ocean. It glowed faintly red. I pressed my body flat against the silver floor as the mist filled the room.

Amani sat back down. The fog faded in an instant.

Cautiously, I lifted my head.

"Okay to sit?" I said.

"Okay to sit," she said. "Good reflexes."

"What would that have done to me?" I said.

She tightened her ponytail. "Major disorientation," she said. "I tricked a bunch of sprites into flying straight into the river. Won't hurt them, but it got them away from a group of Hums, which was the main thing."

"Shouldn't you have, I don't know, other people doing this?" I said. "Why are you fighting sprites?"

"Our law enforcement isn't trained for this kind of thing," she said. "I've got enough magic to make a difference. Until I find a way to break into Kelda's Fountain and deal with her, I may as well help where I can."

I remember Isabelle criticizing Amani for not having her boots on the ground.

I wished she could see this.

"So the room lets you fight them anywhere?" I said.

"It lets me focus my magic," she said. "As queen, I have to be able to be anywhere, any time. That's not physically reasonable, but with this room, I can sort of... project my consciousness and energy wherever it needs to go. The elements support my magic, and the star and moon help me focus it." She nodded up toward the rings that surrounded us. "Earth, air, water, and fire," she said. "This way, when I throw a spell out, most of it gets caught in the rings and stays in the room. I can restore my magic quickly this way."

"Not quickly enough," I said.

She tilted her head at me.

"No offense," I said. "But you look like crap."

"I feel like it," she said. "Even with the room, it still takes time to absorb the magic back in. I know I should just pull the magic straight from the air and let it flow through me, but let's be real. I'm the Faerie Queen. My spells are stronger if the energy's been sitting inside me for a while."

"Whatever works," I said. "You need to make sure to take care of yourself, though."

She pressed her fingertips to the back of her neck and rolled her head back and forth. "I can rest when this is over," she said. "In fact, when this is over, everyone's going to be lucky if I don't just pack up and head to Fiji for a couple of weeks."

I had no idea if we'd survive without the Faerie Queen's presence that long, but it had to be worth the risk. No one should be as worn out from their job as Amani appeared to be right now. Even with the extra boost of my magic, she looked ready to drop.

I propped my chin on my knees and watched her as she closed her eyes and took a few deep breaths, trying to re-absorb the energy she'd just lost. It seemed impossible that she could restore anything that quickly. A single spell like the one she'd just thrown would be enough to knock me out for the rest of the day.

"Amani?" I said.

Her eyelids fluttered open.

"I'm not a good faerie," I said.

She opened her mouth, but I put a hand on her knee and shook my head. The touch seemed to calm her, so I kept my fingertips there, resting lightly in case she needed to pull from me again.

"I'm not," I said. "And I know you don't want me as your heir anymore. You haven't talked to me for months, and I get it. I do. It's okay. And I know I probably can't do anything, but I want to help."

"I can't keep disrupting your life," Amani said. "It's selfish."

"What's selfish is me sitting at Haidar's when you need every Glim you can get to help save this city," I said. "You shouldn't have to be running crowd control on a bunch of idiot sprites. You need to be out there, doing whatever you have to do to deal with Kelda."

I pressed my fingertips down, just gently enough to make sure she knew this was important.

"You're the only one who can touch her," I said. "And you need to go after the cause of all of this, or things are going to get a lot worse. I can't sit by and watch the world that belongs to the Humdrums be destroyed."

"I don't know how to stop it," she said.

For the first time, I saw the fear behind her eyes.

And for some reason, it made me calm.

"I've spent my life wishing I could be one of the Hums," I said. "I've wanted to choose their world since I was a kid. And now Kelda is making it so I won't have that choice anymore."

It was ironic and felt almost impossible, but it was the truth: The Humdrums and their world were the one thing I would embrace my magic to save.

"How can I help you?" I asked. "Tell me what to do."

CHAPTER TWENTY-TWO

She stood and began pacing.

As she walked, the flames nearby rose, as if attracted to her presence.

"You need to let me help," I said. "This isn't just about the Humdrums; this is about my parents, and my brother, and Lucas."

She frowned.

"Lucas," I said. "Sorry, a Humdrum friend of mine."

"Right," she said. "The one the Oracle sucked in. I'd forgotten. That's good. You'll need a Humdrum friend around."

She circled around me, and I leaned back on my heels to watch her. I could see the thoughts racing across her face.

"I need you to go on a quest," she finally said.

It was the last thing I'd expected. I was a godmother. I sent other people on quests. Going on one myself had not been in my plans.

Then again, neither had the rest of this.

"You need to collect three magical objects," Amani said. "They might not be easy to acquire."

"How's that going to help?"

She crossed behind me. The heat from the flames rose up hot against my back.

"We have to perform a spell," Amani said. "A massive, *massive* spell. I've never attempted anything on this scale before."

"And you need the objects," I said.

"If worse comes to worst, yes," she said.

She ran a hand through her hair, practically clutching at her scalp. She looked even crazier than I felt.

"Oh, gods," she breathed. She spun to face me. "I've been trying to negotiate things with Kelda for months. She will not talk to me. Not in any way that matters. And I've been trying to be patient with her, because—"

She stopped and stared at me. Her green eyes seemed enormous in her thin face.

"Never mind why," she said. "Because I'm weak. I have tried everything to avoid this, but she's crossed so many lines." She pulled at her hair again, like she was trying to yank her thoughts out by their roots. "This spell will strip her of her powers."

The words lingered in the air. Even the slowly rotating ring of fog seemed to freeze for a moment to take the words in.

Amani was going to strip the Oracle of her magic? I hadn't even dreamed such a thing was possible.

"Never put your ambitions before your friends, Olivia," Amani said, her voice fierce and low. "Your job, your goals, your politics—none of it is important enough to let the most important relationships in your life fall apart."

She slammed out a hand and sent a fireball spinning into the pool of water. This time, her eyes were fully present. There were no sprites here, just her, me, and what I thought might be her regrets. Lightning crackled from her other fingertips.

"Kelda is so competitive," she said. "She always has been, but I never thought she would do this. Who takes over an entire city just to prove people love them more?"

Amani wasn't talking to me anymore.

"Dear Titania, I don't want to do this," she breathed.

I stood. She trembled. The power thrumming through her body and this room seemed to be the only thing holding her up. Behind it all, she was as lost as I was. Maybe more.

"Amani," I said. I took hold of her shoulders and turned her to face me. "Do you have to?"

She searched my face like it held some way out.

Then, she nodded. The quivering line of her jaw steadied.

"I need an enchanted ring," she said. "Its circle will bind the Oracle. And then I need a golden goblet to hold the energy of the spell. And finally, and this is the part I am sorry for, I need Kelda's wand."

I let go.

Surely, *surely* Queen Amani didn't mean I had to go after it.

"Kelda's wand is a core part of her," Amani said. "It's the only thing that will make the spell last. This isn't just any enchantment. We have to bind her so securely that she can never frighten anyone again."

Fear shot through me.

I had offered to help. I'd thought that might mean fending off a few sprites, or helping Amani plan her next moves.

Stealing the Oracle's wand was a move so audacious that my heart skipped a beat in my chest.

"I would collect it myself, but you have no idea how many spells she has set up against me," Amani said. "She started putting them up when we were fourteen years old and I don't think she's ever stopped."

The glazed look crossed her face again. On instinct, I ducked to the ground. A stream of spells shot out above my head.

"Sorry," she said.

I looked up. She was back.

"You've known Kelda since you were fourteen?" I said.

I clambered to my feet. Beyond my glasses, the gold energies in the room swirled and spiraled around me. It was enough to make me dizzy. I focused on Amani's face through the lenses.

"Longer than that," Amani said. "We were best friends as children. I don't think we are anymore."

"You think?" I said dryly.

Instantly, I regretted the words as I saw the pain flash across the queen's face.

The regret that pulsed from her, so strongly she couldn't contain it, hit me with devastating familiarity.

"She was your Imogen," I said.

Amani's face tightened. She nodded.

"And she's jealous of you."

Amani sighed and sank back to the floor. I sat down across from her again.

"We were always in competition," she said. "Friendly competition, for a long time. But things started to become strained after I was named as Phoebe's heir. She was appointed Oracle not long after, and I was such an idiot. Instead of being proud of her, I just kept our stupid little rivalry going. It was a game to me, but—"

"Not to her."

"She's been getting permissive toward Glims for years," she said. "Trying to win their admiration and loyalty. She allowed people to misbehave more than I thought was appropriate. But I let her get away with it. I knew she needed authority over her own work, and I suppose I wanted her to be loved and admired as much as she did. But it wasn't enough. At the end of the day, I was still queen. We worked together, but I was still her boss."

"And she hated it."

"She hates me," Amani said.

The queen drew her knees up and pressed her forehead to them. She sighed deeply and looked up.

"I've never dared try this on my own," she said. "I've never wanted to, but I've never had the power, either. But I think, maybe, with you, I can do it."

The *no* I wanted to shout rose to my lips, but I bit it back and swallowed it down.

I was only a mediocre faerie. I didn't want any of this. I didn't understand why fate and my own impulses kept throwing me in the queen's path.

But I'd chosen to be here, and in front of me, Amani's face held the weight of a responsibility I could barely comprehend.

"I hope we'll only have to bind her so I can talk to her," Amani said. She let out a trembling breath. "I hope we can stop this there. But we have to be prepared." She shook her head and corrected herself. "I have to be prepared."

We sat in silence for a moment. The flames danced and the water rippled around us. From the top of the room, the mushrooms regarded us like curious observers.

"You'll need to be able to move around the city without being seen," Amani said.

Her tone and posture were suddenly brisk and businesslike. Whatever we had to do, she'd come to terms with it.

I wished I could catch up to her that quickly. The thought of doing as she asked made goosebumps rise up on my arms so hard they hurt.

Amani stood and walked up the black stairs until she reached the level of the pool. She put her hand into the water and closed her eyes. A moment later, something shimmered with a flash of gold, and she pulled out two necklaces on thin golden chains.

"These are for you," she said. "One for you, one for your friend Lucas, if he's willing. You'll need a driver and a Hum will know his way around the city without using any of the rainbow roads."

She came back down and dropped the necklaces into my outstretched palm. They were heavy and still wet from the pool.

"Wear these and they'll do their best to hide you from the sprites," she said. "Or at least, they'll keep you from catching their attention."

I held one up to examine it. I recognized the gold filigree pendant. The image was of Multnomah Falls with the bridge spanning its lower section. I'd seen these in the Humdrum gift shop by the road.

Amani smiled wryly. "The items will be a little harder to find."

She began pacing the circle again. The gold stars set into the walls above us winked as the pale moon changed from crescent to gibbous.

"The first one you're looking for is an enchanted ring," Amani said. She tapped her hands together as she paced, as if keeping them moving would keep her thoughts moving, too. "It's an unusual piece, very old, made of gold and set with a rose carved out of quartz. From what I understand, it was made by a Faerie Queen from when Portland was a new city and it has more charms than a single piece of jewelry should be able to hold."

An image flickered in my mind, of a pink quartz ring on a familiar hand.

"I don't know where it is," she said. "I'm hoping that, if you can help me, we can send out a locator spell."

Seriously? I thought, and the voice in my head sounded on the edge of a nervous breakdown. *Seriously?!*

"No need," I said. I stood and wiped my sweating palms on my jeans. "I know exactly where it is."

CHAPTER TWENTY-THREE

Three twists, and I hurtled from the tunnel outside Amani's studio and back into Haidar's closet.

My head spun, though it was impossible to tell if that was thanks to the unusual mode of transportation or sheer panic at what I was about to do.

I wasn't even tempted to poke through Haidar's stuff. I put the ring carefully back in the drawer and then hurtled myself through his room and back down the stairs.

They were all sitting around the table where we'd had breakfast. Either they'd heard my footsteps or Daniel's faerie gifts had alerted them that I was on my way, because by the time I stopped in the doorway, every face was turned toward me.

"Haidar," I said. "I seriously do need to borrow your car."

He pushed his chair away from the table and stood.

"I'll get the keys."

I could see the questions forming behind Isabelle's dark eyes, but I didn't have time to explain. Instead, I turned to Daniel. The question was one I didn't want to ask, but he'd come this far. He deserved to decide his own next steps.

"Queen Amani just gave me a couple of assignments," I said. "I need to collect some things around town. Do you want to come with me?"

Surprise shifted over his face, as obvious as expressions usually were on faeries but twice as quick.

"Do you need me?" he said. "I've been talking to Haidar and I think I can be useful here, but I'll come if you need help."

"No, stay here," I said. Relief pooled in my stomach. "I'd rather you stay safe."

"I don't know that *safe* is the right word," Isabelle said. "What kind of stuff are you collecting?"

"Stuff," I said. "A ring, a goblet, and something else I don't want to get into right now."

The *something else* was enough to make a tiny scowl appear between her eyebrows. But instead of asking about it, she tapped her fingertips on the table and said, "What kind of goblet?"

"A gold one," I said. "The queen said it belongs to a sprite named Brooke."

Isabelle's fingers tapped harder against the table.

"Brooke?" she repeated.

"Yeah," I said.

She slammed her hand down. "Can I come? I owe that little nightmare a visit."

Somehow, the idea of having an irritated Isabelle on hand didn't make me feel better about this mission.

"You're probably needed here."

She groaned, but we both knew I was right. She pointed at me. "Scare the fountain water out of her for me," she said. "That's an order."

"You got it, sergeant," I said.

"That little water devil stole that goblet from Haidar," Isabelle said. "Half the magic of this manor is locked up in that cup. Any chance he'll get it back when Amani's done with it?"

Haidar strode back into the room, a small chain of keys in hand.

"Get what back?"

"Absolutely nothing," Isabelle said. She folded her arms across her chest and scowled. The air seemed to crackle around her. I peered over my glasses. A storm cloud had begun to form over her head.

"Sleeping Beauty here did not get her eight hours," Haidar said dryly. He ignored Isabelle's indignant look, and so did I.

She may have been grumpy, but Isabelle was no Sleeping Beauty. I couldn't imagine her napping through her Story in a hundred years.

Haidar handed me the keys. There were three of them, all looped on a silver ring with a keychain shaped like a blooming rose.

"What about you?" I said.

Lucas didn't wait for more of an invitation. In a second, he was by my side.

"Liv?" Daniel said. "Be safe."

I wanted to hug him, but I knew he'd never put up with it. Instead, I sent him a push of grateful energy. He offered a smile in return.

Haidar led us to the garage.

The opulence of the house should have prepared me. But somehow, I hadn't expected to find four cars there. One was a blue Honda Accord. Another was a Porsche. I didn't recognize the other two, but it was clear that the insurance alone on those things probably cost more than my college tuition would.

"Whoa," Lucas said. "Is that a Ferrari?"

"FF model," Haidar said. "You're driving the Honda."

Lucas ogled the cars. I felt the fascination that drew him toward the machines.

"We're risking our lives here," I said.

"Honda," Haidar said firmly. He handed me the keys. "Drive safe."

I wasn't sure if his concern was for the car or our safety, but I nodded. I held out the keys to Lucas.

"Can you drive?" I said. "I need to be able to fight off any sprites that notice us."

"You should definitely handle the fighting sprites thing," Lucas said.

His fingers closed around the keys. I met his eyes, and for a moment, we just watched each other.

He shouldn't have been pulled into all this. In other circumstances, he would be going about an ordinary day right now, maybe sitting in class and listening to ludicrous rumors about gang wars or UFOs.

Instead, he was here with me, and I couldn't bring myself to be sorry about it.

The garage doors jolted into movement with a loud creak. I jumped and felt myself blush. He smiled halfway and nodded toward the car.

We climbed in. He started the engine, and it purred to life. Even Haidar's most boring car was the nicest one I'd ever sat in. Judging from the new car smell and spotless carpets, he'd never actually used the thing. Why bother, when a dresser full of magic rings would take him wherever he needed to go?

Anyway, I wanted Lucas with me.

Lucas shifted the car into gear. The tone of the engine shifted just slightly.

"Okay," he said, as if the word alone was a pep talk. "Where to?"

I buckled my seat belt and felt the magic in my body gather into my fingertips, ready to fly out just in case.

"I need you to take me home."

CHAPTER TWENTY-FOUR

I couldn't believe how normal everything felt.

Somehow, the regular Humdrum traffic and cloudy sky unnerved me more than a whole horde of sprites would have. At least with sprites, I could see what I was up against.

The necklaces Amani had given me glinted around each of our necks. We drove in near silence. Magic crackled in my fingertips, and I scanned the world around us for signs of sprites or the Oracle, on the off chance the necklaces weren't enough. Whatever Kelda had planned, though, didn't—or couldn't—involve us being attacked on the way to my house.

It was almost worse this way: The tension of waiting for the hammer to fall was unbearable.

My neighborhood looked ordinary, except for an overturned trash can that could have been knocked over by a raccoon as easily as a sprite. I looked in the window of every fancy house we passed, expecting to see faces watching us, but there was nothing.

Not that Kelda would need to hide in windows. The puddles from an early morning rain gave her enough of a view.

"Stay here," I said. "I need to talk to my mom alone."

"Someone should probably keep an eye on the car," he said. He lifted the necklace that dangled from his neck, then let it drop again.

I nodded and climbed out of the car. I allowed myself one last look at his familiar face before I slammed the door shut and ran into the house.

The door was doubly secured. I unlocked it with my key, then held out my hand to let the enchantment verify that I was allowed to be here. White light pulsed around the door, and then the handle clicked loose and the door opened.

"Mom?"

I shut the door behind me and stepped cautiously into the entrance hall.

Within seconds, she was there, wand drawn. As soon as she saw it was really me, half the tense lines on her face melted in relief. She hugged me. An instant later, the lines were back.

"Where's Daniel?" she said.

I put a hand on her arm. "He's safe," I said firmly. "He's with friends."

It was hard to tell whether she believed me, but then, I wouldn't have believed me either. Anyone who had any clue about what was happening knew no one was really safe in this city today.

"I can only stay for a minute," I said.

"Olivia—"

"Mom," I said.

She fell silent. She wasn't used to hearing that much authority in my voice.

Neither was I.

"Mom, this is important," I said. "Things are bad out there. Like, *bad,* bad."

She pulled me in for another hug. "I know, sweetie. I'm so glad you're okay."

We didn't have time to be glad. Because right now, my being "okay" was a temporary and totally uncertain thing.

"I'm trying to help," I said. "I'm working with someone to try to fix this, but I need something from you. I need your ring. The rose quartz one."

Mom pulled back. She held me by the shoulders and looked at me. Her gaze darted back and forth between my eyes, then into every corner of my face. I waited. I couldn't hide anything from her. I was a faerie, and faeries were terrible at hiding things.

More than that, I was her daughter, and she was worried. Her attention was on me with the kind of focus that would put a laser to shame.

"This is really important," I said.

"I can tell," she said. She tucked a strand of hair behind my ear.

She let go and walked down the hall toward the kitchen. I followed her.

"Have a seat," she said. She gestured toward the island.

I sat on one of the stools. The tips of my shoes rested on the bar beneath the seat and my knees bounced up and down. Impatience to be gone crept and tingled down my arms. I could tell she felt it, but she pulled two mugs out of the cupboard. Her movements were slow and measured. I tried to force my breathing to an even rhythm.

"Lucas is waiting in the car," I said.

"Would you like to invite him in for tea?" she said.

I drummed my fingertips on the sharp edge of the counter.

"No, that's okay," I said.

She dropped tea bags in the mugs and tapped the faucet three times. When she turned the water on, it poured hot and steaming into the cups. She set the full mugs on the counter and came around to sit by me.

I blew on my tea to cool it.

What was I doing here? There was literally an evil faerie bent on destroying our world, and I was sitting in my kitchen, drinking chamomile-peppermint with my mom.

"You going to tell me what's going on?" she said.

She sipped and watched me over the edge of the mug.

There was too much to tell, and nowhere to start.

I tapped my fingernail on my mug. Each tap clinked softly.

Mom let out a sigh that sounded like she'd been holding it for years.

"Do you really not feel like you can trust me?" she said.

"It's not about trusting you," I said.

Though of course it was. No one in my family trusted anyone else. I'd even been glad to leave Daniel at Haidar's place, not because I didn't trust him to be on my side but because I didn't trust him to keep himself safe.

Our whole family was nothing but the things we chose not to say.

Mom set her cup down hard onto the counter, then picked it back up.

I didn't even need to feel her frustration to see it there, in the faint wrinkles between her eyes and the tension in her fingers as they wrapped around the mug.

The tea slipped down hot into my belly. I could almost feel the moment it splashed into my stomach. The warmth should have relaxed me, but I was too deep in this for relaxation.

"Your grandfather was never really there for your dad," Mom said.

I tapped my toes against the bar and resisted the urge to ask what that had to do with anything and could I please take her ring and go, please?

"I always promised myself my children wouldn't feel abandoned like that," Mom said.

Were we really going to have this heart-to-heart *now?*

"I don't feel abandoned," I said.

"Neither did your father," she said. "Haven't you ever wondered why he pushes you so hard?"

"He's Dad," I said. "It's what he does."

My fingers twitched. Every second here was another second the Oracle's sprites were loose on the city.

"Your grandpa always pushed him too hard, too," she said. "Grandpa Edgar wanted your dad to be perfect at everything. When he was perfect, Edgar saw that as the bare minimum. When he wasn't perfect, Edgar didn't consider him worthy of attention."

"Sounds like a jerk," I said.

Grandpa Edgar had died before I started kindergarten, but I had a few fuzzy memories of a reserved man with silver hair.

I hadn't liked him or disliked him. He'd existed, there in the world of the grownups, and it had never occurred to me that he was my business.

"He was a jerk like your dad's a jerk," Mom said.

I raised an eyebrow. It was obvious to anyone who paid attention that my mom didn't exactly think my dad was a teddy bear, but I'd never heard her actually call him names. Not when she knew I was listening, at least.

"I mean Edgar couldn't help himself," Mom said. She set her mug on the counter and waved her fingers over it, letting them take in the heat. "He was busy and he'd never been raised to show affection. He was the kind of person who expressed his love by criticizing."

"That's not how you express love," I said.

"For some people it is," she said. "If you're criticizing, that means you're at least paying attention, right?"

I kept the eyebrow up.

"That took its toll on your dad," Mom said. "It's taken its toll on you and Daniel."

"Mom," I said. "Don't take this the wrong way, but why are we talking about this?"

Mom propped her elbow on the table and rested her head in her hand.

"I don't know," she said. "Never mind. What did you need my ring for?"

I didn't answer. She looked sad—sad and lost. Too late, I realized I probably should have been listening instead of counting the seconds to getting out the door.

I stilled the impulse to text Lucas and let him know I'd be a few minutes.

"Sorry," I said. "Um, are you okay?"

It was clearly the most insightful and empathetic comment in the world.

"I'm fine," Mom lied.

I pushed my mug away.

"I know when someone's faking it, Mom."

A faint smile tugged at the corner of her lips.

"Of course you do," she said. "You fake it all the time."

For a moment, I remembered that she was my mother. Not just the woman who'd birthed me and reminded me to do chores, but also the woman who still remembered my first words and had continued to stick my artwork on the fridge even after I was way too old for that kind of thing.

I crossed my ankles and pressed my hands between my knees.

"I need the ring because Queen Amani needs it to stop the Oracle," I blurted.

The words floated in the air, hanging there like something I'd let escape from a cage and couldn't put back.

And for some reason, she didn't look surprised.

"Okay," she said.

I blinked.

"Okay?"

"The ring's upstairs," she said.

She slid off her stool and walked out of the kitchen. I stared for a second, then hopped down and scurried after her.

"You're just going to give it to me?" I said, jogging up the stairs behind her.

"No offense, sweetie, but you really couldn't take it by force," she said over her shoulder.

"I was thinking, like, pleading or bad excuses," I said.

I followed her into her bedroom. She'd been sleeping there alone for months; when he was home, Dad lived in his office or the guest bedroom down the hall. Her marble jewelry box sat on her dresser on top of a pale cream doily. She waved her hand over the box, releasing the locking charm that held it closed, and lifted the lid.

It took only a second of rummaging to find the ring. It was easy to find. Though it didn't look much different than the other gold and silver pieces in the box, it gave off the unmis-takable zing of magic.

Mom held it out to me.

I wrapped my fingers around it.

"Mom?"

"Yeah?" she said. She closed the box and locked it again.

"Why are you not freaking out?"

"Do you want me to?"

"No," I said. "I just…"

I just what? I didn't know what I had expected. Panic, maybe. Or stern orders to go get Daniel and bring him home. Or maybe at least just a shred of resistance.

"I do divination," Mom said. She stared at me, not like she was trying to figure something out but like she already had. "My visions have been telling me not to underestimate you for a long time."

I felt my eyebrows crinkle. "You do divinations about me?" I said.

"Yes, Olivia," Mom said, in an overly patient voice. "I'm your mother. Most of my divinations are about you and Daniel."

"I thought your divination was for work," I said. "And, you know, your whole 'finding yourself' thing."

Her eyebrow went up. It occurred to me that I'd probably inherited that exact expression from her.

"My 'finding myself' thing?"

"You dyed your hair red and started flying to Argentina," I said.

She rested her palm against the edge of the dresser and leaned in, putting her weight on it.

"I did that for you and Daniel too," she said. "And for me. Do you know how many years it had been since I touched my scrying mirror?"

"I don't know," I said. "A while."

"Thirteen years," she said. "I put it away not long after Daniel was born, because your father thought it wasn't appropriate for me to spend so much time on my craft. He thought I'd be neglecting you."

Anger flared in me. How dare he try to stop her from pursuing her magic, just like he'd tried to stop me from pursuing my goals of studying in the Humdrum world?

How dare she let him?

"Dad's a moron," I said.

"Your dad tries his best," Mom said sharply. But then her face softened. "Reginald didn't understand that I could do more than one thing at a time. Reginald isn't good at complexity."

"Reginald is a control freak," I said.

"That's true, too," Mom said. "I decided I needed to take some of that control back. And I think you deserve a chance to do that, too." She nodded toward the ring. "Whatever you're doing, it's your choice. I'm not going to stand in your way."

I frowned at her. Even though her face was as familiar to me as my own, I felt like I'd never actually seen it before. I looked at her big dark eyes, her tidy noise, her thin lips softened by years of applying beeswax every night before bed, and her weird auburn hair. I'd taken all that in before. But beyond all that, just behind her eyes, I saw fire.

"Thanks," I said. "Wish me luck."

"With that ring you won't need too much," Mom said. "It's been in my family a long time. It's seen adventures no one even remembers anymore."

Somehow, I didn't have to ask which great-great-grandma had owned it first.

"I'd better go," I said.

Mom nodded. The lines of her face tightened, but she didn't stop me.

Instead, she followed me out of the room and down the stairs.

"Olivia?" she said.

I turned around. She stood on the bottom step, looking intently down at me.

She held out her arms. I walked into them, and her arms wrapped around me with the smell of vanilla and cloves.

"Be safe," she said. "And honey? Give her hell."

CHAPTER TWENTY-FIVE

My phone buzzed. My hand shot into my pocket to grab it.

Amani: Found the goblet. It's at Gilt with the sprite.

I groaned. Lucas looked sharply over at me.

"What?" he said.

He turned the corner. We'd been circling this neighborhood for twenty minutes while Amani tracked down the next item for her spell. I'd been ready for anywhere but there.

"It's at this club," I said.

"What's wrong with it?" he said.

"Nothing." I put the phone back in my pocket and pointed ahead, telling him to go straight through the intersection. A single drop of rain landed on the windshield. "It's just, it's a popular place for Glims. A popular place for popular Glims.

And if a sprite is there, I'd say it's a good chance that the popular Glims are now the ones the Oracle has in her watery pocket."

"Probably a safe guess," Lucas said. He ran a hand through his dark hair. It was a nervous habit; he'd been doing it every few blocks since we'd left my house. "Especially seeing as how everyone is supposed to be on lockdown."

"In their homes," I said, finishing the thought. "So we're dealing exclusively with people who have freedom of movement."

"Sprites," Lucas said.

"Fantastic."

I watched him as we drove. I knew the way from here, so I told him where to go. He kept his eyes intently on the road, only taking breaks to check his mirrors or scan the sky for trouble.

He seemed calmer now that he had something to do. Sitting around at Haidar's hadn't been good for him, but out here, alone with me and able to help, his posture and energy had both settled. He shouldn't have been part of any of this, but somehow, he had relaxed into it.

I imagined reaching across the space that separated us and putting my hand on his shoulder, maybe his knee. I wanted to thank him, to reassure him, to tell him how grateful I was to have a friend.

But we were half a block from Gilt, and it was time to park and go in to face the next step of our quest.

"Right here," I said. I waved toward an open space. Usually, trying to find parking in Portland at this time of day was an ordeal. But today, the streets felt empty. Only Humdrums drove down the roads and walked along the sidewalks, and there weren't many of them. A woman hurried past our car. She glanced in our windows and quickly looked away.

I climbed out. Lucas fed the meter while I paced behind him, hugging myself against the chill and hoping Amani's necklaces would hide us at least until we got into the club.

"You should wait here," I said.

He glanced up at the building I'd pointed out to him. It stood innocently, looking for all the world like just another restaurant behind an old brick façade.

"Not a chance," he said. "You're not going in there alone."

I couldn't bring myself to argue. We crossed the street to a plain door that looked like it was only there for deliveries. I tucked my necklace underneath my shirt.

Normally, a bouncer stood outside Gilt, making sure only Glims came in. Today, though, whoever was running the place hadn't seen the need for precautions. The door stood cracked a few inches. I nudged it further open with my wand.

Nothing happened. The staircase was empty.

I nodded to Lucas behind me. His presence here would either help or throw everything into chaos. It was impossible to guess which way things would go.

Unlike every other time I'd been here, no pulsing dance music made the walls vibrate. Instead, I heard only the mellow tones of someone singing to acoustic guitar, accented by the soft burble of conversation. Warm light poured from teardrop-shaped crystal lamps attached to the silvery sage walls.

I waved at Lucas to follow me up the steps.

The door at the top of the stairs led into the actual club. I stopped in front of it and held my wand up carefully in front of me. Behind the door, the voices continued to rise and fall, oblivious to our presence.

What's the plan, Feye? I demanded.

But any voices in my head remained silent.

There was no plan.

I inched toward the door. And then I stopped cold as her voice floated out toward me.

"I give her two more weeks to have this place totally cleared," she said. Her laugh hit my ears, so familiar it took everything I had not to double over in pain. "I can't believe how quickly she's made this all happen. It's, like, beyond crazy."

Lucas pressed his hand gently against my back.

"What's wrong?" he whispered, so softly I could barely tell the voice was his and not just one of my stray thoughts.

I turned back to him and mouthed her name.

Imogen.

Something flashed over his pale face, but I couldn't identify the emotion. My faerie senses were closing in on me, making the world seem too bright and sending the feelings and impulses of everyone just behind that door crashing over me until I felt my knees tremble with the effort of standing.

This one wanted to go home. That one was getting a headache. Another one hated someone else in the room, and someone else was having the time of her life.

And in the middle of it all, Imogen reveled.

Lucas was no faerie. He had no idea what was happening. But he was my friend. In an instant, he was right behind me. He wrapped one arm tight around my waist and the other around my shoulders and held me to him. His heartbeat pounded against my back as the world tilted and blurred in front of me. My knees trembled, and in an instant he was the only thing holding me up.

"You're okay, Liv," he whispered against my ear. "You've got this. Remember to breathe."

I zoned in on his heartbeat. Its rhythmic thump-thump was the only thing in the world I could count on. I listened for it, felt for it, and tried to match my breathing to its pattern.

In, thump, thump, thump.

Out, thump, thump, thump.

In again.

Slowly, the world stopped spinning. The emotions screaming for attention in my head faded back, until all that was left
were the faint conversations behind the door. At the edges of
my vision, a silver shield glimmered, covered with vines.

I let a breath out. My body relaxed. Hesitantly, Lucas let go.

"I'm okay," I whispered.

"You're okay," he confirmed. He squeezed my arm, then
fell back into place behind me.

I crept toward the door and slowly, carefully pushed it open.

She was impossible to miss. Even in a room full of silvery
sprites and crystal chandeliers, Imogen glittered.

She sat at a table with a handful of sprites. Some of them
looked like petite humans with white-blond hair; others let
their tell-tale blue shimmer loose, and still others were translucent and rippling and looked like they'd splash to the floor if
anyone touched them. I pushed down my glasses. Past the
lenses, the room practically swam in shifting blue light.

In the middle of it all, Imogen's magic pulsed warm and
gold. Her aura was bigger than last time I'd seen her, and it
swirled so quickly it seemed frantic. But Imogen herself was
languid. She hung her arm over the back of her chair and
slouched elegantly as she watched the room. Her hair seemed
almost rose gold in the light. It was swept into a French twist
on her head, and her lilac silk blouse made her shimmer.

The dance floor, which was usually empty, now contained several clusters of sofas and armchairs. Sprites slept on a few of them. The ones that weren't sleeping talked softly together. Occasionally, a laugh rose up.

No one noticed us.

I crept into the room. Behind me, Lucas followed. Part of my mind screamed to get him back out to the car where he'd be safe, but I couldn't. I needed him. I held a hand out behind me. He took it and squeezed, and then I let go, raising my hand to throw a spell just in case they saw us and my wand wasn't enough.

"The real holdouts are going to be the ones who've been squatting in the same horrible place for decades, clinging desperately to their rent-controlled apartments," said a sprite at Imogen's table.

I had to squint to see which one was talking. Sprites looked too similar. They all had the same pale hair, the same delicate features, the same big blue eyes, the same slender figures. This one wore a white tunic and blue jeans. It was impossible to tell her age.

"Her Honor doesn't plan on getting everyone out," Imogen said. She looked over the room as though this conversation was too boring to deserve her full attention. "She doesn't need to. As long as people understand the way we do things now, they're welcome to stay."

A couple of the sprites laughed. The others gave each other knowing looks.

"The news has finally started to leak beyond Portland," another sprite said.

"Of course it has," Imogen said. "Even the most obtuse Humdrums realize something's going on. In another week, they won't have to wonder about the details."

"You think it will only be another week?"

"Do you honestly think it will be more?" Imogen said. She looked sharply across the table at the sprite that had spoken. "You know the plan. Get the Glims into lockdown. Scare out everyone who can be scared. Deal with this ridiculous Huntsmen problem. Close the city limits."

"And then we can live as we were meant to live," a sprite said.

"We'll never have to hide our magic again," another said. He held out his hand and a tiny fountain erupted in his palm.

"Speaking of," Imogen said. She waved her hand at the sprites around the table who looked like they could be anyone off the street. "What is this?"

The sprites shifted in their seats, looking almost embarrassed. Shimmering light started to ripple around them, casting blue ripples on their skin.

"I'm not used to that yet," one of them said. "Being able to just *be.*"

I watched as emotions filtered over their faces, confusion and satisfaction and pure discomfort at something unfamiliar. I'd never seen a sprite out in public with their shimmer visible. They weren't like faeries or witches, who could blend into the human crowds with no effort. They were like mermaids and werewolves; their magic was visible and its appearance sometimes couldn't be controlled. That was why most sprites stayed in the fountains—they were only allowed to roam freely once they'd demonstrated they could control their appearance enough to blend in with the Humdrums.

What must that be like? I'd spent my life hiding my faerie side from the Humdrums and my Humdrum interests from my family. But it had come easily. What if I'd had to work at it?

The relief they felt lapped over me, familiar and strange all at once.

Lucas nudged me in the back. I jumped.

We had a mission.

I straightened up and walked into the room. Still, no one noticed us. Whatever charm was on these necklaces, it was a strong one. I twisted my hair up into a bun and jabbed my wand through it.

"The goblet is with someone named Brooke," I said.

"We obviously can't go around and ask everyone's names."

"Can you imagine?" I muttered. "No, we'll have to look. It's here somewhere."

We started walking between the tables together. Everyone here seemed to be drinking water out of plain glass goblets. No special magic seemed to come off of them. After a while, we split up and prowled the room separately. I was tense and looked up every few seconds, waiting to see Lucas wave me over and tell me he'd found it, but the minutes crept past with nothing to show for them.

I avoided getting too close to Imogen's table. I'd been practically attached to her for years, but now, the thought of my energy touching hers was enough to make my stomach turn over.

Her table was the only one I hadn't looked over, though, so I skirted around its edges, avoiding brushing against any of the sprites.

Glass goblets, a couple of cell phones, and a single chewing gum wrapper sat on the cream tablecloth. Around it, a couple of the sprites had purses or handbags, but I didn't sense anything strange in any of them. I looked for signs that any of these people were Brooke—a personalized bracelet, a Humdrum ID that happened to be lying out. But, of course, there was nothing.

I caught Lucas' eye across the room and shook my head. He shook his back.

We were getting nowhere.

When I looked back down at the table to give it one final scan, I jumped.

Imogen locked gazes with me. I stared at her, and she stared back.

"You can see me?" I said.

Almost imperceptibly, she nodded. She glanced around the table and looked back up, the message clear: *They can't?*

"No," I said.

None of the sprites seemed to hear my voice. Two of them kept talking about how they wished the lockdown would hurry up and end so they could get back to shopping at Glim stores downtown.

Goosebumps prickled down my arms.

"Yeah," Imogen said, slowly, drawing out the word like she was unbelievably bored. "Guys, I have some business to wrap up. I'll be in my office. Knock if you need me."

She stood, her thin, lanky figure seeming to unfold from the chair.

"You have an office?" I said, following behind her. "At Gilt?"

Lucas started walking toward us. I waved frantically at him to stay where he was. Imogen hadn't seen me until I was close; with any luck, she'd never know he was here.

Though maybe keeping him away wasn't the best idea. As far as I knew, she'd only dumped him. That was nothing for Imogen. She could dump seven boyfriends in a year without breaking a sweat.

She didn't hate him like she did me.

I crooked my finger at him, gesturing to follow us slowly.

I followed Imogen through a nondescript door. I'd never noticed it before; it looked like a service door Gilt employees might use to bring hors d'oeuvres in from the kitchen during events.

Instead of leading to a kitchen or hallway, though, the door opened directly onto a private office. It was a nice one, too, with pale silvery-blue walls and a gleaming charcoal desk. A crystal chandelier hung in the center of the room. It wasn't turned on, but the charmed crystals gave off a pale white light anyway.

She ignored the desk and waved me to one of two charcoal plaid armchairs set by the tall picture window. The view outside was obscured by sheer silver curtains. She shut the door firmly, leaving Lucas outside.

"I have an office," Imogen said, like I was an idiot, "because the Oracle's heir needs an office. It'd be pretty unprofessional if I didn't have one, don't you think?"

"Imogen," I said.

Too many words fought to be the first out of my mouth. I wanted to apologize, to ask where we went wrong, to tell her everything that was wrong with Kelda, to convince her to come back to the side that wasn't bent on destroying every-thing.

EMMA SAVANT

Instead, I couldn't say anything.

"Have a seat," she said.

Her voice was cool and distant. I sat and tried to look confident.

Imogen walked to a sideboard loaded with bottles and poured herself a glass of sparkling water. She added a pinch of silver fairy dust and walked over to me.

"What are you doing here?" she said.

She sank into the seat opposite me and surveyed me, like I was a mildly interesting specimen instead of her friend, or even her enemy.

"I'm looking for a goblet," I said.

She raised a smoothly manicured eyebrow. She looked different, and older. "Try IKEA."

"A specific goblet," I said. "A sprite named Brooke has it. I need it."

"Why?" she said.

"Seeing as how we're on opposite sides of this, you don't really think I'm going to answer, do you?" I said.

She smiled—not enough to imply amusement, but just enough to let me know that she wasn't threatened.

"Brooke doesn't have the goblet," she said. "I do. She gave it to me for safekeeping." She laughed. "That was her story, anyway."

"Why else would she give it to you?"

"You really have no idea what's been going on here, do you?" Imogen said. "She was trying to impress me."

She rolled her eyes, but I still knew her better than that. Whatever had happened, she loved it.

How had it come to this? We were supposed to be best friends. We were supposed to be helping each other get ready for senior prom and graduation.

"How'd you meet Haidar?" she asked.

She leaned back in her chair and crossed her legs. She sipped her water; the fairy dust in it sparkled and danced inside the glass tumbler.

"You don't need to look so shocked, Olivia," she said. "Obviously you know Haidar. Why else would you be here? Only Haidar would be self-absorbed enough to think all this business between our rulers was a perfect time for him to get his precious goblet back." She swirled her drink. "And only Haidar would be cowardly enough to send a child to collect it for him."

Haidar. She thought I was here for Haidar.

I remembered Isabelle telling me to give Brooke hell for her.

I had no idea what the history was here. But it didn't matter. It had given me an opening.

"Haidar is not a coward," I said. "He's not exactly charming, but cowardice is not one of his problems."

"Why else would he send you?" Imogen said. "It's cowardice or laziness, and I wouldn't put either past him."

"How do you know him so well?"

"Oh, we've never met," she said, waving me off with the drink still in her hand. The sparkling water sloshed inside the glass. "Brooke knows him, though. She told me more than I cared to hear, honestly. Nothing talks as much as a sprite bending over backwards to get your attention."

"Nothing lies as much either, I guess," I said.

"Aw," Imogen said. She gave me the most condescending smile I'd ever seen. "You're defending him. How sweet."

"I'm not defending him, I just think your sprite is making crap up," I said. "Or you are."

I scanned the room. It seemed innocent enough, but the goblet could be hiding anywhere: in a desk drawer, behind the books on the bookcase, in a concealed panel in the walls. I took off my glasses and cleaned them on my shirt. Even without their shield, the only magic I saw in the room was Imogen's.

"That's always been part of the Faerie Queen's job, you know," Imogen said. Her aura sparked. "Defending the so-called 'worthy' who can't protect themselves. Your precious Amani must be so proud."

"She's not my 'precious Amani,'" I said. I shoved the glasses back onto my face. "She's my queen. And yours."

Imogen laughed again, with real mirth this time.

"My queen?" she said. "*My* queen? Seriously? Olivia, have you seen anything happening around you?"

"I haven't wasted my time worrying about it," I said.

I glared at her. How had she gotten so stupid?

"Her Majesty's going to deal with you," I said. "You're going to be nothing more than a sad little footnote in Glimmering history. I'm not worried about it. I'm just here to get my friend's property back."

I folded my arms and scowled at her. I forced all my determination out of myself and through my skin, pushing to make the air around us heavy with anger and stubbornness.

Imogen was sensitive to that kind of thing.

"Good Titania on a cracker," she muttered. She slammed down her drink. "Olivia, you're such a child. The world is changing around you. Everything is changing."

"Don't care," I said. "I said no to Queen Amani, remember? You know, that time she asked me to be Faerie Queen?"

I hated the words even as they came out of my mouth. I hadn't meant to hide Amani's request from Imogen. I hadn't meant to keep secrets or hurt her. I just hadn't wanted her to worry about me, or worse, get jealous.

I hadn't wanted it to get between us.

Now, there was no "us."

"I don't want to be involved in any of this," I said. "I'm just doing a favor for a friend, and then I'm out. You and your Oracle can do whatever you want here. After graduation, I'm done with this world."

"God, Olivia, you're pathetic," Imogen said.

I felt the disgust coming off of her, and she, unlike me, wasn't forcing her feelings out into the air.

She pushed herself up from the chair and walked to her desk. She yanked open a drawer.

"You can have it," she said. She rummaged around in the drawer, not bothering to look up at me. "Brooke stole that goblet years ago and still hasn't shut up about it. It's freaking annoying. Give it back to Haidar if you want; maybe she'll go after it again and it'll get her out of my hair for a while."

She stood up, a golden key in her hand.

"It's not like the goblet's worth much anyway," she said. "You know what it does, right?"

"No idea," I said. "Haidar just said he wanted it."

"I seriously don't know what Amani saw in you," Imogen said.

She went to the sideboard and rearranged some of the bottles and jars of sparkling dust. At the back of the sideboard was a plain old bottle, half-full of some dark red liquid. Imogen opened the bottle, dropped the key into the liquid with a muffled clunk, and screwed the lid back on.

The bottle began to change. Its neck lengthened and thinned, while the body shrank and grew fat. The dull glass grew opaque and clarified to a bright, glittering gold, dotted with rose-shaped gems the same color as the liquid had been. As soon as the bottle had settled into the form of an upside-down gold goblet, Imogen picked it up and righted it. She glanced inside. She blew, and a tiny cloud of dust kicked up.

She didn't look impressed.

"This is nothing he couldn't replace if he were a better wizard," Imogen said.

"What's it for?"

"Brooke said it helps him focus his magic," she said. "That giant house of his is all automated with spells. Magic does the laundry, magic vacuums, whatever. Right now he has to use his own energy to keep it running. Probably what makes him such a grumpy beast all the time, or so everybody tells me. With the goblet back, he won't have to try so hard to keep his house clean."

She held out the goblet to me.

"Yippee," she said flatly.

Put like that, it did seem like a pretty stupid object. It'd probably be easier to downsize to a place that didn't have five million spare bedrooms.

But Amani had said we needed it.

My hand closed around the goblet's hard stem.

"Thank you," I said.

She pursed her lips and raised her eyebrows at me.

In her eyes, I was nothing more than an ugly stain on her chair. But I straightened my back and looked up at her.

"Imogen?"

"What?"

"You don't have to do this," I said.

I felt myself soften. I wanted to reach out for her.

We'd shared each other's clothes once. We'd stayed up until two in the morning bingeing on TV shows and Swedish fish. She'd given me some kind of plant for my birthday every year for almost as long as we'd known each other, and I'd always tried to surprise her with some Glim novelty item she hadn't seen before.

The Olivia that had been unable to buy a T-shirt without Imogen's approval was still inside me.

But no matter how hard I looked, I couldn't see a trace of the girl I knew inside this cold-eyed woman.

"Gen," I said. "Please talk to me."

"Are we done?" she said.

"I thought you were going to Institut Glänzen," I said. "What kind of future is this?"

"I've seen my future," Imogen snapped. "Don't you dare try to tell me what's best for me."

I squeezed the goblet. It didn't feel like it was full of magic. It felt cold and empty, a lot like Imogen and this room and maybe even me.

"Can't you see what she's doing?" I said.

"Can't you see that I don't care?" Imogen said.

For a fleeting instant, I saw a warmth I knew.

And I realized: I should have seen this coming.

Going through boys like they were disposable, dragging me to parties, occasionally blowing her entire paycheck on shoes and phone cases—Imogen leapt first and asked questions later. If something felt like an adventure or promised to make her life more interesting, more dazzling, more special, Imogen was there.

Even so, Imogen—*my* Imogen—would care what the Oracle was up to. My Imogen was strong, and smart, and knew how good she was at her job. My Imogen never would have cheated on her Proctor Exam, and she never would have turned on me like this, no matter what I'd done to her.

My throat closed up.

Imogen was the kind of girl who could ingest tablespoons of fairy dust the night before a big test and not think twice. I was the kind of girl who hid the fairy dust and made sure she drank enough water to flush it from her system.

And I was the kind of girl who hid in the corner and refused to go out, and the kind of girl who got so wrapped up in her own selfish problems that she didn't notice when her best friend slowly started slipping into the darkness.

"How long has she had you?" I said.

Around the stem of the goblet, my fingers twitched.

Imogen crinkled her nose like I smelled bad.

"I've been her heir for months," she said.

"Not her heir," I said. My voice trembled. It was suddenly so important that I say this right, that she listened. "Gen, she cursed you. Not just the night you went into the Fountain. She's been cursing you for I don't even know how long."

Imogen's eyes narrowed.

"Probably since before your Proctor Exam," I said. "I'll bet that's what happened, that she told you about Amani coming to me, and you were hurt, because you should have been." Another wave in an endless sea of guilt crashed over me. "She needed your guard down, just for a minute, and she got in. And I should have been paying attention, but I wasn't, and I'll bet you didn't fight as hard as you could have because you always get so *stupid* when people start telling you how great you are."

I pressed my tongue to the roof of my mouth as hard as I could. Panic rose up in me, panic and guilt and a fury at the Oracle so strong it scared me.

"Come with me," I said.

Haidar had said that my gift was that I didn't give a damn about what other people thought. But he was wrong.

Maybe I didn't care about my parents' opinions. Maybe I didn't care what Queen Amani thought about my potential.

But I cared about Imogen.

I cared that she'd once loved me. I cared that she used to trust me. I cared that she not throw her life away just because the Oracle and all those horrible sprites sitting outside the office door made her feel special on a bad day.

I gave so many damns about Imogen that I couldn't breathe.

"You have your goblet," Imogen said. "You should probably go."

"Gen, come on. We can talk about this."

"Get out of my office," she said. A shower of blue sparks shot out of her fingertips. "I'm not asking."

CHAPTER TWENTY-SIX

Lucas pressed a button on the keychain and unlocked the doors when we were halfway across the street. I slid into the passenger side and slammed the door. My heart threw itself against my rib cage.

It wasn't so much that I was worried Imogen would come after us.

It was that I knew she wouldn't, and the knowing killed me.

Lucas locked the doors and turned the engine on. He looked at me, dark blue eyes taking in more than I wanted him to see.

"Are you okay?" he said.

"I'll survive," I said. But only because I had to.

I leaned against the seat and took a deep breath.

"Where to next?" he said.

Suddenly, the windshield began to rattle. Somewhere outside the car, I heard a voice. I tightened my hand around my wand and rolled the car window down a crack.

The time has come for change, the Oracle's voice boomed. *Over the past few days, many of us have become aware of a movement of Huntsmen who claim that the Glimmering world is something to fear. We have attempted to meet their absurd claims with diplomacy, but those who will not respond to reason must respond to force. Portland now belongs to the Glimmers. The remaining Humdrums will be recruited to serve our cause or will be expelled. Remain in your homes. Do not interfere. Those who violate my orders will be treated as one of them.*

Her voice faded. Lucas and I exchanged glances. And then she started up again, intoning the same lines like a recording at the airport: *The time has come for change. Over the past few days, many of us have become aware...*

I rolled the window back up.

"Seriously, though," Lucas said. His knuckles whitened against the steering wheel. "Where to next?"

A sick feeling I'd been suppressing all day started roiling in my stomach. I let out a long breath, trying to let out my tension with it, but no amount of calm breathing was going to control the kind of fear that prickled through my bloodstream.

Getting the goblet had been bad.

This would be so, so much worse.

"Head toward Forest Park," I said. "I'll tell you where to go when we get close."

He pulled onto the road. We drove in silence. I scanned the skies; Lucas kept his eyes on the road and the handful of cars around us. Portland felt like it was sleeping. Humdrums were out and about, but there were fewer than usual, and they seemed quiet. Above us, I knew the rainbow roads were empty.

Lucas shifted in his seat as we passed deserted brick buildings. Anxiety and adrenaline tingled off of him. His nerves crashed and mingled with my own, like churning ocean waves that never found rest.

I tapped my finger rapidly against the car door.

Lucas' hand shot out and jabbed the radio on.

"Keep listening for all your favorite classic hits," an overly enthusiastic man said. The opening chords of some classic rock from the 80s started playing. Lucas hit the scan button. A Christian pop singer crooned about how Jesus was the only man who'd ever loved her right. A perky woman gushed about her new auto insurance. Someone played a banjo and said "Yee-haw!" Every sound was painfully normal.

And then, a man said, "This situation in Portland is unlike anything we've ever seen, Dave."

"Portland likes to keep things weird, that's for sure," Dave said.

"I don't know what to make of it," the first man said. "You hear about shootings and knife fights, but the kids that belong to this extremist group have a real flair for showmanship. I'm sure we've all seen the videos. Listeners, if you don't know what we're talking about, head to our website. We've got a handful of the highlights on there. You've never seen magicians like this."

"Do you think it's a prank, Joe?" Dave said.

Joe made a noncommittal noise. Dave continued. "The whole thing just seems ludicrous. It's got to be a stunt."

"I hope it is," Joe said. "I really hope it is."

"If not, where's the National Guard in all this?" Dave said. "Stunt or not, this business has people scared and leaving the city in droves. Don't you think it's about time the law stepped in?"

Lucas slammed his hand against the steering wheel.

"This is so stupid," he shouted. "There's a war going on and my side can't even see that it's happening."

I opened my mouth to comfort or console him. But what did I have to say? He was right. His side was being fed lies and shadows, and my side was *awful*.

"Where to?" he snapped.

"Straight ahead," I said.

Our car sped forward, onto a winding road up a hill covered in trees.

My phone buzzed.

Isabelle: The Oracle just formally declared a "difference of opinion" with Queen Amani. Will keep you posted.

A second later, it buzzed again.

Daniel: Oracle & Amani are officially on opposite sides. Gloves are off. Where are you?

Before I could answer, another message came through.

Mom: Dad said the Oracle just made a statement that she's no longer cooperating with Queen Amani. She'll make an announcement later, but I thought you should know. I never thought I'd see this happen.

Mom: Please be safe. Text me back so I know you're okay.

Safety wasn't something I could promise anyone right now, but I quickly texted back: *I'm okay. Thanks. Love you.*

I was going to throw up. I leaned my head against the cool glass of the window and forced myself to breathe.

"Turn right up here," I said.

Lucas nodded without taking his eyes off the road. I could see the thoughts racing in his mind, hidden behind his tense forehead and sharp, darting eyes. But I didn't know what the thoughts were. I didn't think I wanted to know. Chances were too good we Glimmers deserved them all.

"Thank you for helping me," I said.

His jaw softened, just a little bit. He looked over at me, and nestled somewhere in the anger and frustration was concern.

"Sure thing," he said. "That's what friends are for."

I held out a hand across the gap between our seats. He hesitated, then took my clammy hand in his. He kept his eyes on the road, but I felt his skin warm against mine. He squeezed, gently enough that I might have missed the gesture had not all my senses been on edge.

"I want to say it's going to be okay," I said.

But I couldn't. It would be a lie.

He bit the inside of his cheek.

"Me too," he said.

"Have you heard from your mom?"

"Yeah," he said. "She's okay."

I nodded and went back to watching the skies. Ahead of us, the distant blue figure of a sprite leapt between the treetops and was gone. I ran my free hand along the chain that held the Multnomah pendant.

Why had Imogen been able to see me? The other sprites hadn't noticed me, even when I'd been right next to them. I'd even brushed against a sprite girl's hair and gotten nothing. But Imogen had seen me from feet away.

It seemed Amani couldn't protect me from everything.

The road curved and climbed up a hill. The trees grew denser, their branches hung with dripping pale lichens and dense emerald moss. The forests in this part of Oregon always looked mysterious, but today, these clusters of foreboding trees felt almost too normal. What was hidden between them was so much stranger and darker.

"There's a pull-off up here," I said.

I recognized the area from Amani's directions. But when Lucas pulled into a parking space next to a trailhead and cut the engine, I felt that we were in the right place. Above our heads, outside the car, the trees seemed to crackle with warning. I peered up through their branches and into the dense woods, but we seemed to be alone.

The Oracle wouldn't let anyone know what was here; not even her sprites. It had taken Amani years to figure it out.

"I'll come with you," Lucas said.

I shook my head with a vehemence that startled even me.

"No," I said, too loudly. He was already risking too much by being with me.

"Amani's necklaces have hidden us so far," I said. "But the Oracle's more powerful than a whole club of sprites. She's keeping a close eye on me, and probably you, too. That's why Amani hadn't been talking to me, did I tell you? She wanted Kelda to think we'd dropped our connection."

For a brief instant that was gone too soon, I felt calm.

Somehow, on a selfish level I would never admit to out loud, I would rather be in the middle of all this with Amani on my side than be outside of it without her.

Humdrum college was still in my future, and I still wished Kelda had just stayed sane. But this had happened, and the only thing I could do was help Queen Amani until I couldn't help her anymore.

And I had to move quickly. We would only have so much time to help before the Oracle wrecked this city so hard that we'd never be able to conceal the Glim world again. Even now, we were pushing our luck. It would take the Council years to repair the damage.

"I'm going to put an enchantment on the car," I said. "It will hide you better than just the necklace. Make sure you stay in the car. It's going to take me a while to find what I'm looking for."

Underneath my Multnomah necklace, the mirror ring Amani had given me a long time ago still sat. I pulled it off and over my head.

"If I'm not back in an hour, use this," I said. I dropped the ring into Lucas' palm. The silver chain coiled down onto it like a snake. "Put it on your finger and ask for Queen Amani. Hopefully you'll be able to reach her."

He closed his hand around the ring. "I should come with you," he said.

"You have to stay here," I said. "If something happens to me, you have to get the ring and the goblet to Amani. Promise me."

"I will," he said. "Liv, please be safe."

"Everyone keeps asking that," I said.

Between us, the goblet sat in the cup holder, looking out of place and overdressed. Mom's ring rested inside it. I touched its rose quartz surface for luck.

"What are you looking for?" Lucas said.

I pulled my wand out of my hair. Clumpy curls fell down onto my shoulders. Normally, having my hair down drove me a little crazy. Right now, it felt like a cloak, something to hide me and keep me safe.

I pointed my wand up, directing a sharp burst of energy strong enough to suffuse the car ceiling with a rippling flash of white, visible even through my glasses. The flash spread until the entire car glowed with the concealment spell. Over my lenses, the spell continued to shimmer white. Through them, the car faded quickly back to normal.

I reached for the door handle.

"I'm going after Kelda's wand," I said.

His eyes widened in his already-worried face. Even as a Humdrum, Lucas had heard enough fairy tales to know that you didn't touch another faerie's wand, especially a faerie like Kelda. Not if you wanted to live.

Saying the plan aloud felt good, though, in a nutty, danger-ous, have-you-lost-your-mind kind of way.

"Why would she leave her wand out here?" he said. "I've never seen you without yours, even when I thought it was just a thing you used to keep your hair up."

"This is different," I said.

Amani had explained this to me. I'd heard of powerful faeries using talismans before, and this was one of them.

"Amani and Kelda are both really powerful," I said. "They use a crazy amount of magical energy every day. Normally, it's impossible for a Glim to summon and channel that much power, but they have to, so they use a kind of... battery, I guess. They each have a second wand hidden somewhere in the city, in a place that's loaded with magical energy. That wand connects them to everything."

"And you're going to take Kelda's," Lucas said.

I took in an enormous breath and then let it out, trying to release my fear and tension with the air.

It did exactly nothing to help.

CHAPTER TWENTY-SEVEN

A bird screeched overhead. Above me, eldritch moss-covered branches loomed dark and foreboding.

I had always taken comfort in the trees that covered Portland. But here, at the bottom of the ravine, their branches were heavy with menace.

The trail was hidden now, up above me and winding through the lighter part of the forest, where normal birds chirped and Humdrum plants lined the path. I'd known to leave the trail the moment I felt like the absolute last thing I should ever do was wander from its safety. The moment the impulse to cling to the carefully marked dirt path gripped me was the moment I knew exactly where Kelda didn't want me to go.

I stumbled down the steep slope. The ground was thick with ferns and saplings that tangled around my ankles. As I descended, the air grew colder and the sky seemed to darken. Around me, the plants became strange and unfamiliar.

Concealed from Humdrums by the canopy and a repellent glamour, oily black ferns grew underfoot, leaving smears on my jeans as I walked. Prickly bushes scratched my arms; on some, red berries glowed with a light that shouldn't have been possible on such a gray day. Eerie whispers wove through the branches, words I couldn't make out and didn't want to hear. And from everywhere, no matter how quietly I tried to walk, came the sense of being watched.

A creek flowed down the very center of the ravine. Upstream, to my left, the water seemed clear and clean. I heard its cheerful burbling. The plants on either side of the water seemed normal, brown with winter but still healthy and carrying hints of green. Far downstream, the world looked the same —exactly as it ought to be.

But in front of me, the water grew dark, icy not with the season but with something deep and hidden. It was the kind of darkness that collected in dangerous alleys and the corners of basements, the kind of darkness that fed on imagination until you had nothing left but fear.

This had to be the place.

I held my wand out. Of everything in this grim landscape, it was the only thing that hinted at light. It glinted silver amid the shadows.

I knelt at the edge of the creek and rested my fingertips on the oozing dark brown mud that made up its banks. The water slithered and whispered in front of me, black enough to hide anything. Images of leeches and biting fish and venomous snakes filled my mind, and I shuddered.

If only it could have been hidden anywhere else. A tree trunk, I could have handled with the help of a good flashlight. The wet dirt that soaked my knees would have been fine. I could dig.

But water was kind of the Oracle's thing, and it was the only place she'd hide her wand.

A cutting breeze whipped through the ravine. The cold rushed through my bones. I flexed my toes inside my shoes, trying to find balance and warmth.

The tip of my wand glowed star-white as I focused, and I lowered it to the water. The glow reflected on the inky surface, but that was as far as the light would go. Whatever was in there, Kelda didn't want it to be seen.

Tree branches littered the ground around me. I leaned back on my heels and reached for one that seemed solid and just long enough. Its damp surface was clammy and left disintegrating bits of bark against my skin. I braced myself and plunged the stick into the shifting black surface.

It hit the bottom and I scraped it around, tense and listening closely.

Nothing.

The stick slid smoothly across the bottom of the creek. There were no rocks, no pebbles, no normal creek debris. Nothing was down there that would create the ripples that disturbed the creek's surface. And there was definitely no wand.

But Amani had said it was here. And the creepy-as-hell goth nature show around me was backing her up loud and clear.

"*I* am living in a hashtag-Dark-Forest," I muttered.

I wished I had Aubrey here. I'd dunk her in the creek without a second thought.

I was only going to get this one way. I pushed up my sleeves until they caught behind my elbows.

Goosebumps prickled up my arms and the back of my neck. I tensed, then took a deep breath and tried to let the stiffness of fear go.

I touched the black water with the tip of my finger. A shock of ice shuddered through me. The freezing water seemed to make my blood crystallize in my veins. I yanked my finger back and shook my hand, trying to force heat back into it.

But nothing terrible had happened. Doom hadn't come crashing down on my head.

The water was frigid, and this place was creepy as creepy could get, but nothing had actually hurt me.

Before I could think twice, I plunged my hand into the water. I screamed as the cold slammed through me. It was beyond cold; it was ice, it was dry ice, it was the vast reaches of space where nothing could survive, and it was all rushing through my veins so quickly I couldn't do anything to stop it.

Pain shot through my mouth. I became vaguely aware that I was biting my tongue and fought to wrench my frozen jaw apart. My arm thrashed in the water, scraping the slick bottom and desperately searching for the thing that would get me out of here.

I'd never understood terror. Now, it gripped my body like a vise. I trembled and shook, unable to control my body.

I didn't want the wand. I didn't want anything except to run, to get out of here and never look back, to throw myself into the most brightly-lit room imaginable and never, ever leave it. At any moment, I could fall into the water and never come up, and every second I stayed here was a second closer to death and to what I was suddenly sure was the pointless nothingness that came after it.

I was going to die, and everyone I loved was going to die, and none of this would matter.

My stomach heaved and spasmed, and I leaned over the oily water and felt bile rise up in my gut.

My throat closed. I gasped, and felt my ribcage shake with caged panic.

"Amani," I whispered.

Her name was all I remembered. It was a talisman, a glow against this relentless darkness. For a moment, I couldn't remember what it meant, only that it was a word that might protect me—the only word that might mean something out here where every second meant terror and pain.

And then her face formed in my mind, and the mission she'd given me, and what it meant for my family, for Lucas, for Isabelle and Haidar, for Elle and Kyle and maybe even Imogen.

A shudder stormed through me. How did Imogen live with this kind of cold?

"Amani chose me," I whispered, to the water and to myself and to the horror pressing in against my skin from every side.

My stiff fingers brushed against a smooth, long surface. I begged my hand to close around it, but my fingers wouldn't listen. They wanted warmth.

"Amani chose me," I whispered. The words rose to a stream of chants as relentless as the ice in my veins. "Lucas is waiting for me," I muttered. "Haidar gave us his car. Mom gave me her ring. Amani chose me. Amani is waiting."

As I tried to lift the wand, wind whipped around my head. An inhuman, unearthly shriek swept down with it, piercing my eardrums and echoing the cold in my veins.

I screamed back.

Screaming meant I was alive; screaming meant I was still here. Suddenly furious, I forced my hand shut and felt the wand press against my stiff skin.

I wrenched the wand up out of the water. Black droplets sprayed everywhere, landing on my face and soaking my jacket.

It didn't matter.

I had the wand.

The moment it was in the air, the shrieking intensified. Wails and whistles filled the air around me. The wind whipped at me from every side, and an eerie, ghostly blue light filled the menacing darkness.

Dozens of sprites swooped down toward my head. They seemed to pour from the sky, and their insubstantial, watery hands slapped against my face.

But my face was warm again—or at least it felt warm in comparison to the numbing frost of the Oracle's water. I could feel their slaps, and I could move my fingers and my toes.

And that meant I could move my legs.

I gripped Kelda's wand so tightly that nothing could have pried my fingers apart, gripped my own wand with the other hand, and ran. I crashed through the underbrush and up the steep side of the ravine, tripping and stumbling but miraculously staying upright.

And still the sprites came at me, screaming like banshees and trying to make me fall.

But while their hands could touch me, while I felt their stinging slaps and heavy blows, they weren't enough to knock me down. They were like ghosts or memories, enough to scare me and hurt me but not enough to change my course. I threw a spell over my shoulder and kept running.

Amani's gold charm pressed hot against my skin, protecting me and shielding me from the worst of it.

The vicious thorns of overgrown blackberry bushes scratched my arms and tore at my legs, but then I was through them, and through the ferns that lined the trail, and back onto the trail where a Humdrum could have walked every day for decades without ever learning what waited below.

The moment my feet touched the steady surface of the path, I broke into a dead run. The sprites flooded after me. I heard their voices calling my name and ordering me to stop, to return what I'd stolen. I didn't turn. I didn't reply. I didn't even listen, beyond what I could help.

And there, at the top of the path, Haidar's car sat waiting. Above my glasses, it pulsed white and bright against the shadow of the trees and overcast sky.

My lungs screamed for rest and air.

I fought them, too.

Then I was at the gravel parking lot, level with the car. I dashed around to the passenger's side, threw the door open with my wand, and hurled myself into the front seat. I slammed the door and clenched my hand around the wand so tightly my skin tingled.

"Drive!" I screamed. "Go!"

Lucas was one step ahead of me, and the engine had already roared to life. He threw the car backward and peeled out of the parking lot, kicking up gravel behind us. The sprites were caught in a swirling fog of dirt and exhaust, and I watched in the rearview mirror until their choking blue forms were far behind us.

CHAPTER TWENTY-EIGHT

Haidar's gates slid open, a thousand times too slow. The tires squealed as Lucas pressed the gas pedal to the floor. We shot up his driveway and screeched into the garage.

The car stopped with a jolt. We sat in stunned silence for a few seconds while the engine hummed beneath us.

My heart still felt like it was trying to slow down. My chest ached with the pounding. I let out a long, controlled breath and willed my body to be calm. *We're at Haidar's*, I thought, soothing myself like a child. *It's okay, we're safe.*

But I wasn't a child, no matter what Imogen said, and I wasn't about to believe my own lies. We weren't safe. I had the Oracle's wand on my lap. No one would be safe in our position, no matter how strong the enchantments were that guarded Haidar's grounds.

I reached out to open the car door, but Lucas stopped me. He grabbed my other wrist and held on until I looked at him.

"You're okay," he said.

I nodded and tried to let the words sink in.

He was right. At least in this moment, I was okay. If that was all I had to hold onto, I'd do my best to cling to it.

"I can't believe we made it out of there," I said.

I leaned back into the seat and pressed my head against the solid plush of the headrest.

"What happened down there?"

He had the biggest eyes sometimes. They were a dark hazel-green, the kind of eyes that changed color with different light, and there was so much buried behind them. He thought more deeply than most people, and he felt more deeply than he let on.

"I'll tell you about it someday," I said. "I don't want to think about it right now. The Oracle is nasty. That's all anyone needs to know for now."

He leaned his head into his seat, too, and stared across the space between us. I began to hear the silence behind our breathing and the noise of the car. My heartbeat shuddered in my chest and slowed, finally realizing it was protected here.

"I'm sorry you got pulled into this, but I'm glad we're friends," I said.

"I am too," Lucas said.

He rubbed his thumb across my wrist.

"I feel alone a lot of the time," he said. "But not with you."

The first real smile I'd felt in days crossed my face.

"Let's go in," I said. "When all this is over, can we just, I don't know, spend an entire weekend watching cartoons and eating cereal?"

"We can do anything you want," Lucas said. "We'll have earned it."

He gave me a smile that made a tingle rush up my spine. It was exactly the kind of tingle I didn't have time for right now, and exactly the kind of tingle I wasn't planning on having when it came to Lucas. Even so, I welcomed it. The sensation was a reminder that good things existed beyond all this chaos. Maybe we'd get back to them someday.

Lucas carried the goblet and ring inside; I held the Oracle's wand carefully away from mine.

The door from the garage led to a hallway, which eventually opened onto the entrance hall. Something felt different in here; it was as if the lighting had been altered, or a new scent had been introduced, though I couldn't put a finger on what had changed.

I took a careful step forward, listening for the sound of sprites.

"We're back," I called.

Isabelle's voice responded, and though I couldn't make out the words, her tone was casual enough that I could relax. A moment later, she stepped out of the front parlor.

She reached us in three big strides. Her dark eyes glinted at the sight of the Oracle's wand, and her lip curled in disgust. A second later, though, her whole face was transformed by concern as she looked down at me.

"You look awful," she said. "Did anything happen?"

"Stuff happened," I said wryly. "But I'm okay. Where's Haidar? I need to get this stuff back to the Waterfall Palace."

She snorted, and I felt a tiny flare of annoyance come off of her.

"No need," she said.

I exchanged looks with Lucas, but I wasn't as puzzled as I probably looked. The irked expression on Isabelle's face made the strange sensation in the mansion instantly clear.

In the parlor, Amani's swirling gold energy was too pronounced to miss. She'd been scanning the skies through the big bay window, but turned as soon as she heard us enter. She was wearing brown leggings and a long, cream cable-knit sweater. Wrapped in the sweater, she looked protected and safe. I wished I had one.

"You're here," I said.

Haidar snorted from his place by the window.

"We got everything you need," I said.

She waved a hand. Instantly, a small table shimmered into being. I set the wand down and nodded at Lucas. He put the goblet and ring carefully beside it.

"Is that Mom's ring?" Daniel said.

He was sitting cross-legged on the stiff floral couch. Now, he leaned forward and peered at the objects on the table.

"Crazy, right?" I said.

"I always thought that thing was weird."

"And immensely powerful," Amani said. "Your mother is a strong faerie to be able to wield it."

She leaned over and surveyed the items. She picked up the ring and turned the goblet over to examine it, but didn't touch the wand. I didn't blame her. I never wanted to come in contact with the thing again.

Isabelle sat on the couch next to Daniel and watched. She stayed tense and a little ruffled. Between her irritation, Daniel's eager fascination, Lucas' apprehension, and my own fear of whatever would come next, the room thrummed with awkwardness. I couldn't blame any of them. I had a feeling "chilling with Her Majesty" hadn't been on anyone's agenda for the day. Only Haidar seemed comfortable with the thought of hanging out and plotting the Oracle's downfall.

"How's your garden?" Amani asked suddenly, turning on Haidar.

He grinned. The expression was bizarre on his face. "Good as ever," he said. "Takes all my energy to hold the house together, but the garden runs itself like it always has."

"Excellent," Amani said. "You'll be able to cut back on the house stuff if this all goes to plan."

She turned back to the table and turned the quartz ring over between her fingers.

Whatever calm I had found in the car was fleeing fast. Beneath it, all I had to offer the world was the electric web of tension and panic that passed for my skin.

I felt something brush my finger. A second later, Lucas took my hand in his and held it tight.

I let out a long breath. The staticky feeling faded. I felt my heartbeat, soft and steady in my chest.

"I have a plan," Amani said.

She looked up. She didn't seem quite as drained as the last time I'd seen her, but she didn't look on top of the world, either. Dark circles had made a home under her eyes, and her face was strained tight with the effort of keeping everything under control.

"Haidar, I'm going to need your help," she said. She looked around the room, her dazzling green eyes fixing each of us briefly in turn. "Anyone else, you're welcome to go. This is going to be… not safe."

"Our lives are not safe," Isabelle said. Her tone was flat, but I felt a begrudging sincerity behind the words. Amani must have felt it too, because she smiled, and Isabelle looked steadily back, and then Isabelle nodded like they'd come to some kind of agreement.

Haidar watched this exchange between the two women, and a look crossed his face that could almost pass for exasperation.

"We're staying," Daniel said. "I mean, you've obviously already got Olivia in your pocket, no offense, and I want to help if I can."

"Trust me," Amani said. She pursed her lips at him like they were in on a secret together. "Olivia will not fit in my pocket."

Daniel tapped his nose.

"Ah, metaphor!" he said loudly. "I get it!"

I wished I was close enough to elbow him in the ribs. Instead, I said, "Yes, I'm in. Obviously. What do you need?"

Amani looked up in my direction, but her eyes didn't land on me.

"Lucas?" she said softly.

He nodded, and something passed between them, a kind of recognition that he belonged.

"I'm in," he said.

I leaned up against him.

"In that case, here's the plan," Amani said. She glanced around at us again. "I don't need to tell you that this doesn't leave this room."

She walked to the other side of the bay window and looked up at the sky. It was empty except for heavy pewter clouds. Somewhere beyond them, the sun was setting. The end of the day came with no glorious orange sunset, just a slow fade to darkness.

"This house is powerful," she said. "The garden, even more so. Now that the goblet's back, we'll be able to harness that power."

"It'll be enough," Haidar said.

She picked the goblet up and spun its stem between her fingers. The deep crimson jewels on its side gleamed.

"We're going to summon Kelda," she said. "Haidar will bind her to his grounds. I think the garden will be best. Once we have her locked down, we'll talk."

"You're going to all this trouble so you can *talk*," Isabelle said.

Amani held the goblet up and let it catch the gloomy light from the window. She looked at it intently, as though it held the answers to this whole problem.

"Kelda and I have a long history," she said. "Maybe I can get through to her. We'll start with a civil conversation." She set the goblet down with a thunk. "If that fails, we'll take away her powers."

"No biggie," Daniel said.

"There's a good chance that spell will get tangled with Kelda's rage and kill us all," she said. "Anyone who wants to leave is still welcome to do so."

No one moved. I wasn't about to be the first one to head for the door.

Amani let out a deep, exhausted breath. Then her chin lifted and she looked at each of us.

She laid out the plan. We listened intently, each of us memorizing what we'd have to do and when. When Amani turned to Isabelle to instruct her on keeping out the sprites when we let Kelda in, I looked up at Lucas.

"Stay close to me," I said softly.

He looked down, surprised. His floppy hair looked darker than usual against his worry-pale face.

"In the garden," I said. "Stay close. I need you."

He couldn't tell if I meant it. He was no Glim. He was barely allowed into this world.

But today had been all the proof I needed that he could make a difference. He was the only person here today who'd saved me from Kelda's sprites. He was also the only person who'd given me a moment of calm in all this mayhem.

I held tightly to his hand and wished I had the words to tell him.

"We're going to do this tomorrow," Amani said. "Right at sunset. For now, we need to get to sleep."

The room fell silent. Finally, I stood. Lucas followed me out.

I put on my pajamas and brushed my teeth in the bathroom that adjoined my busy green room. My mind raced so quickly as I brushed that I couldn't keep track of the thoughts.

Not all that long ago in the grand scheme of things, I'd been complaining about being a faerie godmother because it dragged me too deep into the Glimmering world. Now, I was in so far that I couldn't remember what the world had been like without warring Glim leaders and sprite armies and creepy tar-black streams.

At the edges of my thoughts, like a threatening ghost, Imogen lurked. It seemed impossible that I'd talked to her only hours ago. Our history ran over and over in my mind. How long had she been under the Oracle's control? Had it begun right before Imogen's Proctor Exam, or had Kelda been working on her even earlier than that? And how had I not noticed?

Imogen had always been the one to dive headfirst into things and worry about consequences later. I'd been the one who made sure she never went too far. That had always been our pattern, and I'd failed her as a friend.

I spat into the sink. I wished I could wash all of this down the drain.

A gentle knock sounded at my door. I dropped the toothbrush on the counter.

"Come on in," I called.

I heard footsteps. When I came out of the bathroom, Lucas had climbed the carpeted stairs to my bed and was sitting on the coverlet. His shoulders were as tense and tired as mine felt, and behind him, the dark window showed the faint golden reflection of the room. A single lamp gave off the only light. I hadn't made the bed this morning, but in my absence, it had made itself. The white-and-green blankets and pillows were once again pristine, as though the bed had been not only made but ironed, too.

He patted the bed beside him. I climbed up and sat down. It should have been thrilling, sitting on a bed with a gorgeous guy, with everyone else in the house too busy to come check up on us.

But I just felt overwhelmed.

I curled up on top of the coverlet, facing away from him. I pulled my hair from the back of my neck and tucked it under my head like a tangled pillow. My heart fluttered like a bird's, but not with excitement or the good kind of nerves that should have come with having Lucas so close to me. Instead, I just felt sick.

"I don't want to do this," I said. My voice came out so soft and timid I didn't think he'd heard me.

But then, I felt the bed shift as he lay down next to me and curled his body around mine. He wrapped an arm around me.

"I don't think anyone would want to do this," he said softly. His breath was warm against the back of my neck. "Queen Amani looked as scared as the rest of us."

I nuzzled my back deeper into his chest. He ran his hand up and down my arm.

"She wouldn't have asked you if she didn't think you could do it," he said. "I don't know Queen Amani like you do, but I can tell she believes in you and cares about you. I don't think she'd risk you if it was too dangerous."

"I don't think she has a choice," I said.

My heartbeat slowed to something in the ballpark of normal as his fingertips tickled my skin. I let my entire body expand like a balloon and then collapse with a deep sigh. Lucas kept holding me and moving his hand across my arm and back until the world took on the soft, velvety gray tinge that came right before sleep.

"I missed you when I moved away," he said softly.

I didn't respond. It felt like too much work to pull myself into full consciousness. But his words still warmed me. I'd missed him, too.

"I was so happy to see you when I came back," he murmured. "Sorry I didn't stay in touch. I had good intentions, but, you know. I suck at texting."

His hand wandered up into my hair. I wished I could fall asleep like this every single day.

"That text you sent me, right after Imogen and I started dating and you guys stopped talking," he said.

His voice was so quiet I had to focus to hear what he was saying.

"I got it," he said. "I never said anything because I didn't know what to say. I'd never realized you thought about me like that. I guess I just didn't think you would. You always seemed too smart and focused to waste time thinking about guys. I didn't realize until that message how much I wanted you to think of me that way."

He must think I was asleep, I realized drowsily. Why else would he be saying all this now? I tried to stay asleep, or at least to act like it.

I wanted this conversation. I wanted to follow it through to every possible confusion.

But not now, when my relaxation was just a Band-Aid over the buzzing dread that filled me every time I remembered the Oracle.

If I tried to tell Lucas how much I liked him *now,* I was such a nervous, half-asleep mess that I'd probably ruin it. And I could not afford to ruin this.

"I guess it's not going to happen now," he whispered. "Dude." His breath burned into the back of my neck. I felt his lips hovering just inches away, and it took everything I had not to lean back and close the distance between us.

"But I just wanted you to know," he said.

His voice faded to only the sound of his breathing, almost keeping time with mine.

I wanted to turn around and kiss him. I wanted to tell him I'd heard everything, and that maybe it wasn't so impossible for us to be together.

But magic was gathering throughout this house. I felt it, tingling and sparking its way up through the walls and out into the garden. I felt the storm brewing, the heavy weight of the Oracle as Amani and Haidar prepared the grounds for her to descend.

I didn't have time to want him.

I sighed and nuzzled further into him. I felt his surprise, then his arm as it came back around me and pulled me close to him.

We must have fallen asleep, because when a gentle knock sounded at the door, Lucas gasped awake and my eyes flew open. The room came into sudden, sharp focus. Late morning sunlight streamed through the curtained windows.

The door creaked open.

"It's time," Isabelle said softly.

CHAPTER TWENTY-NINE

Beyond the garden, the sky hung with pale silver clouds. The clouds had broken apart near the horizon, letting in a few rays of fading evening sunshine.

Below us, in a sunken garden lined with an irregular stone wall, Amani paced. Haidar stood not far from her, rolling the golden goblet between his palms. Whatever this garden was usually, Haidar had cleared it so that only a circular grassy lawn remained. Rose bushes lined the tops of the walls like sentinels, blooming crimson and ivory and letting off enough perfume that it made me dizzy for a moment.

"Go ahead," Isabelle said. "Daniel and I will watch the perimeter. We've locked everything down except this clearing. If any sprites come in, they'll come in here. We'll keep them away from you."

Daniel gave me a thumbs-up. He stood by Isabelle. His face was as white as mine felt, though it was hard to tell how much of that was our milky Feye skin and how much was the sheer terror of what we were about to do.

Lucas put a warm hand on my arm.

"I'll be up here too," he said. "I can't do much, but I'm cheering you on."

His frustration at not being able to help was palpable. I wished for a moment that I could trade places with him. But that wouldn't be fair. I wouldn't send anyone I liked into this mess.

I pulled my glasses off my nose and held them out to him.

"Would you hold these?" I said. "I need to be able to see what everyone's doing."

He took them from me delicately, almost reverently.

With the glasses gone, magic sparked like static electricity in the plants around us. The grass, rose bushes, and trees glittered green, each speck of magic flashing to light and then fading again.

I let out a final sigh, then slipped off my shoes. I walked down the three mossy stone steps into the garden. They were damp and cool. Above me, Daniel walked around the clearing to the far side. They positioned themselves across from one another, Daniel toward the edge of the garden, Isabelle by the mansion. Below them, Amani paced to stand on one side of the lawn and waved me to position myself across from her.

The four of us stood at compass points and stared at each other across the distance. In the background, above us, Lucas hovered behind Isabelle. And in the center of the clearing, Haidar hulked with the goblet glinting in his hands.

I looked at Amani across the clearing. Without my glasses, she stood in a whirl of gold.

For a moment, I could almost hear her voice in my head, as clearly as I'd once been able to almost hear Imogen's.

Are you okay?

I held her dark green gaze and nodded.

I'm okay, I thought.

It was almost a lie, but not quite. I didn't like anything about this, but I stood on my own two feet, and my breathing was measured and under control.

I stepped just barely to the left. The Oracle's glinting silver wand lay at my feet. I didn't need to use it yet, not until—and if —Amani gave the signal.

I hoped I wouldn't need to touch it today, for all our sakes.

"One minute," Amani called. "Haidar?"

"I'm ready," he said.

My stomach flipped over.

Haidar took three large steps backward toward the stone stairs, leaving the dead center of the grassy space clear. He sat cross-legged on the ground and put the goblet in front of him. Around us, magic tingled.

We were really doing this. Not later, not someday, but now. I shivered and held my ground.

Haidar leaned over his goblet. White light began to pour from his hands and into the cup. The air felt heavy and unseasonably warm. Far off, a bird chirped once and fell silent. As I watched, Haidar's goblet filled with light, and then the whiteness began to froth and spill over the brim.

Haidar's bushy eyebrows drew together. The magic grew more opaque and he thrust it deeper into the cup.

The goblet consumed the magic, and then I saw tiny tendrils of white begin to glow faintly, deep in the ground below us. The tendrils pushed out from the goblet's base like blood in veins, and networked across the clearing. White light cast up from the ground onto Amani's face, illuminating her from the bottom as the vague overcast light glazed her skin from the top.

She met my gaze again. I nodded back: *Still okay.*

Queen Amani raised her hands. Across the clearing, I lifted mine and mirrored her. My stomach churned again.

And then she began to chant. I had no idea what she was saying, but I felt the magic, and I felt what she was doing with it. She called down the sky with her hands, reached deep into the air and sent a message all through the city: *Kelda. Come to me.*

I closed my eyes and joined my thoughts with her own, picturing the Oracle as I'd last seen her, shifting and dappled beneath the waterfall.

The air above us filled with a high shriek. Startled, I opened my eyes in time to see a white-gowned figure land hard on the ground in front of us, trailing sparkles and smoke. Her whole body shone with blue light.

She landed in a crouch, then leapt to her feet and whirled on Queen Amani. The skirt of her glittering white gown swirled around her.

"What the hell are you doing?" the woman snapped.

She winced and twisted. The magic glowing in the ground seemed to brighten around her, putting a spotlight under her writhing figure. She wrenched her gown up, showing bare feet and ankles wrapped in white tendrils of magic.

But no matter how she moved or twisted, and no matter what kinds of spells flew from her fingertips toward the ground, nothing could move her.

Kelda was stuck.

Her glittering black eyes landed on Haidar. In an instant, her focus shifted. She grew deathly still and raised her hands. An electric blue stream of light pulsed from them and landed on the goblet. I thought she meant her magic to mix with his, and I tensed, waiting for his spell to rebound or explode or otherwise kill us all.

Instead, the waterfall of white that still poured from his hands began to move silently backward. The white energy leapt up from the goblet and streamed back into Haidar.

The magic fritzed and sputtered on his hands and up his arms. Haidar winced in pain. I flexed my toes, feeling my connection with the glowing ground, and forced myself to stay where I was. Whatever magic Haidar couldn't consume dissipated in the air around him, and still, it kept pouring up. The pool of light that surrounded her began to fade.

The Oracle wrenched up one foot.

"Isabelle," Haidar shouted. Her name tore from his lips like the cry of a desperate animal.

But Isabelle was busy flinging enchantments toward the sky. A tall sprite with white hair hovered in the air above her like a menacing angel. He darted away and then flew toward her again.

I had been so focused on Kelda that I hadn't noticed the sprites that had come with her. One lay motionless on the ground by the mansion, her pale light faded to almost nothing and her white tunic and leggings smudged with mud. Another lay on the ground beside Daniel. My brother loomed over the sprite, sending down the last of a spell with his wand. The sprite twitched and then stilled. I couldn't tell if she was still alive. Her blue light faded until only a faint afterglow remained.

Isabelle jumped aside as her sprite flung an enchantment toward her head.

"Isabelle," Haidar gasped.

He was on all fours on the ground now, clutching the goblet's stem with both hands. My heart thudded in my chest.

Stay still, I ordered myself.

I couldn't watch him. In front of me, Kelda was moving. She raised her hand toward me.

I yanked my wand from my hair and swooshed it through the air. A humming shield sprang up around me. I shoved the wand back into my hair and kept pushing with my hands, mirroring Amani as we strained to hold Kelda where she stood.

In the corner of my eye, Isabelle's sprite leapt toward her. And then I saw a blur run behind Amani, and Daniel was there, pointing his wand at the sprite and sending a solid stream of orange light toward it. The light hit the sprite in the back. He stiffened and crumpled. His long white hair fell across his face and his light, too, faded to almost nothing.

"Go," Daniel shouted.

In two steps, Isabelle was down the stairs and in the garden. She threw herself down in front of Haidar.

"I can't," Haidar said.

Kelda twisted again. I felt our hold on her begin to slip.

Haidar pushed the cup toward Isabelle.

"You've got this," she said, voice crisp. "Focus."

"Belle—"

"Focus," she ordered.

His knuckles were white on the goblet. She put her hands over his and bent down so she could see his eyes.

"This is your home," she said. "Your goblet. Your magic."

His shoulders shook with the effort. But slowly, in sputters and jerks, the white light began to reverse itself again, pouring into the goblet and through it to the earth. New white veins began to push out again, and the circle of light around Kelda intensified.

Kelda threw her hands up toward Amani. But a light I recognized had kindled in the queen's eyes.

She was no longer Amani. She was the Faerie Queen, and the fury of a thousand generations of our race prickled down her arms and made her hair stand on end.

"Now," Amani ordered.

Lightning sparked down my arms and through my fingertips. Together, the three of us slammed our energy toward Kelda, Haidar hardest of all.

Thick green ropes sprang from the ground and threw themselves together above Kelda's head, forming a thick cage. Sharp, thorn-covered branches spread out until the Oracle was completely enclosed. Here and there, blood-red roses bloomed.

Kelda threw a spell against the cage of rose bushes that surrounded her. The magic rattled the stems, but the cage held. Instead of flying out toward one of us, the curse crackled and sparked along the branches and leaves until it wore itself out and dissolved.

I expected Kelda to scream, or panic, or do anything that matched the frantic hysteria in my head.

But Kelda wasn't some third-rate teenage godmother. She was one of the leaders of our world, second only to the queen.

Instead of screaming, she put a hand on her hip and stared at Amani.

The queen lowered her hands. I saw her chest rise and fall, but she, too, held it together.

"Kelda," Amani said coolly.

"Sycophantic bureaucrat," Kelda replied, matching her tone.

I raised my eyebrows. My frantic heartbeat slowed.

This was not what I'd expected.

"How's it going?" Kelda said.

Her voice sounded normal, not the low echo I'd always heard at the Fountain. All I could see from here was her back, but she came across as nothing more than a tall, thin woman in a long white gown. Her black hair was streaked with silver and tumbled down her back; despite the silver, it was clear she was young, or at least not much older than Amani.

The queen walked up to the cage.

"I keep busy," Amani said. "Thanks for making sure of that."

"Happy to help," Kelda said. "That does seem to be my job, doesn't it? Helping you?"

Amani actually rolled her eyes.

"Give it a rest, Kel," she said. "No one's ever made you do anything you didn't want to do."

"No one ever gave me the opportunities to do things I *did* want to do," Kelda said.

Amani sighed.

"We need to talk," she said. "Really talk."

I stepped toward the cage and took a couple of careful steps to the side so I could see Kelda's face. Every other time we'd met, she'd been hidden behind the rippling waters of the Oracle's Fountain. Her round face seemed slightly at odds with her tall, slender body, but she was stunningly pretty. Her faerie aura, as electric blue as Amani's was gold, fell around her in a constant trickle of light. It shifted across her face like reflections from the bottom of a pool.

She saw me, and turned away from Amani to take me in. Her black eyes drew me toward her, and her rosy mouth drew down in a pout.

"Olivia," she said. "Good to see you. I want to talk to you."

"I'm just here to help Queen Amani," I said.

I didn't want her looking at me. I didn't want her to know I'd been involved in all of this. How was I supposed to ever sleep again, having wronged the second most powerful being in our entire world?

"Yes, well, Queen Amani is useless and obsolete," Kelda said. She tossed her hair, sending silver tendrils flying over her shoulder. "She's not worth bothering with. You'd know that if you ever thought for yourself."

I looked to Amani for guidance. Her mouth quirked downward, but she nodded at me.

I stepped forward again until I could have reached out and touched the thorny cage.

"What am I doing here?" Kelda said.

She glanced sideways at Amani and gave her a quick up-and-down. It was exactly the look I'd seen girls give other girls in the halls of my high school, usually right before they muttered something to their friends like, "Hairdo? Looks like a hair don't" or "Control your whoremones, slut."

It didn't warm me to her one bit.

What was more, it made me realize what I was dealing with.

The Oracle, as a role, was a leader of our world. But Kelda? As far as I could see from here, Kelda was nothing more than a nasty, insecure girl who lashed out when things didn't go right for her. Sure, she couched her spite in nice platitudes about uniting our worlds or letting Glims be freely themselves. But

I'd seen the creek where she'd hidden her wand. She was sticky with lies, and I wasn't about to let her take over Portland *or* look at my queen that way.

"Let's get one thing real clear, right now," I said.

My voice came out clear and strong, and so loud that it shocked me. I wanted to step back at the assertiveness in my own tone. Instead, I stepped forward.

"You've been pulling a lot of crap lately," I said. "You've been breaking our laws and doing everything in your power to screw our community over. You want to reveal Glims to the world? Fine. You do that. But you do it with the support of your people, not by bullying the best of them and bribing the worst with special favors or gold coins or whatever you've been offering."

One of Kelda's dark arched eyebrows went up.

"Your pet has teeth," she called to Amani.

"Kel?" Amani said. "Shut up."

I turned to her in surprise. She was looking at Kelda with the most fed-up expression I'd ever seen on a face that wasn't my own. She glanced at me, shook her head, and went to sit on the stone steps leading down to the clearing.

"I'm going to let you in on a secret," I said, lowering my voice. "I think you're onto something, or at least your public message is. I think maybe there is something to be said for letting Glims be themselves in public. Maybe it's time to explore that."

I leaned in.

"But you do *not* get to make that decision for everyone."

She folded her arms and stared at me. She was trying to intimidate me, trying to quash me with the same "ooh, look at the skank's off-brand jeans" expression she'd been giving Amani.

But I'd survived Imogen's disdain. And unlike Imogen, at the end of the day, Kelda meant nothing to me. Not anymore.

"Call off your minions," I said.

It was stupid that I even had to have this conversation. Who had minions? Seriously?

"No," Kelda said.

"You can't just chase people out who don't agree with you," I said. "You can't just kidnap their kids, or unleash fairy swarms on them. That's not how grownups solve their problems."

She grabbed the edge of the rose cage and leaned toward me. A tiny spot of blood ran down from her white hand onto the branch.

"I'm not a grownup," she hissed. "I'm the Oracle."

"And I'm a craptastic faerie godmother," I said. "Yay. We both have jobs. Aren't we special."

Somewhere beyond this little conversation, I heard Daniel snort.

"You're annoying me, Kelda," I said. "You have interfered in my life for months, and I am sick of it. So don't try and get all high and mighty, because I can't even begin to explain to you the number of shits I don't give."

Imogen's face flashed into my head, as it had every single day since we'd stopped talking. We'd been friends once. And sure, I'd messed up by not telling her about Amani's offer to make me her heir. But Kelda had taken that mistake—a mistake that should have remained between Imogen and me—and turned it into a weapon. She'd turned Lucas into a weapon, too—taken a sweet guy who had nothing to do with our world and thrown him in the middle of it, just to play with Imogen and me.

And now, she was interfering in hundreds of lives like mine all through this city.

If I hadn't wanted to leave this all for my nice Humdrum college before, she'd have sealed the deal.

"You know nothing," Kelda said. "You're as arrogant as she is."

She glared at Amani. I felt the anger and hate roll off her.

Her hostility felt familiar. It was the same as the emotions coming off Imogen at Gilt.

I forced the memory away. I couldn't stand to keep thinking about Imogen. Kelda had broken a lot of things in the past few days. Out of all the broken things, though, Imogen and my friendship had been the first.

I swallowed the frustrated scream that was building in my throat. Instead, I mimicked the two rulers in this garden with me and kept my cool.

"You're going to call off your sprites," I said. "You're going to tell them to go home, and you're going to announce to our entire world that you were wrong."

"I'm not wrong," Kelda said.

She looked down at me like I was a child.

Technically, I almost was. But I was not being the most childish person in this garden. That had to count for something.

"You don't even want to be here," Kelda said. "You're a Humdrum, Olivia. All the magic in the world isn't going to change that. You've always wanted to be a Hum. Don't you understand? My plan would let you really be one."

"By wiping out the Hums?" I said. "How exactly is that supposed to work?"

"I never intended to wipe them out," she said.

She blinked a few times at me. Each blink was like watching a lunar eclipse: The pale moon of her eyelids appeared for a moment, and then they were gone again, replaced by her deep black eyes.

"I just wanted them out of Portland," she said. "Portland is a Glim hub. You know that. It makes sense for the city to only consist of Glims and the Hums who truly respect us. I don't want to destroy the Hums; I just want to push them out of the city, into towns where they'll be happier surrounded by their own kind. Haven't you wondered why almost no one's died these past few days? This change could have been so much more violent."

I'd been so busy with the prospect of things happening to the people I cared about that it hadn't occurred to me to worry about the actual death toll.

I glanced across the clearing. Isabelle looked as caught off guard as I was.

"When you go to school, don't you want it to be at a college entirely full of Hums?" Kelda said. "You'll be happier surrounded by people who think and believe as you do. And those of us who prefer to live magically can be surrounded by people who respect that choice."

"You've been rewarding Glims who show themselves to the Hums," I said.

She let go of the cage and clenched her hand into a fist. It wasn't enough to stop the blood from trickling down her hand. A single drop landed on her white gown.

"This will only work if we know about each other," she said.

"Our entire world is based on them not knowing about us," I said.

"Only because of fear," she snarled. "Fear is not befitting to Glimmers. You've been fed a steady diet of lies since you were a child, Olivia. The Hums won't get to catch us and experiment on us, much as they like to poke and prod at anything that doesn't protest loudly enough. By the time Portland is ours, we'll have made it perfectly clear that we're too powerful to be harassed. As long as they respect us, we'll be happy to keep to our own cities and leave them alone. It's an equitable arrangement."

"You just want to separate us," I said.

It didn't make any sense. We'd been preparing for war. We'd been sending Glims to protect the Hums we cared about. We'd been doing everything we could to slow this Dark Forest movement, because the Humdrum world knowing about us would lead to nothing good.

And yet, everything Kelda said made the past year fall into place.

Every move she and the sprites had made had been carefully calculated. The hauntings, the rumors—they were designed to scare Hums into moving out of the city, not to hurt them. No one had died until these past few days. And even those instances had clearly been the result of people who'd gotten too excited, not sprites acting under Kelda's orders.

"I want to give you the world you've always dreamed about," Kelda said. "Would you really have been able to enjoy college knowing that you could run into a Glim in any class you walked into? And that Glim might not be there because they want to escape to the Humdrum world, like you. I'm offering you freedom, Olivia. Freedom to escape to somewhere full of people like you, who love and respect the same things you do. Why have you imprisoned me in a cage for that?"

I took a few steps back.

What was I doing here? Why was I the one having this conversation?

I wanted to go. This garden was so full of magic it made my skin throb. Without my glasses, everywhere I looked crackled with the light of spells and enchantments. My own green aura flowed around me, clinging to me like a mist I could never escape.

What if I could peel it off and leave it behind?

What if there really was a place full of people like me, people who didn't want the strain of magic constantly weighing on them and creating expectations they were bound to fall short of?

I heard Amani shift on the stairs behind me, but she didn't run to my rescue.

Kelda leaned forward until her nose was almost touching the cage. Her gaze bored into me.

"You could find new friends in a place like that, Olivia. Friends who won't betray you."

Her eyes flickered up to look behind me, to where Amani waited in the gathering dusk.

With a snap, the spell of her words broke. The beautiful illusion of a world where I belonged crashed around my ears like shards of glass, leaving only the truth.

"You helped her betray me," I said. "You fed us stories about each other. I didn't know how to tell her about Amani, but that was none of your business. You had no right to turn us against each other."

My hand twitched. I itched to grab my wand and throw something, anything, at Kelda's pale, wide-eyed face.

"And Lucas? He's not even supposed to be here. This hasn't been easy for him, but you don't care. Maybe you liked it better that way."

I heard my voice rising to a yell and tried to rein it in, to keep all my anger and my magic inside me where it belonged. But some anger wasn't meant to sit inside forever.

"You will call off your sprites," I said.

My voice trembled, and instead of fighting to force my fury to sit inside me and fester, I let it flow toward her.

She was a faerie. She was welcome to my emotions, all of them. Let her sort it out.

"You will call off all your Glim supporters," I said. "You will make a public and formal announcement to the entire Glimmering world that you no longer support the Dark Forest movement. If you want to change the way our world works, you will go through the appropriate channels and not resort to threats and bribes to get your way. These are the rules now. You have exactly one choice: You will agree to them or you will deal with Queen Amani."

"And what's Amani going to do?" Kelda said. She gave me a sardonic smile. "Be the Faerie Queen? Forget about me? Make decisions without my input? We've been there and done that a dozen times while you were still in diapers."

For the briefest instant, I knew what it was like to be the queen when her eyes flashed and sparked with faerie rage. I felt the magic and the outrage thunder inside my body, and when it wanted to crash out toward Kelda, I didn't stop it.

I took a few steps to the side and picked up Kelda's silver wand, lying almost forgotten on the grass.

"We have your wand," I said. I held it up. "You have an hour to think about your decision. Should you not comply, Queen Amani will strip you of your powers, and I will help her."

I whirled on my heel and walked away.

EMMA SAVANT

"That's not my wand," Kelda called after me.

For the briefest instant, I froze. But I couldn't let her see me hesitate. I kept walking.

"You really think I'd leave it lying in a creek?" she said.

She laughed, and the sound sank like lead into my gut.

But I still didn't look back. Kelda hadn't earned it.

"Haidar, Isabelle, Daniel, stand guard," I ordered.

I swept up the stairs past Amani. The queen scrambled to her feet and followed.

CHAPTER THIRTY

I went through the arched wooden door Haidar had taken us through when we'd first come to the mansion. Amani came in after me and locked the door behind her. We faced each other in the stone potting shed. Amani's aura lit the space with a faint golden glow.

Even here, I wasn't convinced Kelda couldn't hear us, so I kept my voice to a murmur.

"What does she mean, that's not her wand?" I hissed.

Amani ran a hand through her hair.

"I should have guessed," she said. "Knowing her, she's paranoid enough to have fakes hidden all over the city in powerful bodies of water. Let me see it."

I held it out to her. She took it. Tense anticipation covered her face. She touched the cool metal, then frowned.

"Nothing," she said.

She turned it over and held her other hand over its tip. Still nothing.

She slammed it onto a dusty wooden table covered in bags of potting soil.

"If that was really one of her wands, I wouldn't even be able to touch it," she said. "She'd have powerful enchantments on it to keep it from ever falling into my hands."

"Why does she hate you so much?" I said.

Amani glanced out the window. We couldn't see Kelda from here, but between the branches of bushes and trees, the dazzling blue of her aura glowed.

"We were best friends," Amani said. "I screwed it up."

The look on her face made it clearer than clear that she didn't want to talk about it. But I'd been dragged into all this, and they'd been flat-out weird in the garden. I'd earned a little context.

"What happened?" I said.

"We're both ambitious people," she said. "At some point, I must have decided my ambition was worth more than the friendship. I wouldn't do it that way again."

The increasing tightness in her jaw made it clear I wasn't going to get any more of that story today. I picked up the fake wand and twirled it between my hands.

"Does she have the wand on her?" I said.

"No," Amani said. "She wouldn't bring it here. Or at least, she would have transported it the second she realized what Haidar was doing."

"Maybe we won't need it."

"You really believe that?" Amani said.

I didn't even have to answer. I still hoped, but I knew what empty hope felt like.

There was no way Kelda was going to back down. Even if she could be convinced that was she was doing was wrong, she was never going to give in, because that would mean letting Amani win.

"This is stupid," I said.

"You were good out there," Amani said.

She smiled. I wasn't sure what the smile meant. Was it *You did good out there this one time* or *See, you'd be a great Faerie Queen after all?* I'd take the former, but the latter was never going to happen.

More than ever, I couldn't wait to be gone.

I glanced around the potting shed. The very presence of the bags of soil on the shelves made me calmer. This was where I belonged.

"If I had to bet, and if I could only make one guess, I'd say the wand was in her Fountain," Amani said.

Exactly nothing about that sounded okay.

"I'm going to take a wild shot in the dark here and say we can't just waltz in," I said.

Amani scoffed. "I couldn't blast my way in with an army of sprites," she said. "She has that thing barricaded against me on every level. Trust me, I've tried."

"I'm not going to be able to just walk in, either," I said. "She's got to have all kinds of protective spells on it. And no sprite's going to help us."

"We need the help of someone the Oracle trusts," Amani said. "Someone who's close to her, the kind of person who'd have a standing invitation. But of course, we don't know anyone like that."

She looked at me. I read her thought almost before she'd finished forming it.

"No," I said. "Absolutely not."

"Imogen Dann is her heir," Amani said. "She can get you in no matter what Kelda's set up."

"No," I said. "There has got to be another option."

"It's that or keep her in a cage for the next couple hundred years and hope she doesn't break out and kill everyone out of spite," Amani said. "Your choice."

"That choice sucks," I said.

"So does the one you just gave her," Amani said. "It's a day of rough decisions for everyone." She let out a deep breath and seemed to deflate a little. "Trust me, I know."

"You still care about her," I said.

"I'm about to do the unthinkable to my best friend," Amani said. Her eyes glittered, and this time, there was nothing faerie about it. "You at least still have the option to go talk to yours."

Perspective was the worst. I pressed on the back of my neck, feeling tension collecting and knowing I had no time to deal with the impending headache.

"Fine," I said.

Amani put a hand on my arm. "I ditched her," she said. "And I destroyed our friendship. Don't repeat my mistakes."

"I'm not sure it's up to me," I said.

I handed Kelda's decoy wand back to Amani.

"I'll enchant you there," Amani said.

I waved her off. "I'll get Lucas to drive me," I said. "I need the time to think."

CHAPTER THIRTY-ONE

As it turned out, the drive didn't help me think at all. I was too freaked out to string thoughts together, so I just sat there, staring out the window at the falling night as Lucas drove.

He reached out a few times to hold my hand. I squeezed it and held on every time, but he could only help so much. This was my shattered friendship and my mission. It was up to me to deal with it.

The streets of Portland were eerily empty tonight. The sprites had done their job. An occasional Glim sauntered down the sidewalk or middle of the street like they owned the place. Other than that, no motion besides the flickering leaves of trees interrupted the lamp-lit city. Signs taped to lampposts ordered people to *Join #DarkForest* or *Choose Peace!*, but there was no one to read them.

"Are you sure she's going to be there?" Lucas said. He pitched his voice low, as if knowing I'd startle at anything louder.

I shrugged. "Your guess is as good as mine."

He turned left onto the road that led past the Oracle's Fountain. My shoulders tensed and hair prickled down my arms. We were too close for comfort, and everyone expected me to get even closer. They wanted me to march right inside.

I was insane for agreeing to this.

Lucas pulled into a metered parking spot by the park, not far from the Fountain. Dark trees hovered overhead, taunting us.

"I'm not coming with you," he said.

I nodded. Imogen was wildly unlikely to let me in as it was, and that was assuming she was even here.

"Keep the car running in case we need to leave fast," I said. "I don't know how long this is going to take."

I made a quick, fervent wish that Imogen was still at Gilt so I wouldn't have to see her yet.

Then I wished that godmother wishes counted for anything.

I pulled my wand out of my hair and shoved my glasses up onto the top of my head where they'd be out of the way. I twisted my hair into a ponytail.

Imogen always said ponytails in my frizzy hair made me look like I'd tamed a wild raccoon and attached it to the back of my head. I could stand a little raccoon-taming energy right now. Sad as it was to admit, even that sounded more badass than my current "wanting to hide under a bed in Haidar's mansion" vibe.

"Good luck, Liv," Lucas said. "You just told off the Oracle, so you're probably going to handle this just fine."

It was hard to tell if he was being serious or just trying to make me feel better.

I climbed out of the car, reassured myself with one last look at his steady face, and shut the door.

The Fountain rose out of the darkness within seconds. It seemed to loom larger as I approached, the Oracle's magic and its own imposing architecture conspiring to make me feel about as important as one of the sidewalk slabs under my feet.

I stepped down one of the large amphitheater stairs that led to the Fountain's base.

Water poured from the pools at its top. But it wasn't just water. Here and there, dropping like strands of Christmas tinsel or tiny skinny snakes, streaks of silver magic plunged down to the glittering pools below. Each strand spiraled in the water before dissipating in an explosion of glittering sparks, making the bottom layer of the Fountain look like it was filled with shifting stars.

"Imogen?" I called.

Silence greeted me, but I was too much of a faerie these days to believe in it. This silence was listening to my every word.

"We have Kelda," I said.

I raised my wand, prepared to defend myself in case any sprites came whistling down at this treason. But the silence kept waiting.

"I need to talk to you so we can figure out what happens next," I said. "It's down to you and me."

The tinsel strands of magic began to cluster together, falling more quickly near the center of the Fountain. As I watched, they grew so thick together that they formed a solid rectangle of white light, falling down to create what I thought might be a doorway.

I stepped forward and into the pool. Cold water gushed around my ankles and seeped into my shoes. Closing my eyes did nothing to shield me from the brightness of the doorway; it only made my eyelids glow violent red as I stepped forward. The whispering, burbling sound of rushing water filled my ears as I passed through.

And then, darkness.

I opened my eyes.

It took a moment for my vision to adjust. When it did, I saw dim reflections, not objects. Here, a tall stripe of reflected light stretching to the ceiling. There, a glint that suggested distance. A moment later, the space shifted into clarity as my eyes made sense of what it all meant.

The entire place was black, gleaming and polished. Jet floors stretched out in front of me and disappeared into shadow. Tall inky columns supported the ceiling, which likewise would have disappeared if not for the vague sparkle that emanated from it.

Blue pools of light clicked on abruptly near the floor, spaced every few feet along the walls. The room filled instantly with shifting, luminous blue. It took me a moment to realize the pools of light were literally pools—small silver bowls filled almost to the brim. The water glowed and cast a rippling illumination onto the black surfaces.

The overall effect was beautiful, but it was cold, too.

I looked around, waiting to see Imogen or a door I should go through. But there were no doors here, only more shimmering rectangular curtains of water set into the walls, falling from the ceiling and disappearing into the floor. They whispered in the blue darkness, but no strands of magic indicated where I should go.

Footsteps clicked ahead of me. I spun toward the sound, but it was a moment before I saw her walk out of the shadows. Her hair was swept up and she wore the kind of gown we both would have died over last year, a slinky silver number that made her look like a curvy goddess on her thirtieth jaunt down the red carpet.

"Where's Kelda?" she demanded.

"Hi, nice to see you too," I said.

She threw a hand out toward me. A white ball of magic flew toward me with a crackling sound. I dodged to avoid it; it hit the wall behind me and fizzled out.

I brought my wand down in a sharp motion toward the floor. A shield sprang up in front of me, glistening translucent and barely visible in the darkness.

"That's really not getting you on my good side," I said.

Not that she needed to be on my good side. I needed to get on hers, at least if I wanted her to hand over the wand.

But who was I kidding? The Imogen standing in front of me was never going to help anyone who wanted to hurt her future with Kelda.

"You hate me," I said. "I get it. Can we put that aside for thirty seconds so we can figure this out?"

"Hate implies I care," Imogen said. "I'm indifferent."

"You're a good liar," I said. "But not that good. People don't throw fireballs at people they don't care about. Trust me. I am one-hundred percent apathetic about Mr. Johnson who lives across the street, and I haven't thrown magic at his head once."

I sounded like an idiot. Why was I rambling? I needed to get the wand and get out.

I took a step toward her. "What are you doing here?" I said.

"I think that's my question for you," she said.

I didn't even recognize her face anymore. She looked like Imogen on the surface, but behind it, all her facial expressions were wrong. My Imogen smiled; this one glared daggers. My Imogen was melodramatic and threw herself on furniture; this one swept around like an empress.

It wasn't wrong of us to change. We weren't that far from college and adult life. Some growing was inevitable.

But she hadn't grown. She just looked like a light inside her had gone out.

"What has Kelda offered you that's so good that you'd join her on this?" I said. "Come on, Gen. You can fight this."

The curse that clung to her was so obvious that I was stunned I hadn't realized it earlier. Even so, no curse was so strong that Imogen, of all people, couldn't fight it if she wanted to.

"She has vision," Imogen said.

"She's an insecure, manipulative child," I said.

Imogen's eyes flashed. I took another step toward her.

"You know that," I said. "You have to know that if you've taken one second to think about it. She pitted us against each other. *Us.*"

"Maybe 'us' didn't mean as much as you thought," Imogen said.

She cast an imperious glance down at me, then turned and walked away. I followed her.

"Why didn't you come talk to me?" I said. "When you found out I hadn't told you about Amani?"

Imogen spun on me, and I threw up a hand.

"Which, I know, I should have told you," I said, before she had a chance. "I was wrong."

She tightened her lips into a thin line and kept walking.

"Why didn't you just ask me about it?" I said. "Don't you think it's weird, that you didn't even ask me?"

"Why would I ask someone who was already lying to me?" Imogen said.

"I wasn't lying," I said. "I just hadn't told you yet. I didn't know how. You would have made me feel like crap for not taking her offer, and I already spend most of my time feeling like crap, okay?"

She scoffed.

"What?" I said.

No answer. I grabbed her arm and pulled her to a stop. Her entire body stiffened, and I felt magic crackle along her skin as she prepared to send something else at me.

"Seriously," I said. I let go of her arm. "What?"

She looked down at me. She was already taller than I was, and her glittering, super-high heels made the difference even more dramatic. I felt like a child standing next to a queen.

An angry queen.

"You feel like crap?" she said, like I'd just said the most outrageous, stupid thing she'd ever heard. "You, Miss High and Mighty Olivia, Champion of the Humdrums and youngest faerie godmother in a hundred years, feel like crap? You poor little rich girl."

"I'm the *worst* faerie godmother in a hundred years," I corrected. "And I like the Humdrums because I, personally, am a shit faerie."

She rolled her eyes and kept walking toward the shadowed back of the room.

Where did she get off? Had she not been there during our entire friendship?

"I'm not like you, Imogen," I said. I matched my strides to hers to keep up. "I'm not just magically good at everything I touch. I'm not pretty *and* talented *and* smart *and* popular *and* confident. So yes, I feel like crap."

"Give me a break," she said.

"Sorry if my feelings inconvenience you."

"Oh my god, Olivia, I'm not talking about your feelings," she said. For an instant, she sounded like the Imogen I knew. And then it was gone as her voice took on a hard edge. "I'm not whatever all you just said. That's the stupidest thing I've ever heard."

"Have you met yourself?"

She scoffed again and stopped in front of one of the waterfalls in the wall. As she looked at it, the water began to glimmer white. It parted in the middle, opening like curtains, and Imogen walked through. I followed close on her heels before she had a chance to shut me out.

It only occurred to me after the water had closed again behind us that following Imogen deeper into the Oracle's lair might not have been the smartest move of my life.

But Imogen didn't seem like she was about to lock me up here or throw me into some deep dark pit hidden in this black underground palace. She strode forward. In the center of the empty room, a waterfall stood, lit by bright white lights and falling in a smooth, glassy sheet from the ceiling.

I was getting just a little bit sick of waterfalls.

"I'm just a mediocre faerie," Imogen said. She sounded like she wasn't talking to me, but didn't care anymore whether I listened in. "I'm nothing special. But Kelda accepts me for who I am, and she's given me opportunities that I'd never find anywhere else. This isn't perfect, but I'm not the kind of person who's going to find anything better."

I wanted to smash the waterfall into a thousand pieces like it was glass.

"Did Kelda tell you that?" I said.

She ignored me and walked around to the other side of the waterfall. It fell into a white-tiled circular pool, studded here and there with bright circular mirrors.

"I need Kelda's wand," I said.

Forget about strategy and diplomacy and trying to slowly talk her around to it. I was done—beyond done. Anyone who could take my Imogen and turn her into the cynical, insecure girl in front of me didn't deserve to keep her magic for another single second.

"You have it, don't you?" I said. "Or at least you know where it is."

"What kind of faerie leaves her wand at home?" Imogen said coldly.

"Not that wand," I said. "The one she has hidden. I know it's here."

Her eyes narrowed. "Why on earth would I tell you that?"

"Because you remember what you used to be like before she got her nasty little claws into you," I said.

Not that I could blame it all on Kelda. There was enough responsibility to go around.

I swallowed. "Gen, I'm sorry I haven't been here for you," I said.

"No big deal," she said. She gestured out toward the room. "As you can see, I'm doing perfectly fine."

"You are not," I said. "You're not doing any better than I am. And I'm crap without you."

Her eyes met mine for the briefest second, and for a second, I almost saw the hint of a smile on her lips. But it was only almost—nothing more than a bit of wishful thinking brought on by stress and the way my arms hurt from wanting to hug her.

"What do you want her wand for?" Imogen said. Her voice was lazy, almost bored.

My fingertips pressed against the handle of my own wand.

How had I gotten here?

I was so tired of this game. I was tired of trying to be clever, and tired of trying to act like every second of this conversation didn't kill me. I had to tell her the truth.

"Someone has to stop Kelda," I said. "We can do it, if we have her wand. We'll take her powers."

A flash of shock crossed Imogen's face. I felt the horror that filled her, and I waited in silence for the initial blow to pass.

"Queen Amani gave her a choice," I said. "She can call off everything that's happening out there, or she can give up her powers. It's a no-win situation for her, but people will stop being frightened out of their homes either way."

Imogen wrapped her arms around herself. I realized suddenly that it was cold in here, cold and empty and dark. What would it be like when Imogen took over? I couldn't stand the thought of her living in this chilly silence as the years stretched on.

"I need your help," I said.

She watched me intently, eyes narrow.

"Come over here," she said. "I want to show you something."

CHAPTER THIRTY-TWO

"You don't know what you're doing," Imogen said. "You don't understand what you're giving up."

An urgency entered her limbs as she leaned forward and reached out into the waterfall at the center of the room. The water split around her hand, leaving an arcing triangle of empty space below.

Cautiously, I stepped toward her. The water splashed into the pool at our feet, casting rippling white light up onto Imogen's face. Her skin gleamed like a moon, and for a moment, I saw a hint of Kelda in Imogen's face.

"Stand opposite me," she ordered.

The water rippled between us. Through it, she looked even less like the Imogen I knew. Her pale face shifted, and I saw what her future would look like. She'd stay here, in this dark, beautiful place, and she'd hide behind the waterfall, and her face would ripple and she'd give coins to whomever she thought deserved them.

It was no life.

"You don't have to stay here," I said.

She shushed me. I bit the tip of my tongue and waited.

"Watch the water," Imogen said, voice low. "Watch what you'll be giving up if you do this."

I stared at the water, though really, I was staring at her. She was barely three feet away from me, and yet she felt so distant that I knew I couldn't reach out and touch her no matter how hard I tried.

As I watched, the water distorted her face, melting the pale oval and spreading it in trails of light.

For a moment, the waterfall seemed to reflect my own face. I stood in front of it, and then my likeness backed away and disappeared into shadow.

And then a spot of light stirred. Behind the waterfall, or perhaps in its reflection, the water began to show me images.

I saw myself, sitting on a twin bed in a small room while rain poured outside. Potted plants surrounded me as I read a giant book that lay open on the bed. I looked enthralled and like nothing in the world could distract me from what I was doing.

The images melted and shifted. I was there again, standing in a botanical garden full of bushes exploding with vivid flowers. I examined one of the flowers, leaning in so close that my nose almost brushed against the fuzzy yellow stamens. Another figure walked into the picture; a moment later, I recognized it as Lucas. He leaned over my shoulder. The version of me in the garden jumped, startled, then hit him lightly on the arm and burst out laughing.

The picture changed again. Now, I stood, surrounded by lush green vegetation, with a turquoise sea behind me. I crouched down and snapped a photo of one of the thousands of plants, then carefully clipped a leaf and dropped it in a plastic bag. I stood, stretched, and looked out towards the sea. A stray strand of hair whipped around my face. It had been tugged loose from the breeze; the rest of my hair was up in a ponytail. My wand was nowhere to be seen.

In every image, the look on my face made my stomach flip over.

That was what it would feel like to be happy. Not temporarily happy, or superficially happy, but actually content in a way I suspected not everyone got to experience. The Olivia in these images lived a life of privilege and purpose and joy.

I watched as the picture altered. I was older in this one, and stood in front of a class of college students not much older than I was now. I wrote the words *Ecotourism – pros/cons* on a whiteboard, then waved up toward a photograph projected onto a screen. It showed low, dry-looking trees and a muddy river where a small herd of elephants drank. My older face was lit up, my eyes sparkling in a way I'd never seen in a mirror.

"Trade me places," Imogen said.

I jumped. Her voice brought me hurtling a million miles an hour back to the Oracle's Fountain. I didn't want to come back. I wanted to stay in these worlds. I wanted to step through the waterfall and slip into that Olivia's shoes.

But the pictures were gone. The waterfall was back, and through it, Imogen stared at me.

I moved to her side. She circled the pool opposite me, her shoulders tense and raised like a cat's.

It took only a moment this time. The waterfall shifted, and showed me as I was, almost as though it were a reflection. But in the reflection, I had the Oracle's wand in my hand. The Olivia in the water turned and walked out, and the picture faded to black.

And then I was back. I stood in the garden opposite Amani, and we raised our wands and Kelda's wand together. There was a blinding flash of white-blue light. Again, the image faded.

When it returned, I sat in an elaborate room at a long polished conference table. Amani sat next to me; my dad was there too, and his boring coworker Charles, and a bunch of other Glims I recognized from dinner parties and company barbecues. My stomach dropped and clenched at the sight of them, but waterfall-Olivia's face was intent. She leaned forward in her seat, and her eyes cut across to the face of the woman who was talking.

The image shifted, and there I was again, but this time, I looked different. My aura had changed. No longer green and mild, it had begun to take on curls of gold that swirled around me like curlicue grape vines. I stood in a room I recognized from the first time I'd met Amani. Multnomah Falls thundered by outside the enormous plate-glass window. Amani faced me and tossed a sparking gold spell in my direction. I whipped my wand out of my hair in one lightning motion. I expected to watch myself deflect the spell, or diffuse it, but instead I did something I'd never seen before. I caught the spell on the tip of my wand and balanced it there. A moment later, my wand swallowed the energy down. I grinned at Amani, and she rolled her eyes at me.

My face was different in these ones, too. There wasn't contentment. There was nothing like the happiness I'd seen in the girl who'd bent down to take pictures of island greenery. Instead, my face lit up with a fierce sense of focus. I didn't recognize that any more than I had the contentment.

Another image appeared. This time, I stood alone. I was older, barefoot, wearing a long cream-colored gown. My aura swirled out ten feet in every direction with gold and green. I wore a gold crown in my hair and held my wand aloft. I stood in a forest, and the trees themselves seemed to stretch out toward me.

And though I couldn't see it, I knew somehow deep in my bones that the Glimmering world was safe. With that Olivia in charge, standing alone in the woods, Portland was protected and the magical world beyond the city borders was secure and as it should be. My family was in one piece. My friends were able to pursue their own lives without worrying about taking sides.

These were images of my possible futures, clearly, but neither of them looked like me. In the future, I would be replaced by Botanist Olivia or Faerie Queen Olivia.

No matter what I chose, *I* wouldn't be there anymore.

And I had to choose now. The Oracle's wand was a deeply personal object, imbued with the magic of one of the most powerful Glims in the world. I could walk out of here with it or without it. Either way, the waterfall was clear: My decision would affect everything.

"If you give me the wand," I said, then trailed off.

Being Reginald Feye's daughter was nothing compared to being the faerie who took down the Oracle. And if this happened, the Oracle would be gone. Her magic would disappear, and the whole city—dysfunctional as it now was—would be thrown even more out of balance. If the waterfall's images were right, this would create enormous problems for the Council. As the one responsible for the Oracle's downfall, they would turn to me.

The waterfall was a sharp reality check.

If I took the wand and did this, I would be committing to the Glimmering world.

And if I left it behind, I would never have to deal with any of this again. The world would sort itself out, or at least its problems would take place far from me. If I could be teaching college when my hair started to gray and loving it that much, things must be all right. Amani would take care of Kelda on her own, or maybe Kelda would break free and her crazy plan would work after all.

Or not.

"This doesn't show me everything," I said. "What happens to the Glim world if I walk away now?"

Imogen's voice stayed cool, but an undercurrent of strength ran beneath it that made my arms prickle.

"What do you think?" she said. "There will be conflict, and not everyone will be happy. But then, you can never make everyone happy anyway. Kelda will take us to a different future. I'll help her, and then I'll become the Oracle. By then, the role of Oracle will be important." She glanced down at me. "Much more important than that of Faerie Queen."

"What happens to Amani?" I said.

Imogen shrugged one pale shoulder. "I'm sure she and Kelda will solve things between themselves," she said. "I'll stay out of it. You should, too."

I stepped away from the waterfall. It seemed to hold all my choices, and I needed some distance and fresh air to think.

But there was no fresh air down here. Just shadows and pressure.

If I left, I could have the life I'd always dreamed about.

If I took the wand, I would never go to a Humdrum college. I'd never have a normal career, or work in conservation, or walk down the street without feeling different from the Humdrums who passed me.

If I took the wand, I'd be a walking cliché: the daughter of Reginald Feye, youngest godmother in a hundred years, heir to the Faerie Queen.

But I could do good for the Glimmering community; I could *feel* it, deep in my gut where I'd never felt anything until this last year. I would change things. Maybe we'd come to Kelda's conclusions and decide to be open about our world. Maybe we'd lock everything back down and keep our secrets forever. The decision didn't matter; the only important thing was the knowledge in my bones that wherever we landed would be something we as a people agreed on together.

I'd stop being a godmother, but I'd keep making people's wishes come true. And that would come at the cost of my own.

The tension between my futures made me feel as if my skin was trying to pull me apart.

"You can have what you want," Imogen said. "You've always talked about getting away and doing your plant stuff like a 'normal' person. This is your chance. We can all have what we want."

"What does the waterfall show you?" I said.

I stepped around its glassy curtain to see her clearly. Her gaze was distant, almost soft, as she looked toward its shimmering surface.

Over her shoulder, I could just make out the images Imogen was seeing. They were faded and hard to discern from this angle, but the gist was clear: Imogen would take over the Fountain. Swarms of sprites in every body of water in Portland would attend her and obey her every word. The city would revere her; the world would look up to her as a ruler.

Imogen had never been hurting for glamour or influence, but the look on her face as she stared at her future was that of a starving person.

She'd always been the littlest Dann, the tail end of a family of beautiful, accomplished sisters. She was as smart as any of them, but maybe she didn't see that like I did. She'd cheated on her Proctor Exam, after all. The Oracle had said she'd been afraid she wouldn't pass.

My Imogen had never seemed afraid.

But my Imogen wasn't this girl. It was impossible to tell whether I'd ever really known her at all.

We'd been best friends, but I'd hidden Amani's invitation to be her heir from Imogen. Was it so impossible to believe that she'd been hiding her fears from me?

"I'm supposed to be crowned her official heir at the Rose Galas," Imogen said. "She arranged for me to be Rose Empress, and we were going to use the Galas as a way for me to meet all the right people and solidify my position. We were going to hold a ceremony. She's been sending her sprites all around the city to collect magic from Glims who don't agree with her. They've been quietly skimming power off of people's auras for months, and they've gathered a lot. She was going to give me some of that magic. And that was only the beginning. If you leave here with the wand, nothing ever happens to me. I'm just *Imogen*."

The disgust in her voice made me feel like someone had just kicked me in the gut. I wanted to hug her, but I didn't dare touch her.

"I always liked Imogen," I said.

"Everyone *liked* Imogen," she said. "You can like someone who doesn't matter. You just never respect her."

"Is it worth it, if mattering makes you this miserable?" I said. I stepped toward her, still fighting the impulse to put my arms around her thin, pulled-in shoulders.

She turned away from me, waving at the waterfall as she did so. The images melted away into nothingness. Clear water continued to fall peacefully into the pool like nothing had ever happened.

"I get it if you can't help me," I said. "I do. I want you to be happy."

"If you take her wand, nothing else ever happens to me," she said. "The role of Oracle is dissolved. A committee takes over." She spat the word *committee,* and I couldn't blame her.

If I took the wand, Imogen's dreams were over.

If I didn't, the Glim world was going to suffer. Maybe my family would too, and Lucas, and Elle and Kyle and everyone else.

But maybe that was the price we'd have to pay.

I let out a heavy sigh.

"Keep it," I said.

She frowned at me.

I bit the inside of my cheek and shook my head at her. "I'm not going to take all that away from you."

The water rippled and splashed in front of us. Imogen stared at it as though it held all the answers, though no images played there now. Strain pulled at the corners of her mouth.

I had no idea how I was going to explain this to Amani. But then, maybe I wouldn't have to. She seemed to regret whatever had happened between her and Kelda.

I wasn't going to let us repeat their mistakes. If the whole world had to fall apart, so be it.

"Gen, I just want you to be happy," I said.

This time, I did reach out. My fingertips landed softly on her arm. Silently, I urged her to smile, or turn to me. I watched for any sign of forgiveness, or optimism, or even confidence.

She shrugged my touch off.

"If you don't take the wand, our whole world's going to crash," she said. She spoke so low that I was almost glad we were in the eerily quiet Fountain. The rippling of the waterfall was almost enough to drown out her voice. "Things will be good for me. I'll be one of the only ones."

"Okay," I said.

She turned, a sudden, angry gesture that made me take a step back. The silver gown swirled around her ankles as she walked away. She reached a wall, then began to pace along its edge, back and forth, her arms folded and her strides long. I felt the rage rushing off her in a torrent, filling the room and mingling with my own worry and anxiety for her and the future of everyone I knew.

And then, just as abruptly, she stopped. Her stiff spine softened, and she seemed to deflate.

I recognized the collapse. It had followed every rant of her life. When things were really bad, Imogen stormed and raged. Then, when she'd ranted and fumed herself empty, she usually either dragged me out for ice cream or crumpled on the couch and fell asleep.

But there was no ice cream here, and there was no couch. There was just me and an otherworldly white waterfall.

Imogen walked slowly toward the pool and knelt down at its edge. She dipped her fingertips in the gently churning water.

"*Fil ar ais go dom,*" she whispered.

With a flash, a silver wand fell from the top of the waterfall. Imogen's hand shot out to catch it.

She clenched her pale fist around the wand and held it in the stream for a moment. The pain in her face was visible in the furrow between her eyes, the thin lines of her lips, and the tight smoothness of her forehead.

She held the wand out to me.

"Gen, I can't," I said.

She hissed as if in pain.

"Take it," she said. "You have to take it. Don't make me keep asking because I won't."

I closed my fingers around its smooth surface.

The instant it was in my hand, I wondered how I could have ever believed the other one was real. The power in this thin silver rod made my palm vibrate and my arm grow hot. The room seemed to instantly become brighter; I could see into the shadowy corners and see the lines of magic that snaked their way through the walls like veins.

Imogen clenched her fingers on the tiled edge of the pool and looked down into the water.

"You're going to take her magic?" she said.

"If she doesn't agree to peace, yeah," I said.

She closed her eyes and nodded.

We fell silent. She was only waiting for me to leave.

"Come with me," I said.

She shook her head.

I knelt down next to her and put a hand on her back. Her skin was cool; her breath came in shallow shudders.

"I'm not leaving you behind," I said.

She wouldn't meet my eyes, but she rose and followed me out. The waterfall watched us go, and our footsteps echoed in the cavernous blackness.

CHAPTER THIRTY-THREE

The drive back to Haidar's was tense. Lucas' fingers stayed white on the steering wheel, and he kept glancing into the rearview mirror at Imogen in the backseat. I couldn't tell if his feelings were related to her association with the Oracle or her role as his ex-girlfriend; either way, he was strung tight.

We drove through the still, quiet city. Here and there, a glowing blue sprite flew overhead. None of them seemed to notice us. At one point, we slipped right underneath one sitting watchfully in a tree. I held tight to Amani's necklace as we drove, willing the sprites not to realize we had the Oracle's heir in the car with us, and willing Imogen not to tip them off.

She'd come of her own accord. Whether she would regret that before we reached Haidar's place was anyone's guess.

I saw the light of the enchantment that protected Haidar's grounds long before we reached his gates. My glasses were still propped up on my head. Without them, the undersides of the clouds glowed white-gold with magic.

Would I need my glasses, as the Faerie Queen?

How soon would I become her, and all traces of me disappear?

I shivered as Lucas pulled the car up the driveway. The gates stayed locked tight.

I glanced in the rearview mirror. Imogen sat with her arms tightly crossed. She'd put on one of Lucas' hoodies that had been sitting in the back. It swallowed her up and hid her champagne-blond hair from view.

Lucas looked to me for direction.

I frowned. Normally, I'd call Isabelle or text Daniel to come let us in. But now, I paused.

If I was going to be the Faerie Queen, little things like gates shouldn't matter. Not when the spell was in place thanks to something I was in the middle of.

I pulled my wand out of my hair and pointed it at the barred entrance. Nothing happened. The enchantment and the metal gate stayed firmly sealed against us.

I will be the Faerie Queen, I thought, ordering my will through the wand and through the gate. *You* will *move aside.*

The gate rattled. I furrowed my brow and tried to force as much magic as I could through its thin metal confines.

The gates burst open as magic flooded through me. It poured through my arm and out my wand, a long heavy stream like nothing I'd ever felt before. I gasped and slammed back against the seat.

What had I been thinking, using my magical energy on something as stupid as a gate? I had a freaking Oracle to subdue. The entry was the least of my problems.

Lucas' gaze landed on me, sharp with concern. I felt Imogen watching from the backseat. A tangled knot of emotions twisted around her. I closed my eyes and took a deep breath, feeling for the tendrils of magic that had burst free from me. Carefully, I began to reel them back in.

Lucas edged the car through the gate cautiously, as though he was worried we'd explode if we drove too fast.

The house sat quietly at the top of the driveway. Lucas stopped in front of the garage, not bothering to pull in. He cut the engine and we sat for a few moments. I could hear both of them breathing, and my own heartbeat was a constant thudding whisper in my ears.

"You're really going to do this," Lucas said.

I swallowed and nodded.

"You could probably wait in the house if you wanted," I said, twisting in my seat to look at Imogen.

Her face was hardened in a perpetual frown. I couldn't imagine any other expression breaking through her set lips and tense eyebrows. She shook her head.

"I need to be there for her," Imogen said. "Even if I can't stop you, or won't, Kelda shouldn't be alone."

Kelda hadn't earned that kind of loyalty, as far as I could see, but I kept my mouth shut. I just nodded at her and took a deep breath.

We climbed out. A sharp breeze hit my face the moment I was out of the car. It was as if the magic on the grounds had whipped the weather into a frenzy. Even the dark clouds seemed agitated overhead. They pulsed with magic and sparked with static energy.

A storm was gathering, and we were the cause.

Kelda's wand throbbed in my hand. She had trusted Imogen with her life, to leave this with her. Even at the height of our friendship, it would never have occurred to me to let Imogen hang onto my wand for a while. It just wasn't something a sane Glim did.

Imogen felt it. The pain was almost enough to double her over. I reached out and took her hand. She stiffened, but she didn't let go.

We walked side-by-side toward the garden until we could see down into the clearing. Isabelle's face darkened with a scowl when she saw Imogen standing next to me. I expected

Amani to scowl, too, and order Imogen away, but she only nodded in greeting.

In the center of the garden, Kelda was still trapped in the cage. I expected her to be shaking the bars, calling in vain to her sprites, or screaming at us to let her out, but she stood absolutely still and silent inside its confines. Her gaze was distant, headed out into the darkness somewhere between Amani and Daniel, who still prowled the ground above the sunken clearing. She didn't turn to look at us.

Imogen shrank back.

"I can't," she said.

I nodded. Lucas put his arm around her shoulders and drew her backwards into the shadows of the bushes and trees, away from the cage. I willed him to comfort her, and though I knew comfort was probably impossible right now, I also knew he would do his best.

Amani moved from where she'd been standing by the cage. She flitted across the garden and up the steps so quickly that it looked like she was skimming the ground like a dragonfly.

I held the wand out toward her. It burned my palm. She eyed it, her expression curious and fascinated and calculating, but she shook her head.

"Should I give it to Haidar?" I said.

I didn't need to ask the question; I knew the answer. But I still clung to the hope that I was wrong until Amani spoke.

"You'll need to do it," she said. "You took the wand. It will only work for you."

I thought of a dozen arguments and a dozen more reasons this job should definitely go to Haidar and not to me.

But I'd seen the future in the waterfall. This was part of it, I was sure, and fighting against it would be no more effective than trying to fight the hundreds of gallons of water that plunged by every instant outside the Waterfall Palace. This was my future.

I closed my eyes.

For one last moment, I was Olivia Feye. I was the daughter of an ambitious Glim politician and a woman who'd finally started stepping out of his shadow and pursuing her own talents. I was the sister of Daniel, a sarcastic, emo poet who'd risked his safety to be here with me. I was Imogen's friend, whether she liked it or not, and I was Lucas' friend, too, and they were both here with me because that's what friends did.

And I was me: a plant-loving, Humdrum-loving, aspiring botanist who wanted nothing more than to hang out in Imogen's shadow and daydream about college.

And then I said goodbye, and opened my eyes.

CHAPTER THIRTY-FOUR

The wind whipped my hair around my face. A tangled strand of it brushed against my lips, but it didn't stick. My lips were too dry. I ran my tongue along my teeth, but that didn't help.

In front of me, Kelda stood still as ice and just as cold. She glared at me. It was a black-eyed glare that could cut through diamonds, and I was no match for it. I felt her rage eviscerate me, but that feeling was mine and something I would keep to myself. I couldn't let her see.

Queen Amani stood next to the bars of the cage, just out of reach of Kelda's sharp nails.

"I don't want to do this," Amani said.

"Good, because you're not going to be able to," Kelda said. "I have more enchantments set to protect me from you than you could possibly dream of."

An enormous raindrop landed on my arm. I glanced down at it. The glistening water made my skin sparkle, as if a tiny bit of magic had fallen from the sky.

"I can't trust you if you have your magic," Amani said. "I've spent half our lives listening to you tell me you won't do things, and then cleaning up after you when you do them. When you rig a vote to put one of your sprite attendants on the Council, that's one thing. But now you're openly declaring war."

"Shouldn't that be a relief?" Kelda said. "Finally, no more lies."

"You know I don't believe that," Amani said. "The lies are only getting bigger."

"No deaths," I interrupted. I looked at Kelda, and she glared at me, and I went on. "You said you don't want to destroy the Hums; that's why almost no one had been killed. Was that a lie?"

She didn't answer, just stared at me as though she could obliterate me with nothing more than her gaze. For all I knew, she could. I sent an extra bit of strength to the shielding spell that protected me.

"All I need is a promise that you'll stop this," Amani said. "A sealed promise, one you can't break, but then that's it. You'll be free to go."

Kelda flicked her hand toward Amani. The queen dodged, but the spell grazed her shoulder. Her sleeve was singed away; the fabric smoked, leaving an unpleasant, acrid stench in the damp air.

Another raindrop landed, this time on my hand. Overhead, the clouds hung heavy with moisture and enchantments.

Kelda leveled her gaze at me.

"This one will have to do it," she said. "You can't touch me, Amani."

A ripple of fear shuddered through the garden. I didn't know if it had come from Kelda or Amani, but it was one of them; they were the only two powerful enough that their fear could send cold terror down through my toes.

One of them didn't think I could do this. Maybe both.

Kelda's wand burned like ice in my hand. I fought the urge to drop it.

If I was smart, I'd drop it. If I was smart, I'd run.

But I didn't have time to be smart. Their eyes were on me, and the lives of everyone I loved weighed on my shoulders.

"I have to try," I said.

"With that kind of confidence, who am I to stop you?" Kelda said.

She eyed me up and down, as if she hadn't fully appreciated my mediocrity before.

I eyed her up and down, too, but the end result wasn't impressive. She wasn't about to feel intimidated by me, and I had only given myself even more reason to be scared of her. Magic crackled in her hands like white lightning.

I felt everyone else circling the garden: Haidar, hulking and watchful as he held onto the veins of magic that held Kelda captive; Isabelle, fierce and angry beside him; Daniel, stalking the edges of the stone wall, his body thrumming with power; Lucas, willing himself to be strong for those of us who needed his steady support; and Imogen, trembling and holding onto her courage with everything she had.

They stood with me like branches woven together so thick that nothing could break through their entangled arms. They stood there because they believed in me, or in Amani, or in a better future, or in something else that meant enough to them that they'd risk their lives to be here.

I pulled Mom's ring out of my pocket and slipped it onto my finger.

Then, I stepped forward and pointed Kelda's wand toward her cage.

There were no words to this spell, no fancy gestures. There was only intent, hot and pure and bright as it burned through me.

But not bright enough.

Kelda didn't even flinch. She watched me with her endless black eyes and held as still as an ice carving. The stream of magic that poured from my wand like white fog didn't even touch her. Instead, it pooled around her cage, slid to the ground, and faded to nothing.

"You have to believe that what you're doing is right," Kelda said.

I hated everything about what we were doing. It was cruel and bizarre, to take magic from a Glim. But Kelda's icy gaze and Imogen's faded confidence were enough to convince me that what we were doing needed to be done. I had no idea what would make the Glimmering world a better place, but Kelda losing her powers had to be at the top of the list.

"If I'm sure of anything, it's that this is right," I said.

A surge of magic shot down my arm, noticeable but not enough to make any difference.

Kelda wrapped her pale fingers around the thorny bars of her cage and leaned forward.

"You have to believe what *you're* doing is right," she said.

"I wouldn't be doing this if I didn't," I said.

She blinked at me.

Clearly, I'd missed some kind of cryptic message. But it didn't matter.

I wasn't here for her word games or her opinions on en-chantments. I was here because her willingness to trample on everyone to get what she wanted made me fear for the Glimmering world's future, and because the magic that had surrounded her faux wand had chilled me to my bones. No magic should feel like that, especially not when it came from someone who had control over our world.

I might have opinions about the way Kelda handled things, and I might know in my gut that her magic was evil, but that alone might not have been enough to kick me into action.

What was enough was the way Imogen had swallowed all her fear and hatred and handed me the wand.

Imogen knew this had to happen. She'd made some dumb choices in the past few months, but so had I. Despite everything, I still trusted her. She knew Kelda better than I did. She also knew better than I did that what had to come next.

I had to believe that what *I* was doing was right.

But this wasn't about "I." That would never be enough. Kelda made her decisions with an "I" in mind, and that was the reason she had to be stopped.

If the waterfall's future was going to play out the way I'd seen, I wanted to be the kind of faerie who led with an "us."

Slowly, I lowered Kelda's wand. I turned to Amani.

"I need Imogen," I said.

She nodded. Isabelle was up in an instant, crossing the garden like she had wings.

"I'll get her," she said as she whisked past us.

"Don't force her," I said. "Bring Lucas too, though, if he'll come."

Isabelle held up a hand to confirm she'd heard me. Her figure disappeared into the shadows of the garden.

Now alone, Haidar tensed. I felt the magic in the garden ripple slightly, though not enough to let Kelda free.

A raindrop fell onto my cheek. Above us, Daniel paced.

Amani folded her arms tightly in front of her. The gold from her aura touched her cream sweater with a warm light.

Thunder rolled softly in the distance. I felt another raindrop land on my hand. The water was cool, but the air around us kissed my face with the warmth of the magic that throbbed in the land and the clouds.

I heard their footsteps before I saw them. Isabelle's shadowy figure led the way into the garden, followed by Imogen's. Lucas brought up the rear, and though he glanced up at Kelda, his gaze went immediately back to Imogen. I felt protectiveness rising from him, a sense that he needed to keep her safe. He met my eyes and nodded slightly, reassuring me: *She's okay.*

I held a hand out to Imogen. She hesitated, then, slowly, she crossed the garden to me.

She took my hand. The familiar warmth of her skin pressed against my palm. I leaned in toward her.

"Will you stay with me?" I said.

I looked into her eyes, bracing myself in the same moment to see nothing there but contempt. Instead, I practically heard her voice in my head.

We're in this together, she seemed to say. Her eyes glimmered with deepest blue.

"I can't do this without you," I said.

"I know," she said, low enough that only I could hear her. "You're useless without me. Always have been."

I squeezed her hand so tightly that I expected bones to break. Every muscle in my body yearned for a hug, but her eyes were already on Kelda.

The Oracle's face twisted in rage.

Imogen pulled me a few steps back from the cage.

"You're going to have to act quickly," she said, voice still low, but fast now. "She's powerful, but her endurance is what's really going to test you. She's taken on the energy of the Fountain for years, and fountains just recycle their water over and over and never run out. Her magic's like that. You're going to have to hit her strong and for longer than you think."

"Stay with me," I said again.

"I'm not going anywhere," Imogen said.

I felt the fear and loss that hit her as she spoke. This choice would take everything from her in an instant.

I promised myself in that moment that Imogen Dann would never feel like "just Imogen," no matter what it took. If

I was going to be the Faerie Queen, I was going to give her the world on a silver platter.

"I'm so sorry I didn't tell you about Amani," I said.

She swallowed, but waved me off like it didn't weigh on her every second.

"We're cool," she lied. "But we should probably talk about it later."

I nodded and turned back to the cage.

Again, I raised the wand and pointed it at Kelda.

Take it, I thought, and the magic rushed hot down my arm.

In an instant, pain ripped through me, blinding me with a burning white. My heart was being ripped out of my chest, tearing through bone and sinew, and being twisted and wrenched apart. I felt as my magic touched hers, felt as she cried out in agony, and felt as my soul lost its cohesion.

I was no longer me. Instead, I was a beast that should never have existed. I was Olivia and Kelda, a sick creature twisted from two into one, threaded up and down with Kelda's rage, Kelda's pain, Kelda's power, Kelda's ambition, Kelda's grief, Kelda's hate. In between the threads, I was nothing: just Olivia, a pathetic child of a faerie who had overstepped her strength by being in this garden at all.

I was an insect, crawling in the dirt. I was the smudge on the heel of a shoe. I was nothing, *nothing,* compared to the all-powerful faerie whose magic I had dared to invade. I fell to my knees and cowered before her.

All around me, the world burned white and blue, shimmering like a star combusting with a violent heat I couldn't even comprehend.

Through the fire, all I could see was her face. She towered above me, her black eyes flickering white like glowing coals and her wild beauty shoving me further into the mud at my feet.

Who the hell did I think I was? I was nobody, nothing, a shadow that should never have existed.

Pressure landed on my shoulder. It took what felt like entire dizzying minutes to figure out what had happened. And then, I recognized the touch, and the person attached to it. Imogen stood next to me, glaring at Kelda and tethering me to the world with her hand.

I lifted the wand higher and threw my anger toward the caged faerie.

And then they were all there, their attention crowding into my mind: Imogen, Isabelle, Haidar, Daniel, Lucas, Amani—far too many of them all standing far too close, their thoughts and their energy as vivid in my mind as if they were my own. It was like the first time I'd fully sensed other Glims, at Imogen's sister's wedding, but this was a thousand times worse. Every complex emotion in the garden rushed in on me at once, and I winced and drew in on myself.

"Everyone step back," a voice said.

A flash of silver surrounded me. The voices faded. I shuddered and looked up into Amani's eyes as her protective shield shimmered around us. On my finger, Mom's ring was a single spot of ice amid the fire. I felt it trying to protect me, trying to cool me and take away the burn of Kelda's magic. But what could it do against fury like this?

Amani crouched in front of me, her face drawn and gaze intense.

"Are you okay?"

I nodded. It was the biggest lie I had ever told.

She put a hand on my arm. "They can't help you," she said, loud enough for everyone to hear her. "You can do this. You have to believe in yourself."

"I need Imogen," I said.

My voice was nothing, not even a full whisper. It cracked out of my throat like dust.

"Imogen will stay close," Amani said. "But even your best friends can't do this for you. There are some days that no one can help you through but you."

I had become so focused on the words coming out of Amani's tight lips that I'd stopped thrusting magic toward Kelda. I saw Amani stiffen and fall forward as Kelda's spell hit her in the back. The magic enflamed the air around us. Amani tumbled forward and caught the fall with her arms.

In a second, Isabelle was on her feet. She threw herself at the cage and grabbed Kelda by the throat.

"Get away," I ordered her, before I'd even realized I'd spoken. This time, the words rang through the garden.

Magic crackled up Kelda's body. Isabelle pulled her hand away just in time.

She crouched next to the queen. Her magic wove a shield out of leaves and grasses, translucent and pale as they hovered, wide enough to cover her and Amani.

Haidar shifted, and Kelda's cage grew deadly thorns.

I turned to the Oracle again, and I pointed the wand at her and braced myself.

But there was no bracing myself.

There was only pain. There was only terror. I had never felt them fully before. Now, they crashed over me, a torrent of agony as if all the water fell at once from her Fountain and onto my trembling shoulders.

I lurched to my knees again, the jolt of the ground against my kneecaps nothing compared to the blinding anguish that ripped through my body and mind.

I couldn't do this.

No one could do this, but especially not me.

The wand trembled before me. In the distance, past the rushing of my ears, I heard Kelda scream. Her magic flooded into me through the wand, but mine flooded back into her as well, stronger and faster. I felt my life draining from me, taking my energy and my will with it.

"Help her!" a voice screamed. I almost didn't recognize it as Daniel's. I'd never heard him panic like that.

As if through water, I heard their words rising and falling.

"She has to do this herself," Amani said.

Kelda's laughter bubbled up behind them. She knew she was winning. She could feel it as well as I could, the way my energy was being pulled back into her. I tried to feel for it and grasp the tendrils of magic that shifted between us, but they slipped away from me like mist.

"You're the Faerie Queen!" Daniel said.

"That's exactly *why* I can't help." Amani's voice came out tight, afraid.

"Screw that," Daniel shouted. He came closer. I couldn't see him through the pain, but I could feel him. He was a tornado of desperation.

I heard his footsteps as he stood beside me.

And then, the last thing I had expected.

The sound of a violin pierced through the haze that surrounded me. For a moment, I heard it as clearly as if nothing else was happening: a single, high note that stretched through the air like a rainbow.

More notes followed. These weren't the shrieks and squeals from before. Now, he played as if he'd been playing forever, his magic and his fear helping him coax notes from the instrument that I knew he didn't know how to make on his own.

I latched onto the sound. The long, thin notes sounded like magic, the way they stretched and faded. I held the wand up higher and imagined Kelda's magic as violin strings. I imagined looping the strings around her wand's tip and coaxing them toward me.

Her panic flared. She hadn't expected this.

I pulled on the strings harder. Daniel's music grew louder.

Kelda screamed. A wave of pain slammed into me. I shuddered and fell forward, and dropped the wand onto the soggy ground. The instant her wand left my hand, the pain began to clear.

No.

I grabbed for the wand just as Kelda threw out a hand to summon it to her. It twitched away from my fingers, but I threw myself forward and caught it. I fell back onto the ground. Jolts of electricity shot through my elbows, but I held tight to the wand's slim handle.

I couldn't sit up, but I could point the wand from here.

It wouldn't be enough.

Hands gripped my body. Imogen knelt behind me and wrapped her arms tight around my shoulders, holding me up and pinning me in her embrace. I let myself fall into her and kept the wand leveled at Kelda.

The magic coming through it now was thick, crackling, and strong. Whatever layer of power I'd reached, it was different than the ones before, and it hurt even worse.

"You can do this," Lucas' voice said next to my ear.

Images flooded into my mind. The island where I'd stood and looked out over a sea of growing green things. The college dorm that would never be mine. The expansive sense of freedom that came from making my own choices in the world, and the terror of realizing there was only one path I could walk and still live with myself. I looked up and saw Kelda's dark eyes boring into me.

"Hold tight, Olivia," Amani said, her voice floating in from the other side of Lucas. "You're almost there."

The pain was unbearable. I fought the blackness that crept in at the edges of my vision. I had to stay long enough to protect my mom, to keep Elle's Humdrum family safe, to shield Lucas' mom, to make sure Daniel got to do whatever he wanted with his life.

There was no longer any question in my mind of whether I'd survive this. No faerie should have to do this to another faerie. The price would be everything I could pay.

The Oracle's magic felt like mud now, the last dregs of something being siphoned from her. I had to fight for a few moments longer. Then I could let go.

"You've got this, Liv," Imogen whispered in my ear.

Kelda shrieked, her voice like cold wind whistling around a house during a storm. And then, with a final, horrible throb of agony, the last traces of her magic were sucked into her wand and into me.

Suddenly, I could see.

I had just enough time to watch the Oracle's white-blue light fade from her cage before the dizziness overtook me. Through the blur of my nausea, I watched the rose cage throb and tangle in a sudden wind. Its tendrils dissolved, flapping in the wind until they blew away as dust.

All that was left was a woman, curled up in a ball on the grass, her eyes closed and her breathing irregular and rough.

Amani stepped toward her. The sadness in her body made me want to fall apart.

I felt myself fading out. The pain was receding, but I was going with it. In a moment, I'd dissolve just like the cage.

"Here," I said.

My voice was the tiniest breeze, but Amani turned. I held out the wand. She took it and knelt in front of me. Her eyes held more than I could process.

"Haidar," I said. Daniel was next to me, Amani before me, Lucas beside me, and Imogen still had me wrapped in her arms, but I hadn't seen the other two. "Isabelle."

"They're all right," Amani said. She nodded toward where Haidar had been before. Now, he sat on the grass, Isabelle tangled up in him with her arms around his neck. They looked exhausted but safe.

Everyone was safe. Everyone would be okay.

I let out a breath and let myself slip away.

CHAPTER THIRTY-FIVE

"Rise and shine, daffodil."

The gravelly voice intruded into my consciousness. I didn't know where I was or what was happening, only that I'd been resting in comfortable oblivion and the voice was interrupting. I tried to ignore it.

"Come on," it said. "People are going to realize how lazy you are."

I pried apart my eyelids. They felt sticky, like they'd much rather be shut.

Blearily, I blinked up into a world that was ten shades too bright. Haidar looked down at me, his face almost cheerful.

The expression looked weird on him.

"Good job," he said. "Keep 'em open."

He waved a hand at my bed. My mattress raised itself slowly to a reclined sitting position, like a Humdrum hospital bed but without all the whirring. He held out a small plastic cup filled with green liquid.

"Swallow this."

I took it, getting the distinct feeling that I did not want that thing anywhere near my taste buds. But I could barely hold my head up. I wasn't in a position to argue with anyone, let alone Haidar.

I knocked the liquid back. It tasted better than I'd expected, but still, it burned a trail down my throat and made me cough and sputter.

He took the cup back, nodded his approval, and went back to whatever he'd been doing before he'd woken me up. He had a small table set up near my bed and it was covered in tiny bottles and jars. As I watched, he added three drops of something to a small stone bowl and stirred it. Around us, the magic of the house thrummed soft and deep.

Slowly, my thoughts began to collect themselves. I remembered endless waves of pain, and Daniel's music, and Imogen's arms around me. I remembered Kelda's frail body curled on the grass. The images came in disjointed bursts: a raindrop on rose petals here, the pulsing light of magic against the underside of the clouds there.

"Is everyone okay?" I said.

"They're fine," Haidar said. "City's a damned mess, but if we're lucky that will just keep the Council busy. I'm not the only one who's fed up with them debating elf tariffs to kingdom come just to have something to talk about."

I was sure Dad was losing his mind over the latest crisis. All I felt was relief that he was able to continue his dumb job for another day.

"How long was I out?"

"Better part of a week," Haidar said, not looking up. He added a pinch of something glittery to the bowl. "Everyone's been worried about you, but you'll be fine."

"Thanks to you?" I said.

He grunted, but there was a smile behind it. The house seemed happier, too. Its magic felt stronger than before and came with a sense of deep, steady purpose.

A soft knock sounded at the door.

Haidar slammed a tiny jar down.

"I said I'd let you know when she was up," he called, his familiar scowl back.

The door creaked open. Lucas' head poked in. He ignored Haidar completely. When his gaze landed on me, his entire face transformed with relief.

"Hi," I said. I sounded like a frog.

He looked to Haidar. They scowled at each other for a moment, then Haidar rolled his eyes and waved him in.

"I need to go talk to her mother anyway," he said.

Lucas rushed into the room, his dark hair a mess, like he'd been running his hand through it nonstop for a week.

"Your mom's downstairs," Haidar added to me. "Finally got her to eat something."

Mom was downstairs.

Mom was safe.

Lucas sat next to the bed as Haidar left. I was in a different room than before, I realized. This one had sky blue walls, and my lap was covered with a bright blue blanket with white flowers embroidered on it.

I sat up. My body felt like it weighed a million pounds.

"How are you feeling?" Lucas said.

I shrugged. I had a feeling I looked bad enough to answer the question.

"I'm glad you're okay," he said. "Amani's been worried."

"What happened to Kelda?" I said.

He shook his head. "She's not awake yet," he said. "Haidar says it could be another week. They've been enchanting her memory while she sleeps. They're going to set her up with a good Humdrum life."

I bit down on the inside of my cheek. That was something I would have given almost anything for a week ago. Anything except the safety of people like Lucas.

That life was closed to me now.

I wiggled my foot under the covers, suddenly restless.

"What about Imogen?"

At this, he smiled and leaned back in his seat a little.

"She's out helping with memory glamours," he said. "Most of Portland's needed a once-over to get things back to normal. Aubrey had an entire team assigned to just her."

He closed his eyes for a moment, like the very thought stressed him out.

"Amani's formed a special task force to clean up the worst of it, and Imogen's leading that. And they've got a Dark Forest Coalition going, which is supposed to open up discussion between Glims about the possibility of integrating the Glimmering and Humdrum worlds."

It was beyond weird to hear all those words come from him. A year ago, he had no idea what a Glimmer was or that faeries existed. Now, he was chatting like he'd been raised as one.

"Kelda went about it the wrong way, but Amani figures if that many people were willing to join her, it might be time to re-evaluate," he said.

"That's a big move," I said. "Good for her."

I wasn't sure I wanted to see Amani anytime soon. With any luck, she'd be too busy cleaning up to spend much time thinking about me.

But I didn't know if I'd have luck. I could feel the future rippling in my veins. I hadn't just pulled Kelda's magic from her; I'd pulled it into me. It tingled down my arms and up my spine.

Somehow, in a way I didn't yet understand, I was powerful.

"You okay?" he said. His eyebrows furrowed a little, just enough to create a line between them.

I leaned back into the pillows. They enveloped me. I got the impression that this bedroom, like the rest of the house, hadn't been used much in a long time.

"It's been a crazy couple of weeks," I said.

"That's an understatement," he said.

He reached out and put his hand on my knee. Its weight pressed gently on me through the blanket.

"I don't know," I said. "This is going to take a while to process. Everything I'd planned for is gone."

"Me too," he said.

I frowned at him.

The corner of his mouth quirked a little bit, like he couldn't decide whether or not to smile, and he held out his other hand. A tiny light glowed in his palm. It solidified and formed into a pale purple flower that opened its petals and rotated slowly in his palm.

I sat up straight. The movement made my head throb.

"Wait, what?" I said.

"Apparently, you leaked," he said. His mouth finally surrendered to a smile, and the corners of his eyes crinkled. "You suck at taking magic from big evil faeries, Liv."

"Well, excuse me for living," I said. "I'll try to do better next time."

I leaned forward and pulled his hand toward me. The flower spun in a lazy circle. I plucked it from his palm and examined it. A soft floral scent rose up to greet me.

"So what, you're a Glim now?"

"Maybe?" he said. "I don't know. Everyone in the garden got a dose of her magic when you pulled it out of her, but I got a whole lot extra. Something to do with the necklaces Amani gave us. I'm never going to be the world's greatest faerie or anything, but I'm not exactly a Hum anymore, either."

"Morgan le Fay," I breathed.

"Haidar had heard of the theory, but this is kind of new ground," Lucas said. "I'm going to be a science experiment for a while. A couple wizards have already contacted me for a 'comprehensive energy mapping,' whatever that is."

"You're such a shiny new toy," I said. I laughed.

It felt bizarre to laugh, but so, so good.

"Are you okay with it?" I said.

I watched his face to be sure he was telling me the truth.

He nodded. He seemed calm.

"It's good," he said. "I think I was supposed to be part of your world from the day I found out. It would have been hard to be on both sides of that line forever."

His hand was still in mine. I laced my fingers through his and looked at our hands there together.

"Thanks," I said.

"I didn't give myself magic, you did," he said.

"No, I mean, for helping me in the garden. And before."

He'd risked his life over and over again. He'd helped me collect the wand and bring Imogen out of that icy palace. And he'd been with me in the garden, offering his support so I could make it through.

"I couldn't ask for better friends," I said.

His hand tensed in mine, gently crushing my fingers and pressing our skin more closely together.

"I'm glad I ran back into you," he said.

"Stay in touch next time," I said. I nudged him with my knee.

Downstairs, I heard a door open and close. Voices rose and fell for a moment, and then I heard the galloping sound of footsteps racing up the stairs.

The door burst open.

"Olivia!" Imogen said.

She was at my side in half a second, pushing Lucas out of the way without a glance. She flung her arms around me and squeezed me so hard I coughed.

She didn't apologize for crushing the air out of me. I didn't want her to.

"I'm so sorry I'm such a stupid idiot," she said. "Lucas, go away. She was my friend first."

He rolled his eyes and held up his hands. I smiled as I watched him go.

The heavy wooden door clicked closed, and we were alone.

Imogen slid into his vacated seat. She leaned forward and propped her head on my lap.

"I'm the worst friend in the universe and I'm sorry for being an asshole," she said, looking up at me with her big blue eyes.

Everything in my body relaxed.

"I'm an anxious, anal-retentive jerk with chronic communication failure," I said.

I ran my hand along her hair. Imogen always melted when people played with her hair. She was a needy cat that way.

"Are we okay?" I said. "Can we please be okay?"

"I miss you so much I can't see straight," Imogen said.

Instantly, the back of my throat closed up. I was going to cry, like an idiot. Instead, I leaned over and squeezed her head.

"I'm not trying to shove my boobs in your face; I just love you," I said.

She wrapped her arms around my waist and squeezed me so hard I coughed again.

CHAPTER THIRTY-SIX

FOUR MONTHS LATER

I leaned into Tabitha's office.

"Do you need anything else before I take off?" I said.

She shook her head and tapped a stack of papers on her desk.

"Nope, you're free to go," she said. "Have fun."

She waved, wiggling her long black fingernails at me, and I practically skipped out of the office.

After the whole Oracle situation, Lorinda had almost been in tears at the thought of losing me. That had more to do with my new role as Faerie-Queen-in-training than my mediocre godmothering skills, but Amani and I had agreed the job would be a good experience. I spent so much time talking with the Council and studying magic at the Waterfall Palace these days that filing papers a few hours a week was a relief—especially now that I had my phone loaded up with the awesome botany and science podcasts Lucas had found for me.

Today, though, I was done with Wishes Fulfilled, the Council, and everything to do with leading the Glimmering world.

Tonight, I would just be Olivia.

Imogen met me outside, two Pumpkin Spice mocha iced lattes in hand. She handed me one and I took a grateful sip. A second later, I leaned back.

"Faerie dust? Really? It's three in the afternoon."

"The Rose Galas start tonight," she said. "Don't even think of getting boring on me, Your Honorable Fancypants."

I rolled my eyes at her and took another sip. It was beyond delicious.

A few hours later, I looked at myself in Imogen's bedroom mirror. She'd loaded my eyelids with more glitter than I'd thought possible, and my lips gleamed like I'd been chugging olive oil. Somehow, the overall effect came together gorgeously. But then, Imogen's glamours always turned out well.

"Your dad offered to write me a recommendation letter for my first job when I get out of Institut Glänzen," Imogen said. She leaned over and swept a curl back from my face. "He's turned into such a suck-up."

"He's always been a suck-up," I said. "We've just never been important before."

Out of all the changes the past few months had brought, literally becoming one of my dad's bosses had been one of the best. It wasn't so much that he had to do whatever I told him now. More than anything, it was the way things had calmed down around our house. Maybe he felt like he could finally relax now that our family was on the map. Or maybe he just figured I'd tattle to Queen Amani if my home life wasn't good. Whatever the reason, he was nicer these days. He'd even sat down and watched a movie with Mom the other week like a normal person.

I could only hope it would last.

As for Mom, she'd headed up the rehabilitation of the Oracle's sprites and was doing brilliantly at it. Kelda was gone, safely established in a new Humdrum life in another city, one that didn't come with a risk of triggering her memories. She was happy, Amani told me, although there had been a sadness in her eyes as she'd spoken that I didn't think would ever fade completely.

We'd decided against appointing a new Oracle. Instead, Kelda was replaced by a second Council, this one dedicated to making sure every Glim had a voice in the way our world was being run.

"I got you a present," Imogen said. She scurried over to her closet and pulled something down. When she turned around, a tiny neon green pot was in her hand, spilling over with sparkling pink flowers that spun in circles on their stems.

"What is that?" I said.

Not that it mattered. I was in love already.

She handed it to me, and I leaned in to inspect the delicate, glittering blooms.

"I thought your Council office didn't, you know, have enough *flowers*," she said. The sarcasm in her voice was so thick I could probably chew on it. "This is a pink tanna," she said. "It lets off a perfume only on the day directly after the full moon. I only got it a couple days ago but they say the smell is amazing."

"You're my favorite," I said.

"You talking to me or the plant?" she said.

I stuck my tongue out between my teeth at her. She leaned over me to look in the mirror and pressed her fingertips to the space just under her cheekbones. Her skin seemed to indent as though it were made of clay. A second later, she pulled her hands away to reveal perfect contoured hollows.

"Let's get out of here," she said. "Leave the plant. You can pick it up tomorrow. We have to go!"

I followed her as she flew down the stairs.

I stepped through the door and onto the roof. Imogen was in front of me, already shaking her arms to the beat of the music. A sea of Glims and their Humdrum loved ones spread out in front of us, standing on a floor of sparkling gold. Past our roof, the same glittering net of gold stars stretched across the gaps to every building beyond, and further gold nets stretched past them, connecting downtown Portland in a single web of light. Some of the nets climbed to the tops of skyscrapers; others fell to cover single-story buildings, and every net was crawling with people.

"Whoa," Daniel said behind me.

"They seriously outdid themselves," his friend Devyn said. She took Daniel's hand and pulled him forward. I waved as they disappeared into the crowd, and he lifted his chin at me.

"Is it like this every year?" Lucas said.

I shook my head, marveling at the way the floor glinted and sparkled.

"Sometimes it's held in gardens connected by portals," I said. "One year it was in glass domes at the bottom of the Willamette River."

"This is crazy."

"Welcome to your world."

The rainbow roads shimmered overhead. And off the edge of the building, far beneath the net, I could see Humdrum cars driving by on the street below. The Humdrums didn't quite remember all that had happened a few months ago, but an air of mystery and adventure had floated around Portland since. It was as though the entire city was trying to recall an interesting dream that kept slipping through their fingers.

"I told Mom I'd check in with her," I said.

Imogen stood on her tiptoes and we scanned the rooftop. A moment later, I caught sight of Mom through a crush of people. She was dancing with my dad. He was actually smiling, and they almost looked like they liked each other. I sent a tiny pulse of energy toward her. It was thin and targeted, and it weaved through the crowd and hit her in a way I'd never been able to manage before I'd taken in Kelda's energy.

She looked up, confused for a moment, and then her eyes met mine. I waved, and she smiled and pursed her lips in a kiss. My heart warmed for a second, and then Imogen was dragging me into the crowd.

In the center of the rooftop, a fountain rose up in a spray of water and pink light. In its center was a silver statue of a blooming rose, and water fell from between its petals and into the pool.

I eyed it warily. Fountains were not my thing these days.

But Lucas nudged me and nodded toward its base. This fountain must be okay, because Haidar and Isabelle were sitting on its edge. Haidar had a tiny pink rose in his hands, probably plucked from one of the arrangements that sat on the tables at the edge of the rooftop. He tucked it carefully behind Isabelle's ear. She smiled up at him, and he bent to kiss her forehead. She closed her eyes and leaned in, savoring the touch.

"Let's get drinks," Imogen shouted across the noise of the band in the far corner. On the stage, the guitarist was playing a busy lick on pearly unicorn-hair strings, and the tiny pixie behind him kept flying up in his seat whenever he hit the drums too hard.

The punch bowls and arrangements of champagne in flutes were interspersed with silver vases overflowing with yellow roses. One of the blossoms drooped over the edge, its head too heavy. The poor thing looked thirsty. I flicked my finger and sent a little zing of magic its way. An instant later, I felt the pull as its stem began sucking up water. The bloom floated up toward the sky as though it had woken from a nap.

I remembered what the legends had always said: The Faerie Queen made the grass grow.

"Stefan is here!" Imogen hissed into my ear in an excited whisper.

"What?"

"Stefan!" she said, looking at me like I was hopeless. "Super hot sprite guy? Wasn't really into Kelda's plans? I've told you about him a million times?"

It had been at least a million and a half. I looked to where she was pointing. Like every sprite, he was tall, thin, pale-haired, and ridiculously hot.

She bumped my hip with hers and then she was gone. A second later, she tossed her hair and looked up at him, her aura glittering gold.

Remnants of Kelda's enchantments had clung to Imogen for months. I'd seen it in little flashes of self-hatred, or moments where my normally obnoxiously optimistic friend turned dark and cynical. But those moments were becoming fewer and farther between, and tonight, she was utterly herself. She glowed.

Lucas handed me a glass of punch. I took it and knocked half of it back in one go, loving its rose scent and the way it made me feel instantly a few degrees cooler.

"This looks amazing," he said.

"Whoever designed it deserves a raise," I agreed.

"No," he said. "I mean, this looks amazing." He gestured toward the crowd with his glass. "They're safe. Everyone's happy."

"That's the Allures talking," I said. But I smiled as I looked out over the party. He was right: They were happy. They were safe, at least for tonight.

I followed Lucas to the edge of the roof. We leaned against the railing.

In front of us, a witch stood on tiptoes to kiss her Humdrum husband's cheek. The Humdrum wrapped his arms around the witch's waist and said something to her. She blushed and giggled.

"I've been thinking," I said.

Lucas bent down so he could hear me.

"I agree with a lot of what Kelda was fighting for," I said.

His ear was so close to my lips that I felt the heat rising from his skin.

"I think everyone should be able to be themselves," I said. "Even if that means being openly Glim or being obsessed with Humdrum biology and culture."

He nodded.

"I know that can't happen overnight," I said, as if he'd been about to talk me out of it. "But I'd like a world where Glims and Hums know about each other, and it's isn't necessarily better to be one or the other. I want a world where people can choose. Maybe we'll find better ways to give Humdrums powers, or to tone them down in Glims who are overwhelmed by their magic. I just want people to have... whatever they want."

"You think that's possible?"

I laughed. "I have no idea. I just want to create a world where everyone can pursue their dreams—whatever that means."

His hand closed around mine. I leaned against him and let out a sigh I hadn't realized I'd been holding.

In front of us, a college-aged girl with honey-colored hair almost to her knees walked by. A guy followed behind her, looking at her as if he couldn't see anyone else.

"I feel a Rapunzel coming on," I said. Lucas laughed.

The crowd writhed and pulsed in front of me. The song changed. Overhead, the rainbow roads glittered and the stars twinkled as steadily as if the planet wasn't moving through space at a thousand miles per hour.

And in the middle of all of it, I stood, feeling the magic and emotions of our people sparkling and shifting around me.

A memory of Queen Amani in the Garden of Glims surfaced.

I was never going to choose this, she'd said. *No sane person would. But this work chooses you. I don't regret it. It's a hell of an adventure.*

I set my drink down.

"Let's dance," I said.

I took Lucas' other hand and pulled him toward me as we disappeared into the crowd.

ABOUT THE AUTHOR

Emma Savant lives with her gorgeous husband and adorable cat in a small town in Oregon, where she spends way too much time watching *Star Trek* and eating nachos. She loves fairy tales and once took an archery class in the hopes of becoming more Narnian.

You can follow her online and be the first to hear about new Glimmers stories by visiting *www.EmmaSavant.com.*